WIDOW'S REVENGE

a novel by

K.L. Fogg

Covenant Communications, Inc.

Cover illustration © Alisa Haggard
Cover design © 2007 by Covenant Communications, Inc.

Published by Covenant Communications, Inc.
American Fork, Utah

Printed in USA
First Printing: March 2007 (Softback 2008)

13 12 11 10 09 08   10 9 8 7 6 5 4 3 2

ISBN 978-1-59811-234-4

In loving memory of James Henrie

March 29, 1989 ~ June 12, 2006

1

The Suspension

For the first time since he knew his real last name, Wesley wished he could change it from Mackey to anything else. It was his misfortune that alphabetically, Mackey came right before MacLean, and that meant his assigned locker was next to Dylan MacLean, which was why he was presently crouched behind the science lab door, waiting for an opportunity to safely collect his history book. Trying to get his history book out of his locker now was actually a moot point, because he was already six assignments behind and probably wouldn't be around to explain to his parents why he got an F on his report card.

Wesley snuck out from behind the door right when he saw the beautiful owner of his left-flanked locker arrive. Katie MacKenzie—one of the most popular girls in the eighth grade—opened her locker, and Wesley decided to make a break for it. Maybe the Beast would leave him alone while the Beauty—Katie MacKenzie—was there to distract him.

"Hi Wesley." Katie flipped a handful of silky brown hair over her shoulder.

"Oh, hi, Katie," Wesley said, trying to sound nonchalant.

"Can I ask you a favor?"

"Sure." Wesley forgot he was in a really big hurry.

"Could you give me this week's assignment for Geometry?"

"Yeah, but I didn't know you were in Geometry." He didn't add that only about five geeky eighth graders were smart enough to be in that class.

"I'm not." She smiled. "I'm getting Michael's work for him. He's sick this week."

"That's nice of you." Wesley found another reason to admire Katie, besides the fact that she was really pretty. Michael didn't have many friends. He was a tiny kid who had been born with cerebral palsy. He walked with crutches and had only partial control of his movements. Michael's locker was on the other side of Katie's, and she was always going out of her way to talk to him and be nice to him. Wesley stuck up for Michael and tried to protect him from the beast Dylan, and that was part of the reason he was living in fear for his life right now.

Wesley was in the process of digging his math book out of his locker when an overgrown eighth grader who had been shaving for two years stormed up behind him. Shoot! How could he have allowed Katie to distract him long enough to let his guard down? He braced himself for a confrontation with the ogre. With reflexes he had developed from seven months of abuse, Wesley dodged the fist aimed at his shoulder.

Dylan MacLean cursed as his fist made contact with the cover of *Advanced Geometry*. "You're lucky I like you, Mackey," he said as he shook out his wounded hand, "or else I'd have to kill you."

Words escaped Wesley, so Katie spoke for him. "You're lucky they don't put you in juvenile hall, Dylan."

"Wouldn't bother me." Dylan sneered. "Anything's better than hanging around the weirdos in this joint. At least my mom and dad aren't brother and sister. Did you know that Wesley's mom is his aunt, and his dad is his uncle? Really freaks me out," he said as he shuddered. "And while we're on the subject of freaks— where's the gimp today?"

Wesley straightened up and started to say something, but Katie beat him to the defense. "I'd choose a *physical* disability like Michael's over a *mental* disability like yours any day!" She huffed and stormed off, leaving Wesley alone with the executioner, who was temporarily silenced by the stinging rebuke. Wesley guessed he was probably trying to figure out whether a mental disability was an insult or a compliment.

Dylan twisted the dial on his locker, forcing it, like he forced everyone around him, into submission. "Hey Mackey, your dad out of prison yet?"

"He was never in prison," Wesley defended coolly, picking up the scattered papers Dylan had left in his wake.

"Oh yeah, that's right—he beat the murder rap. I forgot."

Wesley sighed. This conversation was getting old, and his folders had picked a bad time to start falling out of his locker.

Dylan wasn't going to let it go. "I guess when you're rich and famous you don't go to jail."

"When you're innocent you don't either," Wesley retorted as his American History book tumbled out and hit him in the chest.

"Need some help there, Stalker Boy?" The nickname Wesley detested had evolved from "Son of the Snake Stalker," to "Snake Stalker Boy," and then to just "Stalker Boy."

"No," Wesley answered evenly.

"No . . . what?" Dylan demanded as he slapped Wesley in the back of the head.

Wesley blew out his breath. He focused on a piece of peeling gray paint at the edge of his locker. He knew exactly what Dylan wanted. Dylan wanted him to say, "No, thank you, sir," like he'd always done. Normally he would have complied, but for some reason, he just couldn't do it today. He was tired of Dylan MacLean keeping him away from his locker like some rabid pit bull, smacking him whenever he felt like it, and controlling his every action. He was tired of Dylan bullying Michael, tired of him insulting his dad and mom, and especially tired of being called "Stalker Boy." He slowly pulled his locker door so that it made a partition between himself and Dylan. He would ignore the Beast until it went away.

"I can't hear you . . ." Dylan said in a lilting tone.

"Leave me alone." Wesley couldn't believe what he just said.

"What did you just say?" Dylan asked.

It was too late to take it back. Wesley had to move forward. He gave no outward indication that the mechanism inside his brain that held onto rational thought had suddenly become disconnected. That's why Dylan was completely unprepared for what happened next. Everyone at school, including some of the teachers, cowered to Dylan MacLean. They would never have conceived that studious and mild-mannered Wesley would do something so rash. That's why it worked.

In a split second, Wesley jammed the side of his fist against the inside of his locker door and slammed it directly into Dylan's unsuspecting face. Wesley heard what sounded like a piece of celery snapping in half. The crunching noise seemed to awaken him to the dreadful realization of what he'd just done. The only thing he could think of was to run. Like a thief with stolen goods, he abandoned his books and binder. Copious amounts of adrenaline flowed into his body, and he felt strong, almost exhilarated. He had avenged Michael, Maggie, his father, and himself. He'd been pushed to the limit, and he'd fought back. For the rest of his life, he would remember this day as Dylan D-Day.

Or perhaps as something else.

* * *

Principal Crutchfield sat on the edge of her swivel chair and took her glasses from the chain around her neck, placing them on the bridge of her nose.

"I need to tell you, Mr. and Mrs. Mackey, that in the state of Georgia we have a zero-tolerance policy for any type of violent behavior. Mandatory suspension is the only option. And this will go on his permanent record." She gave Wesley a look that expressed profound disappointment. "And unfortunately, at this time, suspension is the least of your troubles."

Jack Mackey, whose attitude betrayed that he had had some of his own experience in the principal's office as a youth, wasn't getting anywhere with his Aussie charm. "I'm sure we can work this all out. After all, Wes has never caused any trouble before this. Seems to me this other kid had it comin' for some time now."

"Mr. Mackey, believe it or not, I happen to be on your side. No one has to convince me that Dylan MacLean is a bully. I'm not at privilege to discuss his history, but let's just say that Dylan is what we call 'at risk.'"

"At risk of what?" Jack shot back. "Killing other students?"

Jack's wife, Maggie, nudged his knee, amicably trying to act as a buffer between Jack and the principal.

Principal Crutchfield was unruffled. "Your son is the one who broke Dylan's nose—not the other way around."

"I know, and we certainly don't condone his behavior. But this is so unlike Wesley," Maggie said, jumping to his defense. "He's never been violent. You know he must have been provoked."

"I'm not saying that he wasn't," the principal said sternly. "But the fact remains that Wesley should have reported this provocation to the proper authorities—not dealt with it by resorting to violence. We have assemblies where we educate the students on how to handle these types of threats. Wesley should have asked for a new locker assignment. He could have requested mediation with Dylan and another member of the faculty."

Maggie bored into Wesley, who was picking at his fingernails. "Why didn't you tell someone about this sooner, Wesley?"

Wesley didn't have an answer.

The principal continued. "On top of the suspension, I'm sure the school and possibly your family will have to deal with a lawsuit."

Jack sighed. "Isn't there something we can do to avoid that? I'll call Dylan's dad and offer to cover all the medical expenses . . ."

Ms. Crutchfield removed her glasses and proceeded with her lecture. "Mr. Mackey, Dylan MacLean has no father. His mother has lost custody of him, and the last I heard . . . well, let's just say I would be very surprised indeed if his guardian would be satisfied with only a simple offer to cover his medical expenses."

Wesley slid lower in his chair and tried to breathe as quietly as possible. The calendar on the principal's desk said March 30. Dylan D-Day wasn't turning out to be so great after all. Wesley was acutely aware of the air molecules bouncing around inside his ears.

"So what do you suggest we do?" Maggie asked.

"I don't know what you can do to avoid a personal lawsuit," Principal Crutchfied answered, "but I suggest you take the six-week suspension, get Wesley a tutor, and maybe we can pull some strings to get him back into the school system next fall."

"Next fall?" Jack leaned forward accusingly. "You mean, he's out for the rest of the year?"

The principal picked up a paper clip and started to straighten it. "Believe me, I would like to make an exception for Wesley. He's a bright student, the teachers adore him, and up until now has never given us any trouble. But the school board will enforce its zero-tolerance policy."

The reality of Wesley's situation suddenly sank in. Permanent suspension. He was over and out. After eight months at Greenwood, he finally felt like he fit in somewhere. He actually had some real friends besides Amanda. How could he blow it all in one stupid, reckless maneuver? What was he thinking? His dad and Maggie were taking it extremely well—after all, they hadn't even gotten his side of the story yet, and they were still trying to give him the benefit of the doubt. Lost in his thoughts, he drifted out of the conversation and didn't realize they had wrapped things up until he heard chairs scuffling and the principal saying, "We'll decide that later."

The car ride home was painful. Somehow describing Dylan MacLean in mere words couldn't convey the true nature of the Beast. Wesley definitely needed a thesaurus to plead his defense. By the time he had rehearsed the story to his parents, he thought if they grounded him for life, he would be getting off easy.

* * *

That evening the extended family gathered in the Mackey living room to discuss the course of action. As usual, everyone had a different take on Wesley's strange behavior. Maggie was disappointed that he hadn't told anyone about Dylan earlier and found his actions appalling. His father was somewhat more understanding, and Wesley sensed he was possibly even proud that his son had taken down the biggest kid in school. His grandparents, who lived next door on an expansive horse ranch, had come over to weigh in on the affair. Grandma Penny could always be counted on to be stern but sympathetic, and Grandpa Walter usually kept quiet.

"I think tomorrow we need to go to Dylan's home and offer him an apology," Maggie suggested, "and try to persuade his guardian not to file a lawsuit."

"What, so they can use our confession as evidence in their lawsuit?" Jack retorted. "You can't just talk to these kind of people!"

"You don't know that!" Maggie argued. "Maybe all they need is for someone to take responsibility—to try and make amends."

"That's true," Penny jumped in. "The best way to get rid of an enemy is to make him your ally."

"You're both crazy!" Jack bellowed. "This is the real world we're dealin' with here. Tell them, Walter."

"Yeah, whose side are you on anyway, Walter?" Penny asked. "You haven't said a word."

Walter leaned forward and cleared his throat. "If you want to know my opinion . . ."

Everyone quieted down to hear Walter weigh in on the issue. "Well, all I have to say is I didn't get to be sixty-one years old by having an opinion."

The discussion was interrupted by the earsplitting sound of a bawling baby.

"Jack," Maggie said, "will you go get C.J.?"

"How do you know it isn't Emily?" Jack asked.

"Can't you tell their cries apart?" Penny questioned, as if he were somehow an unfit parent.

"Okay, so I'm a terrible father!" Jack threw up his hands. "My son beats up kids at school, and I can't tell my six-month-old twins apart when one of them cries from another room." He stood up to leave.

"They're *seven* months old," corrected Maggie.

"I'll get her," Wesley volunteered, looking for any excuse to leave the room full of discordant adults. Before anyone could reject his offer, he hurried down the hallway into the babies' room, which would have been dark if it weren't for the night-light the size of a computer screen.

Just as Maggie had predicted, C.J. was standing up in her crib, bellowing at the top of her lungs. Emily was awake too, lying quietly in her crib while trying to put her foot into her mouth. Wesley would rather have picked up Emily, because she would put her arms around his neck and snuggle with him, but C.J. was the one who needed him. He reached into the crib to grab her, and, as usual, she pushed him away.

"What is it this time, Carly Jane?" Wesley asked. C.J. was named after his grandfather in Australia, Carlson James Mackey. He was Wesley's hero after he saved their lives when they were caught in an ocean storm. Grandpa C.J. was pretty tough until you got to know him. So Wesley hoped little C.J. might take after him and soften up with time. She had a boisterous temperament and tried the patience of everyone in the family. She was the vocal child, the one who constantly demanded food and attention and sucked up any of her parents' precious spare time. With her wisps of blonde hair and her blue eyes, she supposedly resembled Wesley as a baby, but he couldn't see it.

Wesley bounced C.J. roughly on his shoulder as he admired her twin. Now Emily was a beautiful child. Emily had dark hair, long lashes, and large hazel eyes she adored her big brother with. She was usually quiet, and Wesley was certain that it was because she was thinking deep thoughts. He knew it wasn't right to have a favorite, but somehow he already felt a connection to Emily.

He picked up a nearby pacifier and shoved it in C.J.'s mouth. She spit it out.

"You think you have problems?" He patted her back. "You have no idea what *real* problems are!" Wesley tried to stamp out his jealous thoughts. His sisters would never appreciate how lucky they were to grow up with their real parents, not some lady who pretended to be their mother so she could gain control of a business empire. He had missed out on eleven years of being in the best family in the world. Every once in awhile he felt slighted. But then again, there were definite advantages to not being the only child, especially at a time like this, when he had just done something very stupid.

After C.J. fell asleep on his shoulder, Wesley carefully deposited her back in her crib. He gave Emily a kiss and plodded back down the hallway to the family room, but he stopped short when he saw who had entered the house.

Sitting on his living room couch with an unfamiliar man and woman were Katie MacKenzie and Michael from Geometry.

Before he could figure out why they might be there, the unknown man stood up and reached his hand out to Wesley. "You must be Wesley. We're Katie and Michael's parents."

Wesley hoped he muttered an appropriate greeting, because he had just gotten slammed with two pieces of stunning information. First of all, Katie MacKenzie was in his house. Second, Michael was her *brother*. And not just her brother—they would have to be twins. Michael sat next to him in math, and even though Wesley considered him a friend, he had never known what his last name was. Until now.

"The MacKenzies heard about what happened today and have come here to offer us their support," Maggie explained.

"This Dylan MacLean has been a thorn in our sides, too," said Mr. MacKenzie. "We really appreciate all the times you've stuck up for Michael. Frankly, we applaud you for doing what the administration wouldn't."

Wesley smiled. This was a positive turn of events. Maybe he wasn't going to be in so much trouble after all.

Katie piped in. "I'm sorry I wasn't there to see it. It seems to me that Dylan should be the one getting suspended."

Thanks for the backup, Wesley thought.

"Unfortunately, that's not how things work," Mr. MacKenzie added. "You know, his father abandoned him, and his mother has some pretty serious issues. His aunt has custody of him—Janine or Joann Dunford is her name, I think."

Penny perked up. "You mean *Jonelle* Dunford?" She pronounced the name "John-L."

"That's it. Do you know her?"

Penny nodded at Walter. "We certainly do. Beautiful girl—but a rebel through and through. She used to come to the ranch when she was a youngster. Turned her mother's hair prematurely grey when she ran off with the wrong guy."

"Yes, I think she's had some trials, and taking on Dylan is one of them," said Mrs. MacKenzie. "We've already looked into having him transferred, but evidently he's on his last school. The next transfer would be to a juvenile detention center."

"So send him over," Jack said disdainfully. "No use kickin' out the good kids to save the bad ones."

"That's exactly the point we made," Mrs. MacKenzie said, "but the school can't ignore the rules for Wesley, so it looks like the bad kid stays."

"In any event, we'd just like to help you any way we can," offered Mr. MacKenzie. "I'm sorry for Dylan's situation, but I need to look out for my own kids first. It's getting late, so we won't keep you any longer."

"We appreciate you coming," Maggie said as she and Jack stood up to usher them out.

Jack closed the door after they had left and shook his head wistfully. "Ah, the poor girl," was all he said.

"What? Who?" asked Maggie.

"Katie. I can tell she's obviously smitten with you, Wes."

"She was pretty, too," Penny said enthusiastically. "Don't you think so, Wesley?"

Wesley shrugged and felt his face grow hot.

"Yes, she's very cute." Maggie gave them both a penetrating stare. "But what does that have to do with anything? Starting tomorrow, Wesley is suspended. Dylan MacLean's family may sue the school or us or both. The school board can't help us, so what are we going to do about it?"

"If anyone cares what I think," Penny rattled Walter's arm, "I'd like to propose a solution. Walter, wake up!"

"Let's hear it, Mum," said Jack.

2

Befriending the Enemy

Wesley knew he had always led a charmed life when it came to material things, which is why he was disturbed by the sight of the ramshackle houses they were driving past. He was alone in the car with Grandma Penny, and he wanted to ask if they were in the ghetto but then decided he'd better keep quiet. He didn't like the whole idea of coming here in the first place, and his dad liked it even less. Grandma Penny had convinced them this was the best thing to do, and, for some reason, everyone always deferred to Grandma Penny.

"It's a shame what choices Jonelle made," Penny said, more to herself than to Wesley, as she parked on the street in front of a dilapidated old house. The front yard looked like someone was holding a convention for old couches and car parts.

"Are you sure this is safe, Grandma?"

"Sure it is. Jonelle is a friend of mine. Her mother and I go way back. Y'all just let me do the talking and everything will be fine. What do we have to lose?"

Our lives, thought Wesley.

Penny made sure to lock the doors, and Wesley followed her reluctantly up the broken cement stairs, dodging a roller skate and a headless doll. Penny knocked soundly on the door after seeing that the doorbell hung loosely at the end of several frayed wires.

A small toddler with a dirty face and wearing nothing but a soggy diaper opened the door. Stale air from inside the house wafted out, soaking them in a smell that reminded Wesley of a hamster cage.

Penny forced a smile. "Hi there. What's your name?"

The toddler eyed them both suspiciously.

"Could you tell your mommy someone's here?"

An overweight woman with greasy hair ambled to the door. "Get away from the door, Jasmine!" she bellowed. "Hey, can't you read the sign?" She motioned to a plaque that was as decayed as the exterior of the house. "No soliciting."

"We aren't solicitors, Jonelle. It's Penny Scott. Remember when y'all used to come to the ranch and ride horses when you were smaller?"

"What the—? Well I ain't seen those days for awhile." Jonelle patted her stomach.

Penny realized "smaller" wasn't exactly the right word. "What I meant was—"

"Sure I remember. That was the best time I ever had, at the Scott Ranch." She looked as though she might invite them in, but Wesley sincerely hoped that she wouldn't.

"So, what brings you over to the wrong side of the tracks, Penny Scott?"

"I heard y'all look after your sister's boy, Dylan MacLean."

Jonelle hesitated as if she didn't want to admit it. "I do. When he's here, that is. What's he done now?"

Penny pushed Wesley forward. "This is my grandson, Wesley Mackey. He'd like to tell you something."

"I would?" Wesley looked at his grandmother for a hint.

Penny nudged him.

"Oh. I want to say I'm very sorry, ma'am, about what happened yesterday." He hoped that was what Penny wanted him to say.

With her mouth agape, Jonelle stepped back, took a long look at Wesley, then burst into laughter.

"You mean to tell me that it was *you* who busted Dylan's face?" She paused again to cackle. "Well if that don't beat all . . . It's about time somebody let him have it. I know he probably deserved it. Just didn't expect it would be someone like you is all."

Wesley didn't know if he should be insulted or relieved by that remark.

"Jonelle," Penny ventured. "You know my daughter and her husband will pick up all the medical bills."

"Now that's right nice of them, Penny, but it doesn't do Dylan or me and my five babies much of a favor, really."

It sounded like a threat, and it wasn't missed by Penny. She was silent for a moment, and Wesley wondered what his grandmother's course of action would be.

"I agree with you, Jonelle, and that's why we're here. I'd like to make you an offer."

Of all the responses Wesley thought Grandma Penny would come up with, this wasn't one of them.

"You would?" Jonelle was suddenly interested.

"Yes, I would. Y'all know that Dylan is a juvenile delinquent. What he needs more than anything is some parental guidance and structure in his life. Without it, he'll end up in jail or some rehab center or worse. I'm offering to have him come and stay at the ranch for a few months—free room and board. He'll have to help out in the stables, but we'll make sure he has plenty of time for school and homework."

Wesley felt faint. Was Grandma nuts? Did she have any idea that she'd just pronounced his death sentence? She was obviously under the misguided impression that Dylan was a kid who just needed a pat on the back to build his self-esteem. Someone needed to set her straight.

Jonelle was already aligning her. "Penny, you dear woman, I'm sure your offer is sincere, but have you ever *seen* Dylan?"

"In the yearbook. He's a very handsome young man."

"Well let me clue you in. He's about six feet tall, built like a refrigerator, smokes like a chimney, and can pick up your grandson here with one hand. I'd love to have you take him off my hands, but I'm afraid he'd rob you blind then disappear for good."

Penny didn't appear shaken. "So if we accept the liability, you'll agree?"

Two more grubby kids under five came screaming into the entryway, the girl crying, and her brother smacking her with a flyswatter. The way Wesley saw it, the distraction could not have come at a better time.

"I don't know." Jonelle grabbed the flyswatter and tapped the boy on the bottom with it. "I'll think about it." She gave them an annoyed look and closed the door.

Penny marched down the front steps and unlocked the car. "Well, that went better than I expected." There was no hint of sarcasm in her voice.

Wesley leaned against the car window, his head still spinning. His only hope was that his dad would veto Grandma Penny's offer before it went any further. He silently climbed inside the car.

"I know you don't really understand all this, Wesley, but sometimes folks seem bad because they've had a lot of hard knocks in life. I've seen it time and time again."

Wesley just nodded. He didn't trust himself to say anything just yet.

"That's why Dylan hates you, don't you see? Look at that environment where he lives—no mother or father. His aunt can't look after herself, let alone him and five squalling kids. Think of how depressing that would be. You have everything he wishes he had. He can't pull himself up, so he tries to pull you down."

"So you mean he insults me and my family because he's jealous?"

"Exactly. I know that doesn't excuse his behavior, but it does explain it."

Wesley had to admit the psychology sounded right on, but it still didn't mean that Dylan could be rehabilitated. Grandma Penny may be kind and wise, but she totally lacked common sense.

The Navy SEAL

Wesley's history teacher had told her to be prepared for a tutor, but Maggie was still caught off guard when she answered the door. The man standing at the door looked more like a caricature than a real person.

"Hello, um, I'm Harrison Landry," the man said in a timid voice.

Maggie composed herself and put out her hand. "It's nice to meet you, Harrison. You're Wesley's tutor, right?"

"Yes, that would be me." Harrison looked at Maggie's hand as if he wasn't sure exactly what was expected of him. He gave it a weak shake and then pushed his thick-framed glasses toward his face. There was an awkward silence as he thrust his hands into his pockets and waited for Maggie to invite him in.

"Oh. Please come in while I get Wesley."

Harrison carefully stepped inside while Maggie made an unobtrusive observation of the man who would be spending six hours a day with Wesley for the next six weeks. He was wearing high-water polyester pants in old-man plaid, with a white-collared shirt tucked into a belt that was secured a few inches below his ribcage. His mousy brown hair was combed forward, and his stringy bangs fringed eyes that were shrouded in black-framed Coke-bottle glasses. He appeared to be in his thirties and was strapped into a red backpack that showed the outline of at least ten monster-sized books and had enough zippered pockets to harbor every calculating device ever invented.

Maggie called Wesley, and when she saw Jack come in with him, she discreetly pulled her husband aside and whispered a quick warning to him. "Do not comment!"

"Honestly, Mag, you think I don't have manners?"

Harrison appeared even more nervous when he confronted Jack. Jack thrust out his hand cordially. "Jack Mackey. Nice to meet you, mate."

"Harrison Landry. The pleasure is all mine, *mate*." He smiled as if he'd just said something extremely clever, and drew his hand out of his pocket to shake hands. The action pulled the lining out so that he had one droopy rabbit ear hanging out of his pants. He blanched when he noticed it and quickly stuffed it back in.

Wesley also exchanged greetings and appeared unfazed by Harrison's appearance.

"So Harrison." Jack suppressed a smile. "Do you go by Harry?"

"No. Actually, I prefer Harrison."

"Right," said Jack. "Well, have a seat, mate. Can we get you a soda? Some lemonade?"

"No, thank you. I try to stay away from carbonation, caffeine, and sugar. Carbonation decreases the oxygenation of your blood."

"Really." Jack nodded. "What does that leave?"

"Water, milk, and carrot juice."

"You drink carrot juice?" Wesley made a face.

"Yes, I try to drink it every day. It's very rich in beta-carotene."

Jack turned his head. "That explains the orange pallor," he mumbled to Maggie.

"I'm afraid we aren't all that health-conscious around here," Maggie said apologetically. "How about milk or ice water?"

"No, thank you. I'm fine."

"So is it true that you're a Navy SEAL?" Wesley questioned.

"Yes, I am. But right now I'm not on active duty."

"How come?"

Harrison suddenly looked down and rubbed the palms of his hands on his trousers and then pushed on his glasses, looking generally uncomfortable.

Maggie jumped in to save the awkward moment. "Harrison—we've heard you're multilingual. How many languages do you speak?"

Harrison answered eagerly. "Six. Spanish, Portugese, French, German, Japanese, and Arabic." He counted them out on his fingers. "I guess seven if you count semaphore."

"And eight if you count English," Wesley added. "I've never heard of semaphore. What country is it from?"

"Semaphore is actually one of the first visual signaling systems invented for the Navy. You use arm motions and flags to signal ships at short range. It's a bit antiquated, but it's still useful."

"Cool. Can you teach it to me?" Wesley asked.

"Sure." Harrison brightened. "If you want to learn it."

Jack and Maggie exchanged a befuddled look.

"Are you fluent in all seven of those languages?" Wesley seemed intrigued with his new tutor.

"Yes."

"Wow. How did you learn them all?"

Harrison shrugged and pushed on his glasses again. "My dad is in the military, and we moved around to a lot of different countries when I was young. It was pretty easy for me to pick up languages. Then when I was in the Naval Academy, I studied languages before becoming a CTI."

"What's a CTI?" Wesley asked.

"That's a Cryptologic Technician Interpretive—or a code breaker."

"Cool." Wesley was visibly impressed.

"Well, Wes, it looks like we finally found someone who's smarter than you," Jack said. I don't know about you, Mag, but this conversation is already over my head. We'll let these two start workin' on world peace or the next space launch." He tugged Maggie's arm and pulled her down the hall into the nursery, where the babies were crawling around and watching Barney videos.

"Okay," Jack said, "run this by me again. "Who recommended Poindexter?"

"One of Wesley's teachers. Why? You don't like him already?"

"I didn't say I didn't *like* him. It's just that he's a total weirdo."

"So? I don't see why that's a problem."

"The problem is he looks like he's hiding somethin'."

"Like what?"

"I don't know. Calculators, microchips, hydrogen bombs. How do we know he's not a sociopath?"

"Because we did a thorough background check on him. Just because he lacks fashion sense and social skills doesn't make him a sociopath. The man is obviously brilliant, and Wesley seems to like him. And on top of that, he's very disciplined. He has a black belt in karate."

"Yeah, right," Jack huffed sarcastically. "This guy couldn't knock over a traffic cone."

"Looks can be deceiving," Maggie scolded. "If you didn't know I had a black belt, you'd never guess that I could take you down."

"So now you think *you* can take me down?"

"Of course I can."

"I really doubt it," Jack challenged. "Go ahead. Give it a try."

"I don't want to."

"I don't think you can."

"You know I can. Just not in front of the girls. It might upset them."

"I don't see how that would be any more distressing than a giant purple dinosaur dancin' around."

"Could we resolve this issue later? We were discussing Wesley's tutor."

"Scary Harry."

"That's *your* opinion. I think we're lucky to have found him on such short notice. You just need to get over your prejudice."

"That's not prejudice you're pickin' up—it's a warning system." Jack booted a stuffed animal out of his way. "Okay, if you have a good feeling about him, and Wes has a good feeling too, we'll try him out for a few days. But if he gets any weirder, we nix the whole tutor idea, and Wes comes with me to California next week."

"Where he'll be so much safer hunting rattlesnakes with you." Maggie folded her arms and nodded her head.

"Right."

"Harrison Landry will be fine." Maggie put both hands on Jack's shoulders. "Oh, and one more thing I forgot to mention; he can help Wesley with his merit badges. He's also an Eagle Scout."

Jack sighed. "Why does that not surprise me?"

4

The Parachute Story

Maria Perry ended her conversation quickly and hung up the phone before her daughter, Amanda, had a chance to catch the conversation and start a new interrogation about why she had turned down another date. Amanda was constantly hounding her to go out more often. It was obvious she wanted what Wesley had—two parents. Maria couldn't blame her. It wasn't easy being a permanent resident of the guesthouse on the Scott Ranch. The Mackeys seemed to have everything, and lately Maria felt like she should be trying harder to find someone to marry.

But it just wasn't that easy. For the second time this week, she'd made a lame excuse not to go out with some "delightful" man that some well-meaning member of her church had tried to set her up with. "Now, Maria," they would say, "just because he's been divorced three times doesn't mean he's not a really sweet guy." Or "So he's a little older. That just makes him wiser, right?"

No, it just means he's got more issues to deal with. She really couldn't afford to be picky, after all, since she had some baggage of her own. An arrest record for one thing. The Mackeys had been kind enough to forgive her for her part in covering up Wesley's kidnapping for all those years. They were allowing her to move on, so why was she having such a hard time allowing herself to move on?

Then there was the problem that she wouldn't marry outside her faith. And she didn't want to uproot Amanda and move someplace else, so maybe she'd just be grateful with the way things were. Marrying the wrong person was far worse than being unmarried.

Maria heard the door slam and the sound of a backpack thudding on the floor.

"Mom!" Amanda called from the entryway.

"You don't have to yell. The house isn't that big," Maria reminded her, admiring what a beautiful teenager Amanda was turning into.

"Sorry. We're supposed to go over to Wesley's for this big show he's doing with Harrison right now."

"That's not until after dinner."

"They changed it because they want Jack to see it before he leaves tonight."

"I guess Wesley isn't going with him to California then?"

"No, he doesn't even want to."

"Really?" Maria tried not to sound too surprised. "That's a new one. Don't let Jack know."

"I won't. Jack thinks Harrison is a freak."

Without thinking, Maria blurted out, "And what do *you* think of Harrison?"

"I think he's definitely a weirdo, but after you get used to him, he's awesome."

"An awesome weirdo?"

"Yeah, I mean he's a total nerd, but he's really smart and funny—even though he doesn't know we're laughing at him, not his jokes." Amanda looked at her mother suspiciously. "But it's not like you should date him or anything—even though he is a Mormon."

"He is?" This was a completely new piece of information to Maria.

"You didn't know that?"

"No, I'm not up on all the latest gossip."

"Yeah, he's really cool. And he's got tons of really amazing stories—you really should talk to him. We've got to get over there, or we'll miss the show."

"No, we wouldn't want to miss the show."

* * *

Once again the majority of the furniture in the Mackey family room had been shoved into the corner to make room for one of Wesley's magic shows. A large footlocker borrowed from his grandparents' house filled the center of the room. The audience consisted of Maria, Amanda, Wesley's parents, and his grandparents.

"Attention ladies and gentlemen." Wesley rapped his magician's wand on the table in front of him. "The great Weslini, with his trusty assistant Harry Landini, will attempt to stupefy the audience with his latest escape. First, Mr. Landini will tie my hands and feet securely with this rope." He stretched the rope out for visual effect. "He will then lock me inside this trunk, which, by the way, has very little oxygen, and I will attempt to set myself free. If by chance I am unsuccessful, I bequeath all my possessions to my sister Emily."

Everyone laughed except Penny, who gasped. "Good heavens! Next time you ask to borrow something

I'll need to ask a few more questions. I don't think that's a very smart thing to do, Wesley."

"Sure it is!" Walter adjusted his couch pillow. He couldn't have been more excited if he had fifty-yard-line seats at the Super Bowl.

Wesley stepped inside the trunk, and Harrison quickly tightened the ropes around Wesley's wrists and ankles.

"How do we know those aren't fake knots?" Jack challenged.

Wesley seemed to be waiting for someone to ask this. "Dad, please come up and check the knots for yourself."

Jack hopped up and dutifully pulled on the ends of the ropes to make sure they were fastened securely. "Okay, those are real knots."

Harrison helped Wesley sit down inside the trunk. He closed the lid and locked it, showing the key.

Penny gasped. "Is there enough air in there?"

"That's part of the suspense." Walter rubbed his palms together. "This is a really good trick."

Penny didn't have too much time to get worked up, because in less than fifty seconds the lid of the trunk jiggled and Wesley stepped out, his hair tousled and a huge grin on his face. The audience rewarded him with cheers and applause. Even Harrison appeared pleased, although he didn't reveal much with his facial expression.

"Wes, you gotta let us in on how you did it," Walter begged.

"Magicians never give away their secrets," Maggie lectured.

"Sometimes they do," Wesley teased. "And actually, if it's okay with Mr. Landini, I'll tell you this one after I show you my mind-reading trick."

When the audience calmed down, Wesley instructed Walter to write down a word on a piece of paper when Wesley left the room.

"Don't say it out loud, so there's no chance I can hear you," Wesley ordered. "Just make it a person, place, or thing." He opened the front door and went outside. "Come and get me when you're ready!" he yelled before closing the door behind him.

Walter, who was acting like the biggest kid, decided to try to make it really hard, so he wrote, "Neptune." He crumpled the paper in his pocket and hollered for Wesley to return.

Wesley came in and studied the faces of every person in the room. He paced the floor and melodramatically stroked his chin. "I'm getting vibes that it's something big."

Walter tried not to show anything on his face.

"Of planetary magnitude, I believe." Wesley nodded his head. "What you don't know is that I'm reading the clues from all of your faces. He stopped at Walter. "Neptune."

Walter pulled the paper out of his pocket and waved it around. "You've got the skills, Wes. I have no idea how you did that. Do you know how he did that, Harrison?"

Harrison pushed uncomfortably on his glasses. "Maybe."

"So you can do it too?" Maggie asked.

"I suppose," Harrison answered.

"Let's see it!" Jack and others joined in. They sent him out of the room and tried to think of something to trip him up. Walter suggested "salmonella," but someone else wrote down "Tasmanian devil" first.

When Harrison came back into the room, he studied their faces and paced around the room for several minutes. "This may take some time, because it's rather long. But I do believe *Tasmanian devil* is the correct answer."

"I have to admit that's amazing," Jack conceded. "Can you do the trunk escape too?"

"Yeah, he sort of gave me the idea for that one," Wesley admitted. "It all started when Harrison was teaching me some knots for my scout merit badge." He looked at Harrison. "Can I tell them this?"

"If you like," Harrison answered. "It's your illusion."

"Okay, so I'm learning these knots—one of them is called the bowline."

"I can tie that!" Walter raised his hand.

"That's great, Grandpa, but wait a minute. Before I explain all that, you need to hear Harrison's parachute story."

Harrison once again looked uncomfortable but didn't refuse. "Did you want to tell it, or do you want me to tell it?"

"You can tell it better." Wesley nodded.

Harrison cleared his throat. He was obviously unaccustomed to speaking before an audience. The room became very quiet. "As you probably know, I'm a Navy SEAL." He looked around, as though this information might be new to some. It wasn't. "Sometimes we're called up for special operations. Several years ago I got called to do a special reconnaissance operation in an undisclosed location in Europe. They asked me because of my CTI training," he added for credibility. "But we suspected there might be a traitor in our SEAL platoon."

"You're CIA?" Walter asked.

"Something like that," Harrison said, sidestepping a direct answer. "The rendezvous point required that we parachute into a mountainous region so we wouldn't be discovered."

"You jumped out of a plane?" Maria questioned.

Harrison seemed delighted that Maria was interested in his story. "Yes, that's pretty standard procedure for someone in this line of work." Whether he had tried to add a little more animation to his voice or whether it had just come out naturally wasn't clear. "So I strapped my parachute on, like I usually do, but something didn't feel right, and I didn't know what it was."

Harrison paused and took a sip of water. "My partner and I tried to jump as close together as possible, so we wouldn't end up too far away on the ground. Everything was going well at first. We were free-falling when my partner moved in next to me and yelled, 'Sorry, Landry. This is your last mission!' I pulled the rip cord, and my parachute inflated and then separated from me. I realized what the funny feeling I'd had was. My partner was a double agent working for the enemy, and he had rigged my parachute so that it would disconnect when I pulled the rip cord."

"You mean you jumped out of a plane without a parachute and lived?" Penny was in disbelief.

"Obviously I lived." Harrison seemed to be more and more at ease with all the attention he was getting. "But I didn't say I didn't have a parachute. I said I had experienced a funny feeling."

Maria's eyes got wider, and she listened even more intently.

"Before I left, something had told me I should grab an extra parachute. So I did. But it was smaller, and I had it strapped on underneath my coat. So I had to take off my coat first and make a few adjustments before I could release my second parachute. Meanwhile, the ground kept getting closer. I managed to open it just before I hit a forested area. I didn't have much time to slow down. Lucky for me, I ended up strung up in a tree. If I had hit the ground at that speed, I would have broken both legs."

"Which is still better than dead," Walter piped in.

"Yes, I would agree. As it was, I still broke my arm and was pretty scratched up from the trees."

"What happened to the other guy? Did you complete the mission?" Amanda asked.

"Well, I could tell you, but then I'd have to kill you." Harrison laughed at his own joke, but it fell flat. He pushed on his glasses. "All of that is still classified information. That's why I didn't mention any names or places."

"That's quite a story, Harrison," Jack said with skepticism.

"I thought it was so awesome when he told me," Wesley explained. "And when he was teaching me knots, I asked him why he hadn't checked his parachute to make sure it was tied correctly. But he said he had, and it was secure." Wesley picked up a rope and tied a knot around his waist. "See, this is the bowline. Pull on it."

Walter gave it a tug. "It's secure."

"No, it's not. Try again." Wesley offered him the other loose end.

Walter pulled it, and the entire knot unraveled in his hand.

"So that's what Harrison used to tie you up?" Maggie asked.

"Yes, but it was Wesley who made up the knot," Harrison explained.

"A regular bowline won't come undone. But this is like a bowline with a loop in it." Wesley demonstrated for everyone. "So I call it the bowline escape knot. But remember, I still had to get out of the trunk. That was actually a lot harder."

"Don't tell us—you made another one of your Houdini keys," Maggie guessed.

"Or it was magic," said Wesley.

"What I want to know is how you had any time at all to study this week," Maggie said.

"I can't do just schoolwork six hours a day!" Wesley protested.

"Actually, we find ways to incorporate scientific principles into everyday activities," Harrison said.

"And you're doing a wonderful job, Harrison. I hope you're comfortable staying here with us." Maggie referred to the summer cabin accommodations next door on her parents' side of the ranch.

"Yes, I'm very comfortable, thank you." Harrison took off his glasses and wiped them with the handkerchief he dug out of his shirt pocket.

"Hey, can I see those?" Wesley grabbed for the Coke-bottle lenses. "Are you nearsighted or farsighted?"

Harrison guardedly yanked his glasses away from Wesley's grasp, bending the side frame at an angle as he did so. "No!" He quickly plastered them to his face. "I mean, I'm very myopic and can't really see without them."

Jack scooted over to Maggie and asked, "Aren't Navy SEALs supposed to have 20/20 vision?"

Harrison heard him and said, "Yes, actually, they are." He looked embarrassed, and the original discomfort that the group had felt about him returned immediately. "I did have 20/20 vision when I passed the SEAL qualification training. Several years later, while I was on a combat mission, I was hit in the face with

35

some shrapnel." He pointed to a thin scar on his right cheek. "I've needed these glasses ever since."

Maggie stared Jack down to indicate that he'd been extremely rude to ask that question.

"I can relate to that, mate," Jack said, attempting to cover his insensitivity. "I had a little incident myself involving snake venom that affected my vision."

"Yes, and he's supposed to wear glasses, but he won't," Maggie added.

"They make my eyes sweat," Jack complained.

"Can't you get surgery to correct your vision?" Wesley asked Harrison.

"I probably should when I can find the time," Harrison said, and then he adeptly changed the subject.

* * *

Maggie watched as several pairs of rolled up socks came flying across the room and into the open suitcase on the bed.

"I don't understand why you can't trust him, Jack. It's not like he's given us any reason not to."

"Oh, like telling some wild, made-up story about jumping out of a plane with no parachute isn't a good reason?" Jack furrowed his brow and dumped a stack of folded shirts into the suitcase.

"It could be a true story. It might sound pretty far-fetched to some people that you were blinded by a spitting cobra, then got your sight back after getting thrown against a brick wall by two thugs."

Jack huffed a response.

"Oh, and don't forget the next day when we found your long-lost son on a yacht out in the middle of the ocean, got caught in a hurricane, which sunk our boat and left us stranded, only to be picked up by your father and brother who had a 'feeling' they should come over from Australia to help you out."

"Yeah, but that really happened."

"Says you. It sounds like a parachute story to me."

"So you believe him?"

"For the most part. He might have embellished a little."

Jack slammed his suitcase shut and zipped it. "I wish you were comin' with me, Mag."

"So I could get eaten by the rattlesnakes?"

"Rattlesnakes don't eat people."

"Thanks, I didn't know that," Maggie said with a touch of sarcasm as she gave her husband a kiss. "It's only for a few days."

"Yeah, nobody will miss me as long as Harrison's here to entertain them."

"That's it. You're jealous!"

"I am *not* jealous. I just don't see why everyone buys into this guy when it's obvious to me that he's a piece of fiction."

"He's very entertaining. You'd better hurry back before we forget all about you."

"I guess I'm not good enough anymore. Just because I don't speak semi-farse or whatever you call that language no one's ever heard of."

"I think that's *semaphore*."

"Whatever. We'd better go before I miss my plane."

5

Strange Encounters

Maria was not looking forward to having dinner alone with Harrison that evening. The Mackey family usually ate together, and Maria cooked for them twice a week. Harrison joined them about half the time; the other half he ate with Penny and Walter. Fast food didn't fit in with his health food regimen, so he tried to avoid eating out. Tonight, everyone seemed to have somewhere to go except Maria. Maggie had to drive Jack to the airport, Wesley and Amanda were at a church activity, and Penny and Walter were gone on some errand. That left Maria to stay home and tend the babies. Not that she minded, but she did dread having to make conversation with Harrison all by herself. Harrison seemed fine talking with Wesley and Amanda, but he was painfully shy around adults. If he did say something, it was usually a comment or a joke that he thought was funny, but that she didn't get. She hoped he would just eat quickly and go back to his cabin.

When Harrison arrived, he surprised her by helping her get the twins into their high chairs and by microwaving their strained vegetables and slicing a banana for them.

"Amanda tells me you're LDS," she tried as an opener.

"Yes."

Maria sighed. Why did people do that? Give you a one-word answer that always made you do all the work, leaving you with no new information to build on. She tried again. "So she probably told you that we are, too. Amanda and I."

"She did mention it." He pushed on his glasses.

Maria stuffed a heaping spoonful of baby food into C.J.'s mouth. This was going to be even harder than she thought. How did Wesley manage to communicate with him all day?

Harrison picked up the other jar and started feeding Emily. "Amanda tells me you're planning on becoming a teacher."

Wow—a whole sentence. Maria decided to run with it. "Yes, I'm taking some college classes. I hope to teach Spanish in high school. Everyone tells me I'm crazy—that it doesn't pay anything and that everyone hates their Spanish teacher."

Silence again. Harrison was coaxing food onto Emily's chin when Emily decided to throw her banana slices on the floor.

"I didn't hate my Spanish teacher," Harrison replied. He spoke to Emily in Spanish and told her to stop throwing bananas around like a monkey.

The sound of Harrison's voice speaking her native language startled Maria. She knew he was fluent in several languages, but until now he'd never uttered more than a few phrases in any language to her. She started speaking Spanish to C.J., telling her to quit spitting her food out onto her chin. It was a strange, eerily connecting moment.

Maria switched back into English. "Your accent is very good. How did you learn to speak so well? I've been trying to get rid of my accent for years, but nothing seems to work."

"Why would you want to do that?"

"I'm just self-conscious about it."

"Why? Jack has an accent. It doesn't bother him."

"That's because he's Jack Mackey. He gets away with it because it adds to his character."

Harrison seemed uncomfortable with what he was about to say. "So maybe your accent adds to your character, too."

"Somehow I don't think so."

"Maria, could I ask you a question?"

He sounded so serious. "I guess so," Maria answered. She was suddenly terrified that he might ask something too personal about her past. She didn't know what dark secrets Wesley or Amanda might have already told him.

"I was wondering if you could help me with my wardrobe."

"Your wardrobe?"

"I know this may sound really strange to someone who always dresses nicely, like yourself, but I just don't know how to put things together. Well, let's face it—I need some help."

The polite response would be to say that he didn't look that bad, but it wasn't the honest one, and Maria knew it had taken a lot of courage to ask for her help.

"Harrison, I would be happy to help you find a new look. But I hope this isn't because Amanda or Wesley said something to you."

"No, they have very good manners. This is all my idea. It's just time for me to make some changes—maybe fix my hairstyle, too."

"Is there some woman you are trying to impress?" Maria tried not to sound too nosy, but she was curious.

Harrison nudged his glasses. "No. I mean, yes. Well, maybe there could be."

This wasn't the answer Maria had expected. "Really? Tell me about her."

"You'll think I'm crazy."

"No I won't. Just tell me."

"Well, she's smart, and unfortunately for me, she's very beautiful. She's way out of my league. A woman like her would never go out with someone like me."

"You don't know that until you ask her."

"Yes I do. Women always like the tough guys, men in leather jackets who can talk smooth—pretty much the total opposite of me."

"Not all women. Some women are very attracted to kind, intelligent men."

Harrison smiled. Maria noticed for the first time that he had very nice teeth. "Maybe intelligent men with lots of money," he added.

"Well, I can't help you with the money part, but I can help you improve your style." Maria started to feel a little more comfortable talking with Harrison. "Maybe we could go to the mall tomorrow."

Harrison looked as though he might refuse her offer. "That's not necessary. I'm sure you have much more important things to do."

"I'll make time. Hey, maybe we can look at some new frames for your glasses too."

Harrison's hand flew up to his glasses like they were a security blanket. "Maybe we shouldn't make too many changes all at once. It might destroy my delicate equilibrium." He set the empty jar of baby food on the table. "Emily says she's finished and would like some dessert."

"Oh, is that what she said?"

"Yes, it was in Hungarian."

* * *

Jack was used to being accosted on the street by strange women he didn't know—it was all part of being a TV star, but he wasn't accustomed to getting phone calls on his private cell phone from people who had very disturbing information. When he'd gotten off the plane in San Francisco, he'd checked his messages, and one immediately caught his attention. He played it again.

"Hello, Jack. You don't know me, but my name is Whitney. I have some very important information concerning Wesley and the safety of your family. Imogene Vandergrift may be alive. Call me back at this number as soon as you can. I'll be waiting."

It was late, and he already had jet lag from the three-hour time change. He needed to get an early start in the morning and wasn't in the mood for some prankster. The woman sounded young, and she might have found some way to get his phone number off the Internet. Should he blow this off and not respond? He quickly called the number before he could analyze it too much. He remembered when Penny had called him to tell him Wesley was alive, and Steve, his cameraman, had thought she was a deranged fan too.

The phone rang only once before the same sultry voice came on the line. "Jack Mackey? I knew you'd call me back. You feel it, don't you?"

"I can't say that I'm feelin' a whole lot except curiosity about how you got my cell number."

"I just love your accent. I could listen to you talk all night."

"Well, this conversation is going to end now."

"Suit yourself. You'll just call me back because you have questions, and I have answers. Don't you wonder what happened to her that day on the ocean?"

"What are you talking about?"

"I told you in the message."

"It's a federal crime to harass people like this, you know."

"It's also a federal crime to pretend to be dead and live under a false name in another country."

"And I should trust you because . . ."

"I happen to be very close to the source. Have you ever heard the name Genevieve Devereaux?"

Jack felt a stab in the pit of his stomach. He had no problem remembering the name. Wesley had been receiving fan letters and gifts from Mrs. Devereaux, who lived in Zurich, for more than a year, but he had recently commented that he hadn't heard from her in several months.

"If Imogene is alive, then why haven't you taken this information to the police?"

"I have some very good reasons, but I can't discuss them over the phone. As luck would have it, I just so happen to live near San Francisco, and that's where you are right now. Meet me on Pier 41 tomorrow at nine. By the sea lion statue at the ferryboats."

"I can't. I have a shooting scheduled—"

"Tell them you'll be late. Trust me, this will be far more important to you." She hung up.

Jack was angry and curious at the same time. Whoever this person was, she obviously knew what she was talking about. Nobody except immediate family members knew about the Genevieve Devereaux fan letters. He almost hoped this was just a ploy to get pictures for the paparazzi. Should he call Maggie? And what—get her all worried when she was on another coastline and there was nothing she could do about it? Plus, it was almost three in the morning back home. A call to the house phone would wake the babies, and she wouldn't hear her cell.

He sighed and hailed a nearby taxi. The driver had dreadlocks and a nose ring and spoke in a foreign accent so thick that Jack thought he'd been transported to another continent.

"I don't think we're in Kansas anymore, Toto," he said to himself as he ducked inside and told the cab driver the name of his hotel.

* * *

Wesley was opening the door to the stables to take his horse for a ride when he smelled something strange that didn't fit in with the usual barn smells. Cigarette smoke wafted from two stalls over, and Wesley knew nobody in his family smoked. He hoped Amanda wasn't picking up any new habits since he wasn't at school to keep an eye on her. He walked over to find out who was defiling the air on his grandparents' property.

Leaning against the barn wall in the empty stall was a big, smarmy kid wearing a baseball cap and a T-shirt imprinted with a skull and crossbones. He had two black bruises under his eyes and a scab on his nose, and he was the last person in the world Wesley wanted to run into when he was all alone.

"Hey Stalker Boy." Dylan blew a smoke ring in his face. "Your grandma says if I'm good, she'll give me your horse."

"You can't smoke in here," Wesley stammered. "There's hay all over the place."

Dylan took a long, slow drag from his cigarette. "What are you going to do about it? Punch me in the face?"

Wesley couldn't believe that Grandma Penny had done this to him without any warning. How could she be so naïve to think that Wesley would be safe with Dylan wandering around the property? And he wasn't the only one in danger. Surely Dylan would terrorize every living soul around him. Wesley tried to back slowly out of the barn, so as not to aggravate the Beast.

Before he could exit, Penny came rushing into the barn. "Wesley! I've been looking all over for you."

Wesley gave her a look that conveyed his profound disappointment.

Penny strode calmly past him and made a beeline for Dylan. Without an inkling of trepidation, Penny plucked the cigarette out of Dylan's hand and threw it onto the dirt floor. She stared up at him while she ground it into the dirt with the heel of her cowboy boot.

"I believe y'all just broke rule number three." She pulled a piece of folded paper out of her pocket and ran her finger down a numbered list. "The penalty for that would be helping Jamal bail hay for two hours. You might want to get started on that now, before it gets too hot."

Dylan was even more stunned at Penny's audacity than Wesley was. "I'm not doing any manual labor." Dylan sneered. "And who's Jamal anyway?"

"That would be me." An immense, muscular black man strolled into the filtered light of the barn, his body completely blocking the sun behind him. He had a large coil of rope slung over his shoulder. To Wesley, it was like watching the marshall ride up right before the bank robbery. This was going to be good.

Dylan tried to look unimpressed, but Wesley could see that his eyes had bugged out and that he had visibly shrunk a few inches.

Jamal sniffed the air. "I believe I smell smoke in here." He squatted down and picked the cigarette butt off the barn floor, then stood up and walked over, stopping a few inches away from Dylan so that Dylan got the full effect of his massive frame towering above him. "Now what kind of ignorant punk would light a cigarette in a barn full of hay?"

Dylan swallowed but didn't answer.

"Jamal, this is Dylan MacLean." Penny sported a smug grin.

"So, this is him, huh?" Jamal looked Dylan over carefully and shook his head to show his disappointment. "I thought you said he was a big kid."

"Well, relatively speaking, he is," Penny defended. "Dylan, this is Jamal Hoskins. If that name sounds familiar, it's because he's probably the best linebacker the University of Georgia Bulldogs have ever known. He's smart too. Planning to go to vet school after he graduates."

Dylan seemed to have lost his ability to speak.

"Aw shucks, Penny," said Jamal. "If that's true, it's only because of all the work you did on me."

"We're just thankful you come back to help us now and again. You think you can work with this one?"

Penny motioned to Dylan with her head. "Here's the list of his rules." She handed him the paper.

"Not necessary." Jamal waved them away. "Got 'em all memorized." He pointed to his head. "Number one, Grandma Penny is the boss, and you respect her."

"That's right, Jamal. You're in good hands, Dylan. I guess we'll see y'all for lunch at noon." Penny dismissed them like they were small children going out for recess.

Wesley watched Dylan follow Jamal without complaint. He knew that not only would Jamal not put up with any attitude from Dylan, but he also had the physical ability to enforce the rules.

Wesley looked at his grandmother with renewed admiration. He should have known all along that she wouldn't invite Dylan unless she had a plan. Jamal had been coming to the ranch on and off to work for about eight years. He was only one of the great success stories from the Scott Ranch summer camp. He wasn't the first troubled kid that Penny and Walter had helped to rise above his circumstances, and he probably wouldn't be the last either. Wesley had never even considered that Dylan might have the same potential.

"Grandma Penny?"

"Yes?"

"How long is Dylan going to stay here?"

"Two months maybe."

"You think that's enough time?"

"For what?"

"To turn him into a decent person."

"I guess we won't know that until we give him a chance."

* * *

People milled up and down the pier, watching sailboats out on the windy waters. Ferryboats pulled out to deliver vacationers to Alcatraz Island, but Jack wasn't interested in the tour. He studied the people's faces as he kept checking his watch. She was late.

A striking blonde with long, spindly legs in skintight jeans swaggered up to him. If her voice had conjured an image of what she might look like, this was it. She handed him a plain white envelope. "Oh my, it's Jack Mackey—the Snake Stalker! May I have your autograph, please?" She didn't give him a pen.

Jack opened the envelope. Inside was a close-up picture of two smiling women who were very familiar to him. The redhead with large teeth was Imogene Vandergrift, and the attractive blonde next to her was her younger sister Delphina Lockhart—the same Delphina Lockhart who had sued him for the wrongful death of her sister.

"Where did you get this?" Jack demanded.

"Before I answer that, I need to know if you can keep a secret."

Some things shouldn't be kept secret." Jack studied her face. She had the appearance and attitude of a spoiled rich girl. He didn't trust her at all. "What do you want?"

"It's not money, if that's what you think." She snatched the picture back.

"Then what should I think?"

"You should think that I'm a very decent person, Jack, and I'm not at all like my mother. I happen to be a huge fan of your show. I don't want anything bad to happen to you, that's all."

Not like your mother? Jack thought. He looked for some resemblance to anyone he knew. "And do I know your mother?"

"Do I have to spell it out for you?"

"You're Delphina's daughter?" he ventured.

She started walking away from the crowd, and Jack followed her. "Please don't hold it against me; I didn't get to choose my parents, you know. I've always liked Wesley. I just assumed he was my real cousin. I didn't know anything at all about what Aunt Genie did—I was only six at the time. But just recently I've been seeing and hearing things that make me believe she's still alive. Then I found this picture in my mom's house."

Jack noticed she had called Imogene "Aunt Genie," and remembered Wesley saying that Delphina and Imogene referred to each other as "Feenie" and "Genie." He gave her some more credibility points. "How do you know it wasn't taken years ago?"

She pulled out the picture and pointed. "Because I gave my mother that necklace a few months ago for Christmas."

"Where is Imogene now?"

"I'm not sure, but I think she's somewhere in the States."

"Why did you come to me?"

"Because I can't go to the police with this. There's no way they won't find out I ratted her out. I just can't get on their bad side—they can be really ruthless." She looked around suspiciously then suddenly linked her arm in his. "I'm sorry, but just telling you about this has really made me scared."

Jack carefully removed his arm from her grip. He was way out of his comfort zone, but he needed to get more information out of her first. "Listen, mate—"

"You can call me Whitney."

"Whitney, could you let me have that picture?"

"No, you'll take it to the police."

"If I do, I won't tell them where I got it."

"I don't know," Whitney mused. "Do you promise to keep my name out of it?"

"I promise."

"Pinky swear?"

It seemed pretty juvenile to Jack, but if it would put her mind at ease, it was worth it. Jack held up his pinky.

Whitney locked her little finger around Jack's and then without warning, reached over and gave him a quick kiss on the lips. Jack pulled away, stunned.

Whitney shoved the envelope into his hand. "I'm sorry for all this, Jack. You really seem like a nice guy." Then she turned and ran away.

With a sinking feeling that this bizarre exchange was not at all what it appeared to be, Jack slowly opened the envelope. To his relief, the envelope still contained the picture of Imogene, but on closer examination, the date in the corner of the photo said two years earlier. Someone had colored it with a red marker to try and match the color of Imogene's shirt, but he could still read it. Imogene had supposedly been dead for a year and a half, meaning Whitney had made up the whole necklace story. If Whitney was even her real name.

The picture was useless. The fact that this girl had tampered with it—and hadn't even done a good job of it—made him believe she was only a fan looking for some way to meet him in person. He stuffed it in his pocket and scolded himself for being so stupid. He was so angry that he didn't notice the man sitting on a nearby bench throwing breadcrumbs to the seagulls, a zoom lens camera around his neck.

Rattlesnake Rally

Jack didn't fill in Zeke or Steve, his filming crew, on the event that had transpired that morning, knowing they would only chastise him for being duped by some floozy. He didn't need the lecture. Plus, Zeke and Steve had come all the way from Australia for this shoot, under the expectation that this was going to be the best show of their career. Jack highly doubted it. He was having trouble concentrating, and even though they had run into several rattlesnakes already, they still hadn't found any of the rattlesnake nests that hikers claimed to have spotted in the green foothills of Mt. Diablo.

Keep lookin', mates," Jack urged. "I hope it wasn't all folklore. It's got to be around here somewhere. Zeke, can't you use some of your aboriginal charms to flush them out?"

Zeke, Jack's longtime friend and the brains behind the majority of the *Snake Stalker* TV shows, was usually the one who located the wildlife. "It only works in Australia, boss," Zeke answered.

Jack took off his hat and fanned himself. He hadn't slept last night and was pretty tired. "Don't we have enough video to make a full-length feature film out of this, Steve?"

"Nope," Steve answered. "I told you, I don't have my golden shot."

"Yeah, we definitely don't have a golden shot," Zeke echoed.

"I know, I know." Jack knew exactly what they needed. Every show had to have at least one really exciting, over-the-top piece of video in it. It had to be dangerous, thrilling, and unexpected. That's what set his shows apart from the other nature shows and kept his audience tuning in. And his crew always knew when they had this golden shot.

"Shh!" Zeke put a finger to his lips. "I hear somethin'. This way."

Jack and Steve shrugged and lugged the camera gear further into the tall grass. It was a warm day, and Jack was wearing shorts, even though Zeke had advised him to wear long pants for safety reasons. Jack argued that wearing shorts added an element of danger to the show. Zeke countered that he was just trying to show off his legs.

"Over by that patch of boulders." Zeke motioned for them to follow. "Watch your step."

The trio trudged through the grass and prickly weeds until they came to an open space shrouded by an outcropping of fairly large trees. "Who wants to go on a little reconnaissance mission?" Zeke asked.

"Oh pick me, pick me!" Jack raised his hand. He took off his backpack and unwound a coil of rope with a rappelling hook on one end. He threw it up, coiling it around the sturdiest branch he could find. "I'm going in," he said with deadpan seriousness. He jumped up and swung out like a pendulum over an area of grass that to an untrained observer would look completely vacant.

"Zeke, you've found the mother lode!" Jack exclaimed as he swung back and dropped down onto the grass.

Steve and Zeke had already climbed up the nearby patch of rocks to take a look. Sure enough, as Zeke had predicted, there was a massive, writhing pool of rattlesnakes.

"There's got to be thirty snakes in there!" Steve was already setting the camera up for the shot.

Jack studied the area where he had seen the snakes from above. "You'll never get them and me in the same shot if I'm over here."

"Unless you plan on joinin' their little party." Zeke looked through the viewfinder on his smaller video camera.

"Good idea, mate."

"Don't do it, Jack." Steve shook his head. "You've got three kids now."

"C'mon, Steve-o, it's a golden opportunity. I can't let it go to waste. Zeke, throw me my mic."

Zeke pulled a small cordless microphone out of his camera bag and hurled it at Jack, who caught it and attached it to his shirt. "Are we rollin', Steve?"

"We're rollin'." Steve shook his head. "But I wouldn't do it if I were you."

"You can do it, boss," Zeke encouraged him. "There's actually a hole about two meters in diameter right in the center of the snakes."

"I know; I saw it—just like a snake doughnut. Tell me when." Jack looped the remainder of the rope around his shoulder, jumped up, and swung over the pile of snakes again.

On the return swing, Zeke shouted, "Now!" and Jack let go of the rope and dropped into the center of the snake ring. One of the snakes struck at him, but he picked up his leg, dodging its fangs by mere inches.

"Whoa! That was a close one! This is amazing!" Jack knew he wasn't going to have much time, so he started talking right away. "We got ourselves a pile of red diamondback rattlers, and most of these are young-sters." He looked directly into the camera. "I can tell they're young because they only have one or two rat-tles. Now most people think rattlesnakes grow one new rattle every year, but that's not always the case. They can actually shed their skin two or three times a year, and they get a new rattle each time. Also, the rat-tles can wear out or break, so it's unusual to find any snake with more than eight or ten rattles."

Jack took a thin metal rod from around his belt loop and scooped one of the smaller snakes up. "Even though he may be only a foot long, this adolescent is just as ven-omous and even more aggressive than the adults."

The snake appeared agitated and shook its tail, producing a distinctive hiss.

"That sound is one you definitely don't want to hear, mates. It means he's gettin' a little defensive now, and he's sayin', 'back off or I'm gonna strike!'"

"Boss," Zeke whispered loudly, "that's not a bad idea since they're all looking a little restless."

"They've been out of hibernation for a few weeks now, and normally you don't find this many in one spot. Nature always has a way of balancing things out, so—" Jack dodged another strike from behind. He jumped up on the rope, picking his feet up just a foot above the ground. One snake tried to bite his boot.

"Okay, I take it I'm not on the guest list." Jack tried to climb higher on the rope. His grip was slipping, so he wrapped the rope around his fist, and it dug into his skin. The tree limb was swaying under his weight, and Jack knew he'd pushed it past the limit this time. The spot where he was standing seconds ago was writhing with snakes.

Zeke had already assessed the situation and had another rope ready. "Boss, get one hand free and catch this. He threw the rope, but Jack missed it. It whipped into the pile of snakes, distressing them even further. "Can you climb up the rope?"

"If I could, I would have done it already," Jack confessed. "I'm going to have to run for it." He dropped from the rope directly onto a pile of snakes and the rattling went to eighty decibels. Jack didn't hesitate; he sprinted straight for the rock. In two leaps he managed to make it to safety. He paused briefly to catch his breath, looked into the camera, and smiled. "I told you, Zeke. Long pants are for sissies."

Steve put the camera on pause. "Jack, that was great and very manly of you, but something fell out of your pocket in that shot."

"What?"

"Right there at the bottom." Steve pointed to a white envelope.

Jack spied the envelope, and it took only seconds to remember what it was. He sighed and inched back toward the slithering pile. "I really need that."

"Unless that's a million dollars, you can replace it," Zeke stated. "You don't need that."

"I can get it," Jack assured them. He climbed down from the relative safety of the rocks and slowly threaded his way to the edge of the swarming snakes. He had dropped his snake pole, so he needed to get close enough to grab it with his hands. One snake slid right across it. Jack waited while Steve and Zeke stayed absolutely quiet. Steve turned the camera back on.

"Boss," Zeke shook his head, "have I told you lately that you're an idiot?"

"Only three times today," Jack said without breaking his concentration. When a small space opened up around the envelope, Jack reached down slowly and picked it up with two fingers. He delicately slid it back into his pocket and stepped backward up the rocks. A rattler moved in with its tail vibrating. It poised to strike. Jack stood motionless. It was clear that he and the snake were in a standoff. The snake edged forward, and Jack shifted his weight, sending a loose piece of rock tumbling. The snake shot out instantly and closed its fangs on Jack's shin, sending pain signals to his brain informing him that his luck had run out.

After working with Jack for several years, Zeke had learned not to panic in situations like this. He clicked his tongue and started down the rocks to give Jack a hand. "Now *that*," he said to Steve, "is our golden shot."

* * *

The shade trees in the Mackeys' front yard that had been growing for more than a hundred years flanked a rock pond with a small waterfall. Some mallards had adopted the place as their personal abode, which gave Teddy, Maggie's huge black Newfoundland mix, and

Hercules, Wesley's miniature Chihuahua, plenty of amusement. Walter had always called his family's large expanse of front lawn "the football field," and the four-some decided they might as well use it for that very purpose. Wesley, Amanda, Jamal, and Dylan made a pretty motley touch football team, but they didn't seem to notice.

"Great throw, Amanda!" Jamal yelled. "You defi-nitely don't play football like a girl!"

"Unlike Stalker Boy, who definitely does!" Dylan added.

Dylan's comment didn't faze Wesley. He was get-ting used to the nickname and accepted it as Dylan's twisted way of trying to get along.

"Watch it, Dill Man," Jamal scolded, "Amanda's got a better arm than you do."

Wesley laughed as Amanda threw him the foot-ball. She had always been better at sports than he was. She was a great baseball pitcher, so it was only natural that she could throw a football too. He juggled the ball, fumbled it, then lobbed it to Dylan. If anyone had told him a few days ago that he would be playing any sort of game at all in his front yard with Dylan MacLean, he would have thought they were crazy. But it still wasn't as surreal as the vision of Maria and Harrison strolling up to watch them. Harrison had a new hairstyle and khaki pants that actually touched the tops of his shoes. He still wore the same glasses, but he looked like he had just been a contestant on *Extreme Makeover*.

Dylan also did a double-take. He had become much more amicable in the past few days under Jamal's super-vision, but some of his old habits were going to take time to break. Harrison was the exact type of person

Dylan was used to harassing at school. The temptation was too much for him.

"Hey geek, go long!" he shouted, and he hurled the football with considerable force right into Harrison's chest.

Everyone heard the thump. Harrison folded over and dropped to the ground, losing his precious glasses.

Jamal acted so quickly that Dylan didn't even get a chance to laugh at his own prank. He ran full force and slammed Dylan onto the ground, pinning him with his crushing weight.

Meanwhile, Maria helped Harrison to his feet and was dusting him off. His face was red, and he seemed embarrassed.

"Are you okay?" Maria asked.

"Yes, I'm fine. He just surprised me, that's all."

Dylan was focused on the 280-pound weight on his back. He was having trouble getting air into his compressed lungs. "Hey! I thought you said this wasn't tackle football," he sputtered.

"Yeah, well the rules just changed." Jamal yanked Dylan to his feet. "I believe you owe Mr. Landry an apology."

"No way! I'm not apologizing to that wimp. He's supposed to be some army guy, and he can't even catch a pass."

Jamal grabbed Dylan's right arm and wrenched it behind his back. "Excuse me? What did I just hear you say?" He pushed him roughly over to Harrison, who seemed to dislike this exchange even more than getting decked by a football.

Dylan winced in pain. "I said I'm sorry."

Jamal tugged his arm again. "I don't think he heard you."

"Ouch! I'm sorry, Harrison, that I threw the football at you."

"It's okay, really." Harrison looked like he wanted to run away and hide. He picked up his glasses and tried to focus on them. One of the lenses was broken, so he stuffed them into his shirt pocket. He hung his head as though he'd been totally stripped of his honor.

Maria shifted her weight from side to side, pretending not to notice that Harrison had just been humiliated.

Jamal manhandled Dylan back over to the pond, where he could give him some more coaching. "Rule number fifteen. Treat *everyone* with the respect they deserve."

Dylan scowled, but like an animal, he knew it was futile to fight with anything bigger, faster, and obviously more skilled than he was.

Harrison watched Dylan as he made a face behind Jamal's back. He walked slowly over to the stranded football and picked it up. He studied it for a moment, deep in thought. Then he squinted his eyes and locked in on Dylan, who was standing about thirty yards away.

"Hey, Dylan!" he yelled in a voice that sounded like someone else's. "Would you like your football back?" He pulled back and released the football with torpedo force. The bullet pass headed directly for Dylan's stomach. Dylan didn't have time to prepare himself to catch it. The football sped right through his hands and ricocheted off his sternum, knocking him off balance and forcing him to take several steps back. The football bounced into the pond, causing a flock of squawking ducks to exit quickly.

Jamal looked at Harrison and then at Dylan in disbelief.

Harrison said nothing as he pulled his broken glasses out of his pocket and put them back on. He walked hurriedly past the stunned onlookers and disappeared behind the house.

7

Secret Rendezvous

Walter was acting like a six-year-old on Christmas morning. He kept telling Wesley that he was in for a really big surprise, but that this was something he had to keep between the two of them. The two had ridden their horses out to the old Shaffer barn, about three miles from the house. Wesley had been out here before with Amanda, and basically there was nothing of interest besides an old rusted truck on blocks and an ancient woodpile with enough spiders guarding it that no one with an ounce of sanity would approach it.

"Grandpa, I hope you aren't planning on fixing this barn up," Wesley said hesitantly.

"No siree." Walter grinned as he hopped off his horse and led Wesley into the barn. "That would be work. And we are here for pleasure. Wait till you see this!" He walked into the barn and motioned over to a lumpy mechanical object covered with a sheet. "I've been working on her for about two months now, and I think she's ready to go." He removed the sheet with a dramatic swoop, like a sculptor unveiling a statue.

Wesley gaped at the dilapidated old truck. It was so rusty it was hard to say what the original color was—could have been red or black. The entire vehicle was decrepit-looking, except for the set of four somewhat new-looking tires attached to the axles.

"Ever seen a '66 Chevy?" Walter beamed. "This was a hot little item in my day."

Wesley tried to look impressed. "It's a classic."

"Now I know she still needs a little paint and some upholstery work and whatnot, but I got Dylan to help me get some old parts, and I think we got her running pretty good now."

"You had Dylan get you parts? They're probably stolen."

"No, I paid for them—it's all good."

Wesley didn't want to get into the fact that Dylan had probably purchased them from some chop shop where all the parts came from vehicles that were stolen to begin with.

"I've been trying to get you out here for a week now, because you get to be the first one to take her for a spin."

With anyone other than Walter, it would have been just a ride in some nasty old truck, but with Walter it was a great honor. Wesley climbed in the passenger seat, and then Walter stopped him and handed him the keys.

"You want to drive her?"

Wesley was stunned. "I guess so." He looked at the gear shift. "But I don't know how to drive a clutch."

"Piece of cake—you're a quick study, Wes." Walter shoved him over and sat in the passenger seat. "I'll teach you. You'll have to back out, and after that, everything will be easy."

Wesley started the engine, and it sounded like a freight train with tuberculosis. "Are you sure it isn't going to blow up or something?"

"Nah, she just needs a new muffler, that's all." Walter rubbed his hands together. "Okay, ease up on the clutch and try not to hit the door on the way out— liable to take the whole barn down if you do. Not that anyone would care, but we don't want to get dusty."

After about three attempts, Wesley managed to ease the clutch enough to pull the old truck out without hitting the barn or the horses.

On the dirt road, the old jalopy jumped around while Walter told stories about how he would take Penny for rides in this truck when they were first dating. "I remember we had our first kiss in this truck." He toyed with the radio. "Radio still works! I think we only got one station out here back then," Walter reminisced while Wesley drove, stalled a few times, and started the truck up again. After an hour they thought they'd better head back home.

"Now Wes, you can't let on to your Grandma or Maggie about this. They'll shut this operation down in no time flat."

Wesley nodded. "That's for sure. I won't tell anyone, not even my dad. Can we come again tomorrow?"

"If you can sneak away from that blasted tutor, we'll make it an adventure."

"I'll figure out something. I'm a quick study, right?"

* * *

Maggie was hurriedly placing her groceries on the conveyor belt in the checkout line when her eye caught one of the tabloid headlines: *Snake Stalker Secret*

Rendezvous! She snatched up the newsprint magazine and felt the blood rush to her head when she realized that the picture on the cover showed her husband kissing another woman.

Maggie thumbed through the inside pages only to be assaulted by three more photos of Jack walking along the pier arm in arm with a very young and beautiful blonde.

"Will that be all, ma'am?" the cashier lady asked.

She didn't answer for a moment. "Yes—I mean, no." She handed the tabloid facedown to the cashier. The woman scanned it without comment. The bag boy put her groceries into the cart and followed her out to her vehicle.

"You have a nice day," the bagger said as he slammed Maggie's groceries into the back of her Land Rover.

"Thank you." Maggie climbed into her SUV. "But that won't be possible."

* * *

The taxi dropped Jack off in the driveway, and he limped up to the front door. His trip had been plagued with one disaster after the next, and he had finally decided to come back one day early on a standby flight. His flight had been delayed two hours, he had just traveled through three time zones, and he wanted nothing more than to be back in his own home. He had forgotten to charge his cell phone, and when he had tried to call Maggie, his battery was dead, so he had no way of letting her know he was coming home. He found her in the kitchen stirring a pot of soup for dinner.

"Mmmm . . . chicken soup—my favorite."

Maggie whirled around. "Jack! You're back!"

"Hey, that rhymes. I'm Jack and I'm back." Jack looked genuinely happy to be home and gave Maggie a kiss. She didn't appear to be as happy to see him as she turned her back on him and poured some seasoning into the pot.

"So is there some reason why you've been unreachable for the past two and a half days?" Maggie asked.

Jack didn't realize it had been that long. He was going to have to start at the beginning and tell her the whole story. "Well, yes, as a matter of fact, I do have something to tell you. I've got some good news and some bad news."

"Let's hear the bad news first."

Jack rolled up his pant leg and showed his bandage. "One of the rattlers got me."

"Really." Maggie wasn't usually overemotional, but she seemed bitter, almost like he had gotten what he deserved. "So what's the good news?"

"I didn't die."

"Is that it?" Maggie bored into him as if she thought he were holding something back.

Jack was confused at her reaction. "What do you mean is that it? Gettin' bitten by a rattlesnake is a pretty big deal for some people."

"Well, maybe if it's such a big deal, then you could have shared it with someone. Your mouth still seems to be working properly. Did you forget our phone number?"

"I was in the hospital. And then I forgot to charge my phone. Mag, I'm detectin' some anger from you."

"You would be detecting accurately."

"What's wrong?"

"What's wrong, you ask?" She went over to the desk drawer, pulled out the tabloid newspaper, and threw it on the kitchen table. "This is what's wrong."

Jack gaped at the picture and then let out an agonizing groan. This was the epitome of a worst-case scenario. "Okay, this looks really bad."

"Do you *think?*"

"There is a really good explanation. I swear to you, Mag . . . she ambushed me."

Maggie flipped to the page with the scene of Jack and the same woman walking along the wharf arm in arm. "This doesn't look like an ambush to me."

Jack had no idea where to begin. His decision to not tell Maggie what happened that day was definitely a bad one. "She told me Imogene Vandergrift was alive. Mag, I didn't believe her at first, but then she showed me this picture." He dug around his shirt pocket and produced the wrinkled photo. "She claimed she was Delphina Lockhart's daughter, and that's how she knew . . ."

"Wait, wait, slow down. What's her name?"

"Whitney—something. She even said she knew Wes." Jack went on to explain the mysterious phone call and rendezvous, and how she'd grabbed his arm and planted a kiss on his unwilling lips, and how he'd discovered that the whole thing was a hoax.

"So why didn't you call me right after this episode?" Maggie wasn't letting him off just yet.

"Mag, I was going to, but I didn't want you to be worried. Plus, I don't know, it all sounds pretty deranged—like some parachute story."

"You didn't trust me to believe you?"

"Well, I—do you believe me?" Jack raised his eyebrows.

"Whether I do or don't is not the point. The point is you chose not to share some very important information with me. What if Wesley were in some serious danger? What if he still is? You can't be sure there isn't some truth to her story."

Jack hung his head. "I'm really sorry, Mag. I should have told you."

"Does Delphina even have a daughter named Whitney?"

"I don't know."

"You mean you didn't even check?"

"I was going to, but I was already holding up the camera crew, and then the snake bit me, and I sort of got focused on the excruciating pain."

"Let me see that." Maggie crouched down, yanked up his pant leg, and unceremoniously peeled off the bandage, along with all the hair on his leg. It made a ripping noise.

Jack screamed in pain. "Ouch, Mag! That hurts worse than the bite."

Maggie examined the two swollen fang marks and clicked her tongue. "I guess the Snake Stalker is losing his touch."

Jack smoothed Maggie's hair. "You do believe me, don't you?"

"About the snake bite? That's obvious."

"No, about those tabloid pictures."

"You wouldn't be standing here with all your teeth if I didn't. Frankly, these past few days I've felt like I stepped into the twilight zone. This is just about par with everything else that's been going on around here."

Jack hobbled over to the kitchen table and sat down. He pulled Maggie along with him. "Tell me, Mag."

"Okay. First of all, Wesley has a new friend."

"That's not unusual."

"It is if his name is Dylan MacLean."

"The slammed-in-the-face-with-a-locker Dylan MacLean?"

"The same. He's been living at Mom and Dad's for the last four days and will probably be here for several weeks. In fact, he and Wesley were playing football in the front yard together yesterday. And right now they have the girls in backpacks and are taking them for a hike over to the lake."

Jack put his palms on the table to steady himself. "And you're okay with that?"

"Sure. Jamal and Amanda are with them, too."

"Well, that's good," Jack sounded relieved. "We know our kids are safe if Amanda's with them."

"You remember Jamal, don't you? He was here last summer."

"Yeah. Football player. About seven feet tall." Jack stretched his hand several inches above his head. "Jamal's a good mate; reminds me of Zeke—on steroids. Your mum is a sly one bringing him on. But I have to agree that it is unusual."

"But that's not all," Maggie added. "Harrison is dressing like the cover model of a *GQ* magazine and has a date tonight."

"You're kiddin', right? How can he find a date? He doesn't even know anyone around here."

"Yes, he does. He knows Maria."

"That was nice of her to set him up with one of her friends."

"No. Harrison is going out with Maria."

Jack slapped himself in the face. "Wake up, Jack. It's just a dream."

Maggie picked up the tabloid from the counter. "I really wish *this* were a dream."

"I know, Mag. I'm really sorry."

"Well, you might want to figure out how you're going to explain all this to the family." She motioned to the newspaper. "Better to hear it from you before someone else tells them. Oh, and by the way—welcome home. I missed you."

* * *

Wesley studied the tabloid photos of the woman who claimed to be Delphina's daughter. His grandparents were invited to the family gathering, where Jack gave a full explanation of what happened. No one seemed to doubt his story. This wasn't exactly his first run-in with the media getting the facts twisted. Jack had been accused of kidnapping Wesley, murdering Imogene, and using a stunt double for his TV show. His family knew he wasn't guilty of any of these crimes, although some of them agreed a stunt double might have come in handy in the filming of his last episode.

"What do you think, Wes?" Walter prodded. "Is it Delphina's daughter?"

Wesley nodded. "Her name is Whitney Ray. If that's not her, it's someone who looks exactly like her."

"So maybe I'm not so gullible then?" Jack commented.

"But the question is, if Imogene isn't alive—what's her motivation?" Maggie picked a pillow off the couch and punched it behind her back.

"Money or fame," Walter offered. "That's what everyone's after."

"Or," said Wesley, "maybe Imogene really is alive."

"I doubt it," Jack said. "I think your former cousin probably got paid by the paparazzi. They get big bucks for exclusive photos like this."

"That photo of Imogene is dated two years ago," Penny added. "Even if she is alive, we don't have any proof."

"Wes, do you still have those letters from Genevieve Devereaux?" Jack asked.

"Maybe a couple—depends on the last time I cleaned out my drawers. But they're all typed anyway."

Jack scratched the back of his neck. "How would she know that name?"

"There are plenty of sources," Maggie answered, "including the testimony in your grand jury hearing."

"But Whitney wasn't even there," Jack argued.

"But her mother was," Maggie countered. "Delphina is the one who brought up charges."

"Zeke's right. I'm an idiot," Jack said.

"It's okay, Jack," Maggie said. "I forgive you. You didn't have time to think about it."

"So you would have done the same thing?" He brightened.

"No," Maggie said directly. "I would have called you immediately and then cancelled the shoot until I had some more answers. But that's just me."

8

Learning Curve

The picnic table on the Scotts' back patio proved to be one of the most popular places to study, especially on days with good weather. A weeping willow kept it shady, and the swimming pool wasn't too far away if you wanted to cool your feet off. Dylan was straddling the picnic bench, his arms folded across his chest. "So I finished my chores. Why can't I ride the horses today?" he challenged Penny.

"I've been over to your parent teacher conferences, and Mrs. Gilroy says if you can manage to get As and Bs on your next three exams, you can get at least a B in English."

"So what."

"So, if you would like to stay on with us here—and I'm hoping that you do—you need to have passing grades."

"D is passing."

"Not to me, it isn't. You've been with us for three weeks now, Dylan, and I *know* you're capable—you just don't apply yourself. Now, sit yourself down, and Mr. Landry will be right over to help you with your vocabulary words. You should be grateful that we just so happen to have one the brightest linguistic minds right here at your disposal!"

"Yeah, just watch me dispose of Mr. Linguini," Dylan mumbled under his breath.

Penny ignored his comment as she marched over to the pool cover and peeled it back. "And if you study hard, you can go swimming tonight."

"Oh boy." Dylan punctuated his lack of enthusiasm by clasping his hands together in mock excitement. He rattled his pencil on the picnic table as he spied Harrison and Wesley coming over to meet him.

"Hey S.B., what's up?" Dylan called out.

For Wesley, S.B. (short for Stalker Boy) was like a term of endearment coming from Dylan. Lately Dylan had taken up using initials for all sorts of things, especially swear words. Penny and Jamal had insisted he clean up his foul mouth, and for Dylan, this proved to be more difficult than quitting smoking. Penny suggested he start by using just a letter instead of the whole word. Dylan tried it as a joke at first just to humor Penny, but now he seemed to have replaced all his curse words with initials.

"Not much," Wesley replied. "Harrison is forcing me to study with you. Hey Grandma, are you heating up the pool?"

"Yeah, it's about time, don't you think?" Penny puttered around for awhile, and then went inside, leaving the unenthusiastic trio to their studies.

Dylan dug through his binder for the list of vocabulary words and handed them to Harrison. "This is what I'm supposed to study, but it's all Greek to me."

Harrison scanned the word list. "Actually, it's not Greek but Latin," he explained. "Take for example this word: *torpor*. It means "a condition of mental or physical inactivity or apathy." It comes from the Latin word *torpere*, which means "stiff." Just remember, *stiff* is also slang for a dead body, and that's what a person in this state resembles."

"You're a stiff," Dylan mumbled under his breath.

"Quintessential," Harrison said. "What does that mean?"

"How the H should I know?" Dylan threw his legs up onto the patio table. "Who uses any of these words anyway?"

"Educated people," Harrison suggested.

"Well, I'm not one of them, and I don't want to be one of them," Dylan stated.

"Then you," Harrison said resolutely, "are the quintessential fool."

"What did you call me?" Dylan sat up straight.

Wesley started laughing. "I think he called you the quintessential fool."

Harrison pushed a ten-pound dictionary over to Dylan. "Although I find your pugnacious attitude quite innocuous, others may not respond to such insolence with approbation."

"What?" Dylan made a face.

"Wow," Wesley commented. "I don't know what he said, but he just used four of your vocabulary words in one sentence."

"Tell you what, Dylan," Harrison said matter-of-factly. "This is wasting my time and yours. You want to fight? Why don't we have it out right now?"

"You're kidding, right?" Dylan picked up a ruler, just in case he needed to use it as a weapon.

"I'm challenging you to a duel. You can have Wesley on your team to make it more even."

Dylan smiled. "Sure thing, but I don't even need S.B. on my team."

"For this you will, because we'll be using words as weapons. Let's see who can deliver the most insulting blows using this list of twenty-five words." Harrison placed a vocabulary list on the table in front of Dylan. "Anything goes, except profanity, of course."

Dylan thought for a moment. "Deal. But first you have to tell me what you said a minute ago—in English."

"I said that I find your aggressive attitude quite harmless, but others may not approve of your bad behavior."

"That's it?" Dylan tore a page from his notebook and grabbed a pencil. "Okay S.B., two bucks says we can take him."

* * *

An hour later, Amanda came up to the table carefully holding what looked like one of Penny's canning jars with some twigs stuffed in it. "You guys, look at what I caught!" She put the jar breathlessly on the table. Harrison, Wesley, and Dylan were completely uninterested in her show-and-tell jar. They all looked inside, expecting to see a butterfly or some ladybug.

Dylan was the first one to actually see what was inside the jar. "What the—?!" He stood up and knocked his picnic bench over in the process. "Is that what I think it is?"

"That's awesome!" Wesley was duly impressed but not nearly as surprised as Dylan. "You better keep that away from Maria, or she'll freak."

Harrison didn't quite know what to say, so he stated the obvious. "Amanda, are you aware that you've caught a black widow spider?"

"A mammoth black widow," Dylan added.

"No kidding!" Amanda said as if she were talking to a group of imbeciles. "That's why I caught it. I've got my science project all figured out. Look behind that leaf—there's an egg sac in there too." She pointed to the shiny, black-sectioned body the size of an unshelled peanut, with pointed legs tapering out from the side. "I'm calling her Black Betty."

"You caught that yourself?" Dylan asked incredulously. "And put it in the jar, just like that?"

"Yeah." Amanda gave him a challenging look. "There are more out in the woodpile if you want one."

"Are you crazy?" Dylan laughed. "What kind of *girl* are you?"

Wesley motioned to the spider in the jar. "The kind who will put that in your bed if you keep talking to her like that."

"What I was wondering," Amanda continued, "is if you guys could keep this in your room for a few weeks. Not on your nightstand or anything, but just keep it in a corner somewhere until I can get my project done."

"Keep it in your own room!" Dylan ordered.

"I would, but if my mom sees it, she'll probably faint. She screams if she sees a teeny tiny spider that's not even poisonous. She's terrified of them."

"I'll keep it for you," Harrison offered, "as long as Penny doesn't have any rules against keeping poisonous arachnids in the barracks."

"Really? Thanks!" Amanda said gratefully.

"If it's for a science project, how can I refuse?"

"You're the best, Harrison."

"Wait a minute!" Dylan barked. "That's in my room too."

"It's in a jar, you sissy." Amanda rolled her eyes.

"A *glass* jar that can break!"

"Well then don't break it." Amanda walked over to Dylan and stared him down. "Or you'll have to catch me another one." Amanda looked over at the pool. "Is that warm enough to go swimming in tonight?"

"I think so. You want to swim, Dylan?" Wesley asked.

"No."

"So you eschew swimming?" Wesley decided to use one of their recently learned vocabulary words.

"Whatever." Dylan was defensive. "Maybe I didn't have a rich mommy to take me to swimming lessons like some people."

"Well, sometimes that doesn't even help," Wesley retorted.

"Oh yeah, like you didn't learn to swim when you were four?" Dylan demanded.

"No, actually I learned last year. I had some pretty big issues with water. I'm still not a really good swimmer," Wesley confessed. "Do you want to learn?"

Dylan hesitated. "Not really."

"Why? No one cares."

"Don't have a swimsuit."

"Grandma Penny has about a thousand in the lost and found."

"Don't have time."

"I think he's recalcitrant," Harrison declared.

"I'd rather be recalcitrant." Dylan narrowed his eyes. "Than obsequious, you pedantic anomaly."

Harrison looked shocked. "What did you just say?"

"You heard me."

Harrison clapped his hands. "Congratulations, Dylan. That was an excellent excoriation, and I concede defeat." He pushed on his glasses. "What was the wager?"

"Two bucks." Dylan threw out his hand.

Harrison pulled out his wallet. "Here's two, and I'll double it if you can get an A on the test tomorrow."

The glory of winning made Dylan smile smugly. Wesley noticed it and smiled too. Somehow the nerdiest guy he'd ever met and the biggest bully he knew were starting to become friends.

* * *

Dylan wasn't the only person who was getting along well with Harrison. Maria seemed to be making all kinds of excuses to come to the house and hang around their study sessions. She caused quite a stir when she asked Harrison out to a picnic lunch by the lake— alone.

Harrison seemed a little uncomfortable with the proposition, but then Harrison was pretty uncomfortable around a lot of people. Compared with the first few days, though, he was looking and behaving much more within the social norm. This noticeable improvement didn't escape anyone's attention, and sometimes the family would refer to Harrison as "Maria's project."

Maria spread out the blanket on a level spot under a large maple tree by the lake on the Scotts' property. Bob the cat came up to pilfer a piece of chicken, and Maria obliged him.

"So do you like cats?" Harrison asked.

"I never really used to like them when I was little, because the cats around our neighborhood were wild, but Bob has changed me." Maria scratched Bob's neck as he purred. "How about you?"

"Well, I do like Bob." Harrison stroked his back. "But I don't think Bob is really a cat."

"Why is that?"

"Well for one thing, he eats Doritos. He can smell the mailman coming from three blocks away, and he chases the dog around every chance he gets."

"I know, he always picks on Hercules. Bob's twice his size."

"I wasn't talking about Hercules. He was chasing Teddy."

Maria laughed. "That's nothing. Have you seen the *Purrminator* movie?"

"No, I can't say that I have."

"Well, Bob is the star. Wesley and Amanda followed him around with the video camera one day. They have footage of Bob attacking Hercules, knocking over every piece on the chessboard, scratching the couch, and destroying Penny's flower beds. They just recently started filming *Purrminator 2*, and I hear it contains a very violent episode with a goldfish. But I haven't seen it yet."

"Sounds entertaining. I'll have to rent it one of these nights."

Maria took a sip of her soda. "Did you notice I spiked your carrot juice with Sprite?"

"No wonder I'm feeling a little tipsy."

Maria threw a crust of bread to one of the ducks swimming on the lake. "You're doing amazing things with Dylan. He's getting all As in English now. The change in him is unbelievable."

"Well, it's not me. Penny and Jamal are the real heroes. You can see that he was really a good kid in a bad environment. He's smart, too. But he's starving for attention." Harrison went on to tell Maria about their insult challenge the week before. "And then he calls me a pedantic anomaly. That was so accurate—I had to admit defeat."

"You'll have to translate. I only speak English and Spanish."

"Well *pedantic* refers to someone who concentrates on book learning but can't apply their knowledge to real life. An anomaly is something out of the ordinary—or abnormal. That about sums me up."

"You must be so proud." Maria laughed. "Dylan really respects you now."

"I think I'm like the nutty professor to him. He just humors me—and Jack does too."

"No, Jack likes you, really. He's just never known anyone like you." Maria paused for a moment. "And neither have I."

"What do you mean by 'someone like me'?"

"I guess you are pretty out of the ordinary. I mean, you're a genius, but at the same time you're . . ." Maria searched for the right word. "Mysterious."

"*Mysterious* is just a fancy word for weird. And I am definitely not a genius."

"Come on, admit it. You are."

"Just because I know a few languages doesn't make me a genius. I had the benefit of living in a lot of different countries. I'm pretty inept when it comes to some things."

"Like what?"

"Like how to be normal, basically. I don't have people skills. I don't know how to make people feel comfortable around me."

Maria smiled. "I'm comfortable around you."

"That's because you have that talent, Maria. You fit in wherever you go. You make people feel at ease and you bring out the best in them. It's a gift, and I wish you could teach me how to be that way too."

"Harrison, you're fine just the way you are. I like that you're not a carbon copy of every other person on the planet. Don't try to change your personality to please other people."

Harrison looked as though he didn't believe her.

"I'll tell you a secret." Maria moved closer to him. "You are the first man that I have ever asked out to lunch before."

Harrison touched his glasses. There was a piece of duct tape on them where he had repaired them two weeks ago. "Really?"

Maria studied his face for a response and then slowly reached up and took his glasses off. "How well can you see me without these on?"

Harrison squinted and then replied, "It doesn't really matter. I have your face memorized."

"Okay then." Maria leaned over and kissed him. At first she thought he might jump up and run away, but then he awkwardly put his hand on her shoulder. At least he didn't back away.

"I'm sorry, you must think I'm very forward," Maria said.

"No, no, I like that you're forward," Harrison managed to stutter. "I mean, I don't think that you're forward. I just . . . uh, like the way you are." He reached for his glasses and put them in his front shirt pocket. "Would you like to go for a walk?"

Maria nodded while trying not to laugh at Harrison. He was actually fairly handsome without his glasses. With the sun on his skin, she could detect a slight trace of freckles. They stood up to walk, and Maria wasn't sure if Harrison reached for her hand or she reached for his first.

They walked quietly along a path that wound through the thickest part of the forest until they came upon an enormous oak tree with a scarred trunk.

"Is this all the Scotts' property?" Harrison asked.

"No, I think we're on public land now. See this tree?" Maria touched the trunk. "For some reason, everyone carves their initials on it, and they're destroying the tree. It's a shame. I think people who deface beautiful things like this ought to be shot."

"As in the death penalty?" Harrison asked.

"You know what I mean. It's just sad, that's all. What's the purpose in announcing some high school crush that will last two months on a tree that has been here for hundreds of years?"

"Well, it looks like one of the perpetrators is in love with you." Harrison motioned to the trunk where someone had carved, "Jason loves Maria."

Maria shrugged. "Too bad I don't know anyone named Jason."

"And it's a good thing for him, or you might shoot him."

"Well, he would deserve it."

9

Back from the Dead

Wesley ran into the house and screamed at the top of his lungs, "Maggie!" He was sweaty and out of breath. "Maggie!" he shouted again before she bolted into the room and told him to keep it down.

"Wesley, I'm right here!" Maggie answered. "And I just got both girls down for their naps.

"It's an emergency," Wesley huffed. "Rocky ran into some barbed-wire kind of over by the old Shaffer barn, and his front leg is pretty mangled. Grandpa untangled some of it, but you have to come right away."

"Where are they exactly?"

"I'll show you."

"I can't leave the babies alone."

"How about Grandma?" Wesley asked.

"She's not home. Just show me where they are, and then you can ride back to the house. Which horse was Grandpa riding?"

"Lightning."

"We can double-ride her." Maggie went to get her vet kit while Wesley ran out to get on the horse. When they were situated on the horse, Wesley held the bag of supplies with one hand and held onto Maggie with the other. Maggie rode as fast as she could without bumping Wesley off the back. In a few minutes, she was disheartened to see her father trying to unravel what looked like a thorny tumbleweed from Rocky's front leg. Maggie could see from several feet away that the wire was imbedded, and she would need to surgically remove it.

"I got most of it, Maggie Sue," Walter explained, "but I think this piece is going to take some skill."

"It's okay, Rocky," Maggie said soothingly to Wesley's horse. "Just be still, and we'll get you fixed up." She scavenged through her medical bag and pulled out a large set of tweezers. "I'm going to need both of you to hold on to him. And stay away from his back legs."

"I may not be a vet, but I do know how to avoid a horse's hindquarters," Walter lectured.

Several minutes passed while Maggie was engrossed in work she was very adept at. She hadn't really done much veterinary work since the twins were born, and she had to admit, even though she would never leave the kids, she still missed her old job. She was getting ready to put in a few sutures when she suddenly remembered the babies at home.

"Wesley," Maggie said while she poured some disinfectant on the wound. "I need you to go back and check on the girls."

"They're alone?" Walter questioned.

"They're both asleep. I didn't exactly have time to call a babysitter."

"I can get back in a few minutes," Wesley volunteered. He hopped on Lightning and rode back to the house.

* * *

This situation was impossible. Wesley wasn't panicking just yet, but he was about ready to. There were several people who could have just walked into the house and picked her up. It could have been Maria, or even his dad might be back from his doctor appointment early. Whoever took Emily out of her crib was probably looking for Maggie right now and was wondering why she would leave the babies alone. After fifteen minutes of searching and coming up with nothing, Wesley knew something was very wrong.

Wesley knew his grandpa never carried a cell phone, or he wouldn't have sent Wesley back to the house to get Maggie. He tried to call Maggie, but he heard her phone ringing in her purse on the counter. He called his dad, and there was no answer. He tried not to sound upset when he left the message: "Dad, it's me. Can you call back right away? I can't find Emily . . ." he started to explain, but his voice sounded too unsteady. "Just call me as soon as you get this."

Wesley couldn't risk leaving C.J. alone to run out and get someone, and he was supposed to meet Harrison for tutoring in about ten minutes. He was about ready to call 911 when there was a knock at the door. He ran to answer it, hoping it was someone who knew where his sister was.

Harrison was at the door, but he didn't have Emily.

"Harrison!" Wesley was truly frantic. "Emily is missing, and I don't know how she could have gotten out of her crib!"

"What?"

"I mean, Maggie had to leave for a few minutes—my horse got tangled in barbed wire—they were both asleep—I can't find her anywhere!"

"Slow down, Wesley." Harrison put two firm hands on Wesley's shoulders. It wasn't the type of thing Harrison would normally do, but it helped Wesley feel that there was an adult in charge now. "Are you sure someone from the family doesn't have her?"

"I'm positive," Wesley confirmed. "I called Grandma Penny, and she's on her way home now. Grandpa is with Maggie and my horse. Maria's not here, and Amanda and Dylan are still at school. My dad's at the doctor . . . unless he came back and picked her up."

Harrison removed his hands from Wesley's shoulders and followed him down the hall to the nursery, where C.J. was still sleeping. The bedroom window was open several inches, and the curtains blew eerily in the breeze.

"Wesley." Harrison's shy awkwardness seemed to melt away, and he was suddenly very confident. "Go get Maggie, and I'll stay here. I'll try to reach your dad, and then I'm calling the police."

* * *

"How could I have been so stupid?" Maggie said between sobs. "I left them alone. It was only for fifteen minutes, but I never should have done it. I'm the worst mother in the world!"

"I don't understand it." Penny shook her head. "This is so bizarre. It's not like we live in some suburban neighborhood. There's nobody out here but us!"

C.J. was sucking her thumb and leaning on Walter's shoulder. "There's always a chance," Walter addressed the group, "that she climbed out of her crib and crawled somewhere. I think we need to keep searching the house. Remember that time Maggie Sue was about a year old, and we found her asleep in the cupboard with the pots and pans?"

"I know, but we've torn the house apart." Maggie was inconsolable. "I've never seen her climb out of the crib before."

"I think we need to treat this as a kidnapping," Harrison interjected. "It's been almost an hour, and there's no sign of her."

Everyone blanched at the word *kidnapping*. Even though they had all been thinking it, no one dared speak it out loud.

Maggie threw up her hands and paced back and forth. The phone rang, startling the group and giving them hope at the same time. There was no number on the caller ID, but Maggie lunged for the phone anyway. "Hello?" she answered, her voice breaking as she wiped her face with her hand.

"She is an absolutely beautiful baby," a woman's voice said.

Maggie pushed the speaker button on and steadied herself on the desk so she wouldn't fall over. "Who is this?" she demanded. The room went silent.

"I don't think you would believe me if I gave you my name, but I do think that I have your full, undivided attention. Am I right?"

Wesley shuddered at the sound of the voice on the telephone.

"Where's Emily?" Maggie demanded.

"So we did get the right one. Your daughter is being well taken care of at the moment, but if you'd like for her to remain your daughter, I suggest you listen very carefully."

Wesley didn't have to break the news to Maggie. He could tell she already knew who the caller was.

Maggie took a deep breath. "I'm listening, Imogene."

Penny gasped.

"You're perceptive enough to figure that out but not perceptive enough to keep an eye on your children. I think you have some misplaced priorities, Maggie."

"You won't get away with this, you horrible woman!" Penny yelled. "Where is she?!"

"I suggest you not interrupt me, *Penny*," Imogene continued. "Or you might miss some very valuable information. You see, Maggie, I know exactly what's been going on for the last twenty months while you and your adolescent husband have been taking care of Wesley. Although I use the term *care* very loosely here. I know that Wesley has been traveling into the uncharted territories of Australia and riding dangerous wild horses, and that just recently, he was permanently suspended from a school so pathetic I wouldn't send my dog to it. Then you have the audacity to let him mingle with any riff-raff you can pick up off the street at that halfway house you call a ranch. But the most appalling thing of all is that you're just stupid enough to believe that a former gang member has been rehabilitated just because he plays football! I don't think anyone will be surprised that your gross negligence has resulted in your 'misplacement' of one of your daughters."

Tears rolled down Maggie's face, but she kept her composure. She had to keep Imogene on the line as long as possible. "Tell us what you want."

"I'm sure you already know what I want. But I'll spell it out anyway. I'd like to make an even exchange. Wesley for Emily. From what I understand, she's the quiet one. Good temperament, healthy, beautiful features. There are so many childless couples in the world. They would give *anything* to become parents. You have two—more than you can handle, obviously. It doesn't seem right, does it?"

"You're sick," Maggie said with disgust. "It isn't fair to barter with people's children."

"Fair? Didn't anyone ever tell you life isn't fair? Now, the decision to make the exchange is an easy one. Wesley is fourteen, and Emily is only eight months old. She's not an identical twin, and babies change so quickly at this age. That picture on the bulk mailer will be out-of-date in no time."

"You're a very deranged person, and you need help. You can't lock Wesley in a cage, and he'll never agree to stay with you. You know we'll hunt you down, and we *will* find you," Maggie asserted.

"I feel your pain, Maggie. Really I do. I've felt the very same way for a year and a half now. Think about it for a while. Call the police, of course. They are always *so* helpful. Have them search for bugs . . . trace this call. File a report or two . . . I'll be back in touch. Just remember one thing: the minute I see or hear this story on the news will be the minute I end these negotiations, and you say bye-bye to Emily for good."

The line disconnected.

Maggie sank to her knees and put her head in her hands. The room was spinning around her, and she felt like she was being sucked into the floor. Within minutes, Jack came busting through the door, begging for an explanation.

Maggie couldn't tell him what had just happened. She thought Harrison was explaining it all, but the words she heard didn't make any sense through the haze. They had been through this before. Lightning never strikes the same person twice—isn't that what they say?

* * *

Wesley stared blankly ahead as his life rounded the highest peak of the roller coaster; there was no place to go but down. People were talking, and he heard words, but it all sounded like gibberish to him. *She's back.* He thought. It was a dizzying mantra that kept sounding inside his head.

The worst part was that he had inadvertently been an accessory to the kidnapping. He was the one who had pulled Maggie away from the house to tend to his horse. And the fact that he and Walter were headed out to one of their clandestine driving expeditions made him feel even more guilty.

In his semicoherent state, Wesley was aware that Police Chief Hicks had arrived, summoned to the house at Harrison's insistence. He was a "local yokel," as Walter liked to call him, but he also had previous training with the military and the FBI. Penny and Walter had known Cordell Hicks and his family for years.

The chief took out his handkerchief and swabbed his balding head for the fourth time in ten minutes, the creases in his forehead like little shelves with pools of water dripping from them. "So the suspect—" Hicks began.

Maggie cut him off. "Imogene Vandergrift."

"Or someone *pretending* to be the deceased," Hicks interjected.

"She *isn't* deceased," Maggie said impatiently. "I recognized her voice, and so did Wesley. She didn't even try to pretend she was someone else."

"All right, then." Chief Hicks still didn't seem convinced. "Did this *alleged* Imogene Vandergrift give you any sort of indication how or when the transfer of Emily and Wesley is to take place?"

"No, she said she would contact us later."

Wesley willed the phone to ring. He could negotiate with her. He'd had many years of practice and knew her weaknesses. He would volunteer to go if she would give Emily back. Knowing Imogene, she would force them to wait in suspense until they were desperate enough to give in to her demands.

Maggie was gripping Jack's arm with one hand and sipping from a bottle of water in the other, the color completely gone from her face. "I'm telling you everything," she insisted. "She must have the place bugged. She seemed to know every detail of Wesley's life since we've had him back."

"We're sweeping the place for bugs now, but it's going to take some time." Hicks motioned to the detective, who was pulling out couch cushions and running some sort of scanning device over the furniture.

"Look, Chief Hicks," Jack pleaded. "Maybe you could start talkin' to some other people that know somethin' we don't—like Harrison Landry."

"Nobody is above suspicion, Jack, and I've already talked with Harrison. He's actually the person who called us here. Detective Sweeny has checked his record again, and it's spotless. Quite frankly, he has a higher security clearance than we do, and if we want to dig any deeper, we're going to have to get it from the commander in chief. Besides the fact that he's a decorated naval officer, he has an alibi."

"What, that he was the first person at the house after Emily was missing? That's not an alibi—that's circumstantial evidence!" Jack spied Harrison across the room. He was talking to Maria while cleaning his glasses with a handkerchief. "Someone's got to be feeding Imogene her information."

"Well," Hicks brushed Jack off, "we can assume that Imogene has been corresponding with your son under the name of Genevieve Devereaux for more than a year."

"But she mentioned Wesley's suspension and things that happened in the last three weeks," Maggie argued. "And she managed to walk into our home in the middle of the day and steal our daughter!"

"I'm sure it wasn't Imogene herself who came in here," Hicks reasoned.

"That's right." Jack nodded. "She's got to have someone workin' on the inside, and it's plain as day who it is."

"No, it isn't, Jack," Hicks cautioned. "You have two other young men living next door who came here at the same time as Harrison Landry. There are also a handful of people who work here on a temporary basis. Like I said, until we know more, everyone's a suspect, and that also means the two of you."

"I'll take a lie detector test right now." Jack scowled. "Just give one to *him*, too!" Jack's phone was vibrating, and he flipped it open. "Hello," he said hopefully.

His face turned ashen, and he set his phone on speaker and placed it on the table.

"You really didn't think I would be stupid enough to call back on the phone you just tapped, do you?" the caller said.

Wesley wanted to pick up the phone and hurl it at the wall, but he knew that wouldn't solve anything.

"I guess I'm not the homicidal maniac I was made out to be," Jack said belligerently. "But right now I wish I were."

"If we can't speak to each other civilly, then I don't think we need to talk at all."

"He's sorry," Maggie jumped in.

"That was sweet. Do you always let your wife talk for you, Jack?" Imogene goaded.

"Only when I'm about to say something inappropriate to an evil woman," Jack jabbed.

"So, I guess we're through talking, then."

Jack bit his tongue. "Just tell us what the plan is."

"It's a very simple one, really. You'll need to bring Wesley to the drop-off point that I'll disclose in a moment. After he takes the transportation I've provided, and I've received him on my end without any tracking devices, I will call you and tell you where you can pick up your daughter."

Jack was shaking his head in disagreement. "Just hypothetically, if we were to agree with your request, what guarantee do we have that you'll return Emily?"

"My good word, Jack. And the fact that you really don't have any other choice."

"Your word is no good, and there's always another choice," said Jack.

"Suit yourself. I hold all the bargaining power here, if you didn't notice."

The police chief pushed through the crowd and spoke into the phone. "Imogene, this is Police Chief Hicks, and I'd like to have a few words with you."

"And you must be the hostage negotiator who's trying to gain my trust. How presumptuous of you to assume we are on a first-name basis."

"We would like to reach a mutually beneficial agreement, Ms. Vandergrift."

"Yes, of course *we* would! And we already have. Let me tell you what *we* can do, Chief. Keep your pathetic little patrol cars as far away from Wesley as possible, and I won't make you spend the rest of your lackluster career looking for a baby you'll never find. Now, for this to work properly, you'll need to move quickly. I want Wesley at the Atlanta airport in exactly one hour. He won't need any luggage. He will board the plane alone. There will be someone to pick him up and bring him to my location when he lands. When I see him, you'll get your phone call. Not a moment sooner. Do I need to repeat that? Oh, and this is the important part: I don't want Jack or Maggie to drive him there."

"How do you want him to get there?" Hicks asked. "Wesley isn't old enough to drive himself."

"I *know* how old Wesley is, and I believe I'm finished talking with you, Chief," Imogene said curtly. "Maria will drive Wesley in her car. She probably still has that tacky red Camry, doesn't she?"

Maria jumped when she heard her name.

"What if Maria isn't here?" Jack asked.

"Then whoever is wearing that hideous turquoise shirt looks exactly like her."

Maria opened her mouth and clamped a hand over it.

"Don't look so shocked. I've had twenty months to plan this," Imogene gloated. "Which means I've covered all the bases. Now I'm a very generous woman, and I always make good on my promises—provided the people I'm dealing with don't double-cross me. Tell Maria to get in the car now, with nothing but Wesley and her cell phone, and I'll be in touch on the arrangements. Are we clear?"

Wesley leaned across the counter and locked eyes with his father. Jack nodded slowly. "We're clear."

Imogene hung up.

"What? You can't give in to her like that!" Chief Hicks roared. "Call her bluff! Make her meet your terms! Keep her on the line!"

"Quiet!" Jack barked. "You're officially off the case now!"

"You can't fire me! I work for the government."

"Stop talking!" Maggie cried. "She's listening to everything we say."

Wesley stepped in between Maggie and Jack. "I have to go. It's the only way to get Emily back."

"Wes, we don't know that." Jack patted his shoulder. "Maybe Chief Hicks is right, and we should call her bluff. Get this all over the news, and there won't be any place she can hide."

"Dad, she's really good at hiding. She's been hiding for almost two years now." Wesley stretched and then fanned himself. "She knows everything that's been going on in my life. It's really hot in here. I think I need some fresh air." He ran to the door, opened it quietly, and stepped outside. It wasn't more than a few seconds before Jack and Maggie came out and joined him.

A warm breeze blew onto the porch. The ducks were swimming, and Hercules was chasing his tail on the front lawn. It didn't seem possible that normal life could go on amidst the trauma.

"Dad, listen," Wesley entreated. "You have to let me go."

Jack started to speak but was interrupted by Harrison stealing onto the porch with them. "I don't believe we invited you, Harrison," Jack said curtly.

"It's okay, Dad. I did."

"When?"

"Just now. I don't have a lot of time to explain, but remember the mind-reading trick we did for everyone?"

Wesley didn't wait for a response but hurried on. "Well, Harrison and I can communicate using that sign language called semaphore. We can make the signals look like random movements so no one can tell."

Harrison was holding his glasses in one hand. "And he's very good at it. Jack and Maggie, if you'll send me with Wesley, I can tail him without being seen. I've done similar operations dozens of times. I'm trained to do it, and I have a way to communicate with him."

"But Imogene specifically asked for Maria," said Maggie.

"We're not going to send Wes," Jack said as if the point were obvious. "I just told her that to buy some time. I won't send him back to that mad woman."

Maggie started hyperventilating. "Jack, I believe her. If she doesn't get her way, she'll sell Emily to someone who wants a baby."

"Mag, we can't just trade one kid for another. She's a liar, and we're just givin' her the chance to keep both of them."

"I'm not *choosing* between the kids." Maggie started to cry again.

"Maggie's right," Wesley said. "She doesn't want to keep Emily; she's just trying to force you to send me. But you wouldn't be sending me. I'm volunteering to go."

"I'll take him." Maria stepped through the crack in the open door. "I believe she'll give Emily back if you do as she asks. I've known her for a long time."

Jack shook his head and looked at the ground.

"Please, Jack," Maggie pleaded. "It's our best option."

"We don't know what the best option is." Jack's voice broke.

"I have to do this for my sister," Wesley implored his father. "Let Harrison follow both of us. I trust him. He has a lot of skills."

"But Imogene will know if we have someone tail them," Maggie said sternly. "I don't know if we can risk that."

"I won't follow them in a car," Harrison explained. "Maria will drive Wesley, and I'll ride in the trunk. She won't suspect that."

"No, never." Jack said sarcastically. "No criminal has *ever* thought of hiding in the trunk before."

"With all due respect, Harrison," Maggie said, wringing her hands, "I'm sure you're good at what you do, but you have no idea who we're dealing with. If we're going to send someone, it should be me or Jack."

Chief Hicks stepped through the door and joined the group. He made no secret that he'd been listening in on the conversation. "That would be the worst mistake you could make," he stated. "Then what happens when Imogene calls to tell you where to pick up Emily? If either one of you is missing, it will give her a reason to go back on her word."

"We aren't askin' for your help here," Jack said sourly. "We know you have rules to obey, but we won't get our daughter back if we follow them."

"I absolutely agree. Imogene will be expecting us to send one of you or one of our undercover officers. That's why we don't. For all she knows, Harrison is just Wesley's tutor, if she even knows that much."

"She knew what color shirt Maria had on!" Jack threw his hands up. "Of course she knows about Mr. Navy SEAL." He motioned to Harrison with his head. "That's all anyone talks about around here."

"Do you really think we should have Harrison go with them?" Maggie asked Chief Hicks.

"Absolutely," Hicks said. "Normally we're supposed to use our own people. But right now I think it's our best option to let him help us find Emily *and* keep track of Wesley."

"Please, let him come with us," Wesley pleaded. "I'll feel a lot safer, and Maria will too."

Maria nodded her agreement. "But if Imogene is watching us, how will I let Harrison out of the trunk?"

"Don't worry about me," Harrison said airily. "As long as you stop for a few minutes, I should be able to get out by myself."

"He's the great Harry Landini," Wesley backed him up.

"I don't like this," Jack said. "But if you're willing to go, Wes, and you trust Harrison, then let's do it."

There wasn't time to weigh all the pros and cons. They had to get on the road immediately. Imogene had said one hour, and they were already going to be late. There was barely time for Harrison to disconnect the light inside Maria's trunk and stow away under an old picnic blanket.

"Wes." Jack hugged his son. "I promise you, we're going to find you. Just like we did last time, remember?"

"I know you will," Wesley said. "Don't worry, Dad. I can handle this."

Maggie grabbed Wesley's hand. "That promise goes for me too." She kissed the top of his head. "You are the bravest person I know."

Maria was talking to Amanda as if she were just going to visit an old friend. She seemed to be pushing the group to hurry up and let them be on their way.

"It's going to be okay, Wesley," Maggie said with forced conviction. Then she buried her head in Jack's shoulder as Maria drove away in the car, carrying Wesley and Harrison to a fate no one could imagine.

10

The Shell Game

Maria had never even been to the Atlanta airport and didn't know how to get there. Her hands were shaking on the steering wheel, and Wesley, who had a good sense of direction, had a map out and was navigating.

Wesley pointed to the road sign. "It's the next exit."

"I'm really sorry, Wesley," Maria blurted out.

"What for? This isn't your fault."

"If I had been home today, I could have watched the girls, and this wouldn't have happened."

"If I would have been paying more attention, I could have steered Rocky away from the barbed wire, and it wouldn't have happened."

"Maybe not this time, but she would have found another opportunity."

"Yeah, probably." Wesley sighed. "It was weird to hear her voice again, wasn't it?"

"It gave me chills. Are you scared?"

"I'm scared for Emily, not for myself. Imogene will return her, won't she? I mean, she just wants me, don't you think?"

Maria nodded. She wanted to tell Wesley that she never imagined Imogene could do something so awful, and that if she had been a better judge of character to begin with, he could have been returned to his father when he was a baby. But she said nothing, knowing that he was probably thinking that anyway.

Maria's phone rang, and she picked it up as she was turning off the freeway. It wasn't Imogene, but it sounded like a man whose voice was electronically altered. She envisioned one of those protected criminals that were interviewed on TV with only a black outline for a face. He told her to pull up to the terminal curb and drop Wesley off.

"But I can't just leave him there alone!" she protested.

"You'll do exactly as you're told if you want the baby returned safely," the robotic voice said. "You've already broken the rules. And you're late."

Maria swallowed her fear and tried to look impassive for Wesley's sake. "I'll do what you ask." She pulled the car up to the designated terminal and squeezed Wesley's hand. She looked at him and gave him a weak smile.

"It's okay, Maria. I'll be fine. Just promise me you'll do what she says."

"I promise." Her hand slid out of Wesley's to wipe her eyes as he stepped onto the curb. He looked oddly out of place with no luggage or backpack and with just a light jacket on.

Maria had no time to ponder the scene as the voice barked orders at her.

"Keep moving! Under no circumstances will you stop this car until I say so."

"What about traffic signals?" Maria couldn't see how she was going to obey this order.

"There won't be any where you're going."

"Where am I going?"

"I'll give you directions. Just keep moving."

Maria looked at her gas gauge. It showed three-quarters of a tank. She was the type of person who never let her tank go below half. But then Imogene would know that, and that's why she'd selected Maria to drive. But what rule had Maria supposedly broken? She wondered if they knew Harrison was in the trunk. She wished she could signal him somehow. Could he hear her conversation? Her mind feverishly tried to come up with some sort of plan. She just wasn't good at this sort of thing. The ugly voice was talking to her, and she had missed part of it. With a sigh of resignation she decided she would stay focused and not let her desire to protect Harrison get in the way of Emily and Wesley's safety. She knew Imogene would try to use any measure of disobedience as an excuse to go back on her word. Emily, Wesley, and then Harrison. It was a horrible thing to have to prioritize the people she cared about, like some sort of errand list.

* * *

"I am not taking a sedative." Maggie threw the bottle of pills on the floor. "Two of my children have been kidnapped, and I'm not going to just go to bed and hope they reappear in the morning!"

"Maggie," Chief Hicks consoled. "I realize this is a lot for anyone to handle, but you need to calm down . . ."

"Obviously you don't know my wife," Jack interrupted. "It'll take more than a few pills to calm her down."

Chief Hicks gave up and turned his attention to Jamal and Dylan, who had been summoned to the

Mackey house for interrogation. "This isn't an official line of questioning because we can't go to the station right now. Technically, I'm not even here, because if we put this through dispatch, we are required to issue a kidnapping alert, and in this case it may not yield the best results."

"So am I a suspect?" Dylan asked.

"Yes, and no. Until we get some more information, all of you are," Hicks answered. We're just trying to put all the pieces together. Did either of you observe anything strange or out of the ordinary?"

"Besides Harrison, not really," Dylan answered.

"What do you mean, besides Harrison?" Jack jumped in.

"Well, he's definitely strange and out of the ordinary, don't you think?"

"We know that, but is there anything specific?" Maggie prodded.

Hicks had dropped out of the conversation now and was writing notes on his clipboard.

Jamal opened his mouth to speak, scratched his head, and then began again. "Okay, this may not be important, but I saw something the other day that really messed with my head."

"Tell us, Jamal. It could be important," Maggie assured him.

"You may have seen us tossing the football around a few days ago."

Maggie nodded.

Jamal glanced at Dylan. Well, Dylan threw the football at Harrison and knocked his lights out."

"It was an accident!" Dylan defended.

"Pipe down and let me finish," Jamal scolded. "Anyway, I persuaded Dylan to apologize. Harrison accepted it and then threw the ball back to Dylan. Well, I know I'm not the smartest guy on the planet, but I do know something about football. That pass looked like it might have come from Steve Young. Perfect spiral, thirty-five-yard bullet, right at Dylan. Only Dylan isn't Jerry Rice, so he didn't catch it. Anyway, later when I asked Harrison where he learned how to throw like that, he pretended like it was nothing and said they used to throw the ball around at boot camp. I just thought it was really strange, that's all."

Jack and Maggie looked at each other.

"I hear you, mate." Jack nodded his head. "I've been tryin' to tell Maggie that something about this Harrison character just doesn't add up."

"But we know he's a SEAL," Maggie jumped in. "It's no secret that he's had some pretty intensive physical training. That's why we allowed him to go along." Maggie started walking off her nervous energy, and everyone noticed that this direction of conversation was making her more agitated.

"Don't get me wrong. I'm not saying anything against Harrison," Jamal added. "I really like the guy. He's been great to share the cabin with—pretty quiet and keeps to himself. I really doubt he's pulling something over on us."

"If he is," Dylan added bluntly, "then he's doing a really good job."

"And why is that?" Hicks stopped scribbling in his notebook and looked up, as if he were tallying up the pros and cons of Harrison Landry.

"Just that he's the quintessential goody-goody."

"Quintessential?" Jack looked at Maggie and raised his eyebrows.

Everyone looked at Dylan like he was an alien, so he elaborated. "You know, the perfect model of someone who obeys all the rules."

"I know what it means, mate," said Jack. "I was just makin' sure you did."

"I've never even heard him use a swear word," Dylan remarked.

"Have there been any unusual visitors to your cabin?" Hicks asked.

"Just the regulars," Jamal answered.

"I'm going over with a team to check things out right now," Hicks said. "We'll check for bugs and anything else we can find."

* * *

Wesley had been expecting to board a plane and fly several thousand miles to some deserted island Imogene had purchased in the middle of the ocean. For as long as he could remember, he and Imogene had never thought alike, so he should have known that she would do exactly the opposite of what he expected. A young woman with extremely pale skin and a frumpy hairdo came up to him and handed him a plane ticket. The destination was Phoenix, Arizona. "Gate 17" was scrawled in red pen.

"Hurry up, Wesley," she said in a low, throaty voice. She had strangely transparent blue eyes that were icy and unfriendly. "Your flight is boarding. Follow me closely. I am your aunt, and you are coming home with me for a visit. Remember, if you alert anyone that something is wrong, your sister will not be returned. Do you understand?"

Wesley nodded and followed the young woman. She was wearing an overcoat and smelled like cigarette smoke. He almost wished she was packing a gun, so she'd be detained, but she came out of the metal detector clean. But afterward, the fake aunt headed in the opposite direction of gate 17.

"We're going the wrong way," said Wesley.

The woman was silent and kept walking. Wesley tried to think of what Grandma Penny would do in this situation. She always had the answers to life's problems. Who would have guessed that she could turn a hopeless case like Dylan into a hardworking, nonsmoking friend of Wesley's in a matter of weeks? He decided to try Grandma Penny's befriend-your-enemy technique.

"Do you have a name?" Wesley asked.

"Everyone has a name. You don't need to know it."

"Well, then, can I call you whatever I want?" Wesley was hoping this woman wasn't really a bad person, just someone who had a lot of bad breaks in life. "How old are you? You look about nineteen."

"Look, kid, I'm older than you think, and I'm not your friend, got that?"

"Sure, but gate 17 is back that way. I don't want you to be responsible for me missing my flight. That would be bad for both of us." Wesley had to break into a sprint to keep up with her.

"You won't. We're not getting on a plane." Wesley's "aunt" stormed down the adjacent terminal, back out of the airport, and into the covered airport parking lot, all the while ignoring Wesley's pleas to stop and get a smoothie.

"You are some annoying kid." The woman shoved Wesley into the backseat of a forest green jeep that was driven by a muscleman with a crew cut. Her tone wasn't any nicer when she addressed the driver. "Get out, Andy—I'm driving."

"I'm already driving, Simone," he whined back at her.
"I said get out."

Even though he was twice her size, the man she called Andy cowered to her order. He got out of the driver's seat, walked around the car, slid into the passenger seat, and sulked.

Simone removed her wig, revealing spiky, coal-black dyed hair that was only a few inches long. She shucked the overcoat and peasant skirt and threw them into the backseat. Underneath she was wearing a black tank top and army fatigue pants.

"Hurry up! You want the cops to see us?" Andy said impatiently.

Simone sat in the driver's seat, gave him a cold stare, and opened up a duffel bag. She pulled out a black eye pencil, twisted the rearview mirror and proceeded to trace around her eyes with thick liner. Wesley got the impression she was purposely trying to make Andy angry. She took a moment to see if her artwork met with her satisfaction. "Now I'm ready."

Wesley caught her reflection in the mirror as she backed out of the parking stall. She looked like a fair-complexioned Egyptian.

The car was quiet as Simone lit a cigarette and dangled it out the window. Wesley hated the smell of cigarette smoke.

"You know that's really bad for you," he said.

"Yeah, so are a lot of things," Simone answered. "Like talking when you shouldn't."

"Do you know who you're working for?" Wesley asked.

There was no answer.

"She's a really dangerous lady named Imogene Vandergrift, who thinks she's my mother but she's not.

Do you know that she kidnapped my baby sister? She's only eight months old."

"I don't care," Simone replied.

"Well, you should because you won't get away with this. My dad is Jack Mackey. He's the Snake Stalker, just in case you didn't know. Last time he found me when he was blind," Wesley bragged. "Out in the middle of the ocean on a boat." Wesley looked out the window. It was starting to turn to dusk.

"Listen, kid," Simone's voice grated like a saw. "Nobody feels sorry for you—got that? Some people aren't lucky enough to have two people fighting over who gets to keep them. Some people have parents who don't even want them."

Wesley slouched back in his seat. Some people had issues, and it was pointless to try and reason with them.

* * *

The longer Maria drove on the deserted old highway, the more anxious she felt. Two hours had passed since she'd dropped Wesley off at the airport. Her gas tank was getting low, and she wondered if Imogene's intent was to get her as far away from civilization as possible before she ran out of gas. The distorted voice kept her on her cell phone and checked in with her every ten minutes or so to make sure she was following instructions and not stopping. She tried not to think about how Harrison was faring inside the trunk. He was probably wondering why she hadn't stopped to let him out. She hoped he wasn't exaggerating with all those undercover-agent stories. The sun was just disappearing, along with her spirits and her gas.

A car pulled up behind her and started following closely. She maneuvered onto the right shoulder to let it pass. The road was curvy, but the car could have passed her easily if it wanted to. Instead, the car flashed its brights into her rearview mirror. She could see the outline of the vehicle against the dark sky. Either it had a luggage rack on top, or it was a highway patrol car. She checked her speed. She might have been going five miles over. The last thing she needed was the police trying to gun her down for some minor moving violation. Several minutes later her worst fear materialized. The flashing lights in her rearview mirror left no doubt as to the tailgater's identity.

Maria picked up her phone, and the man was still waiting on the other end. "There's a police car behind me," she told him. "It has its lights on."

"If you think calling the cops will get you out of this, you're very stupid. We still have the baby. You stop this car, and the deal's over."

"I didn't call them! How could I call anyone when I've been talking to you for the last two hours? Besides, I don't even know where I am." She thought it might have been Harrison who alerted them from inside the trunk. But unless he could see through metal, he wouldn't know where they were either.

"Lose them," the voice commanded.

"I can't lose them! I'm the only car on the road! I can't outrun a police car."

"You can, and you will. Turn off your lights, and turn right onto the next dirt road, past the deer-crossing sign."

Maria's head was spinning. How was she supposed to see the road when her lights were off? Cautiously she switched off her lights and pressed the accelerator to the floor. She couldn't see more than a few yards in front of the car, but she didn't think the man would be sympathetic to her cause, so she didn't say anything. The sound she heard immediately after that might have been a police siren or some panic alarm inside her head. She couldn't tell. She sped down a gravel and dirt road, leaving a giant plume of dust behind her. When the dust settled, the police car was still with her. Should she pull over now and tell the police everything? Would Imogene really keep Emily if she did? It wasn't worth finding out. She kept steady pressure on the gas and fishtailed down the road. There was absolutely no artificial light on the road, and she had only the dim moon to illuminate her way. At any moment she could drive right off the winding road and straight into a tree.

After a few minutes had passed under these stressful conditions, she checked her rearview mirror. It appeared that the police car had given up the chase. Either that, or the cop had been called away to something else. There was no one on the phone, either. Her phone was out of range for service. She was lost in the middle of nowhere.

Maria eased up on the gas pedal but didn't dare turn her lights on yet. Checking her rearview mirror again, she was fairly sure no one was following her. Her gaze might have lingered too long, because when she returned her focus to the front, she thought she may have wandered off the road. Just ahead she detected the outline of a structure, and she was headed straight for it. She swerved to avoid what she assumed must be a barn. It wasn't until the front of her car made contact with wooden railroad ties that she realized she had just turned her car down a steep embankment to avoid a bridge. Too late for any corrections, her front left tire made contact with the guardrail and two tires lifted off the ground, careening her into a river. For the two seconds that she was suspended in the air, she thought of how she'd failed everyone she was trying to help. The passenger-side front fender hit the water first, and Maria felt her seat belt jerk tightly before her head struck the driver's side window. There wasn't time for her to take a breath before she lost consciousness and the rest of her car tumbled into the water.

* * *

Wesley didn't know how long they had been driving because Andy had confiscated his watch and had thrown it out the window along some deserted highway. He was wondering how much longer they would be driving out where there was a total absence of civilization. They had long since been off the highway. It was pitch black, and they were winding along some deserted dirt road in the mountains. He was starting to feel queasy but didn't think his request to sit in the front seat would be honored.

Finally Simone stopped the car and let him out. The smell of pine needles and the great outdoors was a welcome change to the smoky interior of the jeep, but Wesley was under no illusion that this would be like scout camp. Simone and Andy led Wesley up to the front door of a dimly lit log cabin surrounded by a thick forest of pine trees. He figured Imogene would be waiting for him in a moat-encircled castle in some European country—that this place was only a stop to throw everyone off before they traveled to their final destination. Simone gave four even knocks on the door and then opened it with a key.

Andy ushered Wesley in. The lights were on, and he saw that the small cabin, with its unpolished wood floors, was anything but lavish. Wesley felt the adrenaline pumping through his body when he recognized the woman sitting in a wingback leather chair, looking regal and confident as always. Her red hair was a burning contrast to her cold, gray eyes.

"Wesley, come in and let me look at you. Don't linger in the doorway."

He walked slowly toward her. He hadn't expected her to be here in person. But then, he never guessed right when it came to Imogene.

"You've grown a few inches, I see. But you look a bit thin. I guess the food isn't quite what you're used to."

Wesley resisted the impulse to tell her that Grandma Penny was the best cook in the whole world.

"I've missed you so much," Imogene said. "You know that, don't you?"

"Kidnapping my sister isn't the way to get on my good side," he stated.

"Don't worry, she'll be returned very soon." Imogene spoke as if his sister were an unwanted wedding gift. "Come and sit down." She patted the armrest of the adjacent couch. "We have so much to catch up on."

"You expect me to be okay with this?" Wesley walked over to the worn leather couch and hovered in front of it. "Do you think I'll just forget about my dad and Maggie and want to live with you again?"

"No, of course not. I know I can't force you to stay. I just want to spend some time with you. That's all."

"How much time?"

"We'll discuss that later. Right now I'm sure you must be very tired and disappointed, too, that your parents were so quick to choose your sister over you."

"They had to. She's a baby."

"Yes, and she will always be younger, more fragile, more *important* to them, don't you think?"

"Stop twisting things like you always do."

"Wesley, I'm just stating the facts. They didn't raise you—I did. Naturally, it's too late for you to ever form the same kind of bond with them that we have."

"We don't have any bond."

"Oh, but we do, Wesley. I am the only mother you've ever known."

"Only because you stole me when I was a baby."

"I saved your life." Imogene folded her hands in her lap. "And I'm going to save it again." Imogene checked her watch. Wesley saw that it was encrusted with multiple diamonds. "You can go to bed now, and we'll talk again tomorrow when you're rested. All I'm asking is that you give me a few days, Wesley. Listen to what I have to say, and then you can make your own choice."

"And if I choose to go home, you'll let me?" Wesley studied her face.

Imogene nodded her head slowly. "Promise me you won't try to leave for at least a few days, and I'll promise to let you go home if you want."

Wesley didn't want to make any deals with Imogene. She could always be counted on to bend the rules to fit her agenda. Not wanting to make her angry, he stalled for time. "I need to call my parents first."

Imogene nodded again. "They'll be contacted soon."

* * *

Jack, Maggie, Chief Hicks, and Amanda were the only people left at the house now. They had sent C.J. over to Penny and Walter's because all the commotion was agitating her, and Hicks had sent two men to keep guard over them. It was 10:45, and they had heard nothing for five hours. When the home phone rang, Hicks answered it on the speaker.

"I want to know everyone who is there right now," Imogene barked.

"It's me, Maggie, the police chief, and Amanda," Jack answered. "Is Wesley with you?"

"He is."

"I want to talk to my son now."

"I don't have that much time before this phone call will automatically disconnect. I think you'd better concentrate on picking up your daughter first. See, I am willing to keep my end of the bargain. But just to keep you from setting up the troops, I'll be sending the three of you to different locations. Do you have a pen and paper?"

"Yes," Hicks said.

Imogene gave them three different addresses, none of which sounded familiar to anyone. Chief Hicks scribbled them down on a piece of paper. "You could all take one car," Imogene suggested. "But it would be faster if you split up."

"Where is my mom?" Amanda shouted into the phone.

"Amanda, you poor, dear child," Imogene said in a disparaging tone. "I think it's past your bedtime. I gave Maria the opportunity to drive Wesley because I hoped I could count on her. I do hope no one did anything to jeopardize Emily's safe return. As long as she followed my instructions, I can assure you that—"

The line disconnected.

"Too short." Hicks looked at his watch. "We can't trace it."

"I knew we shouldn't have sent Harrison!" Jack slapped the table.

Maggie shook her head. "Let's look up these addresses right now. Amanda, do you want to stay with Penny and Walter or come with one of us?" Maggie asked.

"She'll stay with them," Hicks decided. "We don't want her to be used as bait for another kidnapping."

"I want to be here when my mom comes back," Amanda said.

"Whoever finds the baby will call the other two." Hicks was typing the addresses into his laptop. He printed out three sets of maps. "As soon as we confirm that we have her, I'll send out my team for an investigation. "Maggie, this address is a hospital. That's the safest place, so you go there. Jack, I have no idea where these two places are. They could be a private residence or some back alley. It's up to you—we can send our detectives, or you can go alone."

"Go alone," Maggie and Jack said in unison.

Hicks handed Jack one of the direction sheets and kept the other for himself. "One thing I can say for this Vandergrift woman—she really knows how to cover her tracks. We are dealing with a very skilled criminal."

* * *

When Maggie called Jack from the hospital for the third time, he had been searching an elementary school playground for twenty minutes. There was no sign of Emily at either location.

"Jack, I've been sneaking in and out of people's rooms looking for her. I checked pediatrics and asked everyone here, and they're about ready to admit me to the psychiatric ward if I don't quit bothering them. I think it's time to issue a kidnapping alert."

"I hate to say it, Mag, but we should have done that hours ago. Hicks is on a wild goose chase too. The address she gave him doesn't even exist."

"How could she do this?" Maggie screamed a whisper. "I really thought she would honor the bargain."

"You can't use the words *honor* and *Imogene* in the same sentence. Maybe Hicks called in the SWAT team after all and scared her away. I think we should head home. Something about this whole thing doesn't make sense, and maybe Hicks isn't being straight with us."

Maggie argued that they needed to wait longer, that maybe they should check the addresses again, but for some reason she knew it was futile. "She's had enough time. She wouldn't even let us talk to Wesley. Jack, she lied to us and set us up. We were desperate, and we walked right into her trap. And who knows what happened to Maria and Harrison?" Maggie's voice got louder and some members of the hospital staff were coming over to usher her out. "I don't know what to do or who to trust—I just want Emily and Wesley back!" She looked at two orderlies coming straight for her. She dodged them as she slammed her phone shut and ran down the hospital corridor. Her heart was pumping so fast she thought she might go into shock and they'd have to wheel her back in.

The cool air outside helped her calm down a bit. She fumbled for her car keys as her cell phone vibrated. It was Penny. She sounded as out of breath as Maggie felt.

"Maggie, we have Emily!"

"Really? Mom, where are you?"

"At your house."

"Is she okay?"

"She's perfectly fine."

"I'll be home as fast as I can drive."

* * *

"I don't understand it." Jack scratched his head. Maggie was on the couch next to Penny, with Emily asleep in her lap. C.J. was asleep in a playpen, and Walter was pacing the room with Jack. Amanda was curled up in a sleeping bag on the floor. "Someone just brought her here to the house, broke inside, and left her in her crib within fifteen minutes of when we left and no one noticed anything?" He spoke quietly and looked over his shoulder so that Hicks and his detectives, who were questioning Dylan in the kitchen, wouldn't overhear.

Penny nodded. "Thank goodness Dylan found her right away. He came over here because he saw the light on and thought y'all were back. He heard her crying and could see her through the bedroom window in her crib. The door was locked, and no one answered so he ran over and got me and Walter."

Maggie folded a blanket over Emily. "They just left her here, all alone."

"So why did she send you out to three different locations?" Walter asked.

"I don't know," Maggie sobbed. "Why does she do anything she does?"

"There has to be a reason," Walter muttered.

"I've got it!" Jack snapped his fingers. "Imogene was playing the shell game with us."

"What?"

"You know when a magician hides an object under three different cups, then scrambles them around and you have to guess where it is. But the magician palms the object and it's really under none of them, so the guesser is never right."

"You're absolutely right, Jack," Penny agreed. "She wants to be in control."

"Right now she *is* in control," Maggie admitted. "She has Wesley, and I'm scared to death. She has our house under surveillance, and I don't think we should stay here tonight."

"Mag, we've got a whole police force in our kitchen," Jack said to assure her. "We have to try and get some sleep so we can start lookin' for Wes in the morning."

"And just where are we going to look?" Maggie asked angrily. "Imogene isn't even pretending to tell us where Wesley might be, and we have no idea what has happened to Maria or Harrison."

"Chief Hicks has some leads on a flight to Phoenix," Walter said weakly.

Maggie was too fatigued to argue with either of them. She knew that Jack was right and she needed sleep, so she propped a couch pillow under the back of her neck, and without removing Emily from her lap, she leaned back and closed her eyes.

11

Rude Awakening

Maria was cold and shivering, but somehow she felt hot and sweaty at the same time. There was a bright light shining through the window, and when Maria awoke, her first thought was that she must have a wad of cotton lodged in her throat. She was lying on some strange bed in unfamiliar surroundings with someone else's clothes on. It took her a moment to realize that the bright light was the sun. Her hair was damp and matted, and when she lifted a heavy hand to her head, she felt a large lump. She had no memory of what happened, where she was, or how she got here. There was a deep gash on her arm, but it wasn't particularly painful. She moved her neck and felt a stiffness, along with a dull ache in her shoulder.

The events from the night before came trickling in randomly. She had been driving alone in the dark on a desolate road. Emily had been kidnapped—no, Wesley had been kidnapped. They had both been kidnapped. And Imogene wasn't dead. The man on the phone had told her not to stop the car. She'd been in some sort of accident. She'd been the only one in the car. Her heart started beating rapidly. She hadn't been the only one in the car.

Harrison was in the trunk!

As her memory slowly came back into focus, it came with the horrific realization that she had driven her car off a bridge and into a river or lake and killed Harrison in the process.

The policeman behind her had probably rescued her, but the police would have no way of knowing there was a person inside her trunk. She wondered if Harrison had hit his head and been knocked unconscious or whether he'd drowned while struggling to unlatch the trunk from inside. This couldn't have happened. It wasn't possible. She had finally found someone she cared about, and within weeks she was responsible for his death. How could she live with herself after this? She would rather have drowned than go on with that burden for the rest of her life.

Maria attempted to stand up, but she was still feeling woozy, and as she tried unsuccessfully to gain her balance, she sunk back down on the bed. The door to her room opened, and the person she least wanted to see on the entire earth stepped in. She had felt sick to her stomach a moment ago, and the vision in front of her intensified the feeling.

"Maria, how very *unexpected* to see you here," her former friend and employer said caustically.

Maria tried to speak, but the words caught in her throat like a piece of dry cracker.

"You're looking very well for someone who has come back from the dead," Imogene commented as she stepped closer. Maria scooted back further on the bed.

"Unfortunately, I can't say the same for you," Maria said as she found her voice.

"Now, now, there's no need for resentment."

"Resentment?" Maria leaned forward and grabbed Imogene's wrist. "That's what you think this is? You just kidnapped *two* very important people in my life and *murdered* another, and you think I might feel *resentment?*"

Imogene yanked her wrist from Maria's grip. "I can't be held responsible for other people's inability to keep track of their children. And I can assure you, I haven't murdered anyone."

"There was someone in the trunk of my car!"

"Really?" Imogene sounded unconcerned. "Are you sure?"

"Yes, and he's dead because of you."

"No, on the contrary, if anyone is dead, it would be because you didn't follow my orders. I told you to come alone."

"I don't answer to you anymore!" Maria shot back. "You knew he was in there! That's why you wouldn't let me stop the car." Maria had enough guilt of her own without Imogene adding to it. "Who pulled me out? How did I get here?" Maria's anger was giving her strength, and she felt worked up enough to stand.

"Patience, Maria." Imogene smirked. "I see you haven't lost any of your petulance. I'll introduce you to your knight in shining armor, but first, let's get some breakfast, shall we?" Imogene strode confidently out of the room.

Maria followed her reluctantly into the kitchen area, where a table was set with a variety of muffins and juices on a lace tablecloth. A large picture window looked out through tall pines that bordered a small lake. "It's really rather peaceful out here, isn't it?" Imogene said. "No phone lines, Internet, or cell phones to disturb the pristine beauty. Nothing but trees and mountains for miles and miles. When is the last time you really had a vacation?" Imogene motioned for Maria to sit and then sat down herself.

"Where's Wesley?" Maria demanded.

"He's here. Sleeping very soundly. I gave him a little something to help him sleep last night. I think it's best to let him rest, don't you?"

"Have you returned Emily?" she asked hopefully.

"Yes, in spite of your failure to follow the rules, she's at home. Everyone is exactly where they belong now. Except for you. Where do you belong?"

Maria suddenly realized that she had unwittingly followed Wesley. If she and Wesley were both here, they could make their escape together. But then she thought of Harrison and started to cry as she took a sip of the orange juice that burned her throat. Imogene probably interpreted her crying as the response to her question about where she belonged.

"Maria, we've washed your clothes, and they should be dry by now. Maybe you'd like to have a shower and change before I let you in on the good news."

"What good news?"

"Oh, just something that I guarantee will make you very, very happy."

"There's nothing you could say that would make me happy right now."

"You would be wrong again." Imogene dabbed the corner of her mouth with a napkin. "Oh, all right. I guess this can't wait." She got up from the table and disappeared down the hallway into another room. She returned a moment later, beaming, as if she were ready to announce the next game show contestant.

"I have someone I would like you to meet. He is the one responsible for pulling you out of your car and saving your life. Allow me to introduce you to Peter Jaworsky." Imogene raised her eyebrows and stepped aside, uncovering the mystery guest.

Maria felt an adrenaline rush, and then she felt faint. If it was possible to feel anger and elation at the same time, she was feeling it now. She blinked to make sure her eyes were focusing correctly. "Harrison?"

He nodded at her and gave her a half smile, one that she couldn't understand.

"Oh yes," Imogene added. "Peter is also known as Agent 11, Harrison Landry, and probably a host of other aliases. Come now, admit that this is a wonderful surprise!"

Maria's relief at seeing Harrison alive was tainted by her confusion with the whole situation. "I don't understand . . . how did you get out of the trunk, and how did you get *here?*"

Before Harrison could respond, Imogene cut him off. "I'll let you two get acquainted momentarily." She sighed. "It seems that I am a better matchmaker than even I could have imagined."

"What?" Bile rose in Maria's throat. She shot Harrison a punitive look. "You work for *her?*" She spat out the last word with venom.

"Don't look so shocked, Maria," Imogene said. "You worked for me for twelve and a half years. If I remember correctly, we were quite good friends. That is, until you decided to give my only child to complete strangers."

Maria was so distraught that she couldn't respond to Imogene's ridiculous accusation. Her eyes begged Harrison to contradict what Imogene was saying.

"I'm sorry, Maria. This isn't how it was supposed to happen," Harrison said in a voice that belonged to a stranger. "I was going to tell you eventually. I never meant for you to find out like this."

"I trusted you." Maria's eyes were full. "I thought you were just different, but Jack was right all along. You're the mole. You've been feeding her information this whole time! And you're as bad as they come."

Imogene seemed delighted with the conversation. She shook her head knowingly. "Yes he is, isn't he? Maria, you are so predictable! You always did like the bad boys, didn't you? You think you've changed—that all you want is a nice young man to settle down with. But didn't I tell you, Peter? She would fall for the one she thought she could help. Always trying to 'fix' people—to help them with their problems." She turned to Maria. "It's so satisfying to be absolutely right all the time."

"You disgust me. You're wrong, and you won't get away this time. Now that you've exposed yourself, the police will hunt you down and find you—and me and Wesley too."

Imogene dismissed Maria with a wave of her hand. "Yes, the police are so capable, aren't they? I practically gave them my name and address, and they still couldn't find me. You have so much to learn about life, Maria, that I'm afraid even someone with my skills cannot begin to teach it to you."

Maria was silent. She looked at Imogene and then back at Harrison.

"I know exactly what I want and how to get it," Imogene continued, obviously enjoying the sound of her own voice. "What about you, Maria? What do you want out of life? Security? A dashing man with a mysterious past—not unlike your own. Wesley and Amanda? Maybe another baby? Wouldn't that be nice?"

"I have that already." She glared at Harrison. "With the exception of the man, and that is something I can definitely do without. What I want is for you to let Wesley and me go home."

"You're free to go. I'm not stopping you." Imogene motioned to the front door.

"You're not going to stop us if we try to leave?"

"I said *you* are free to go. If you don't mind walking alone. It's a forty-mile hike out of here if you know which direction to go. There's also a bit of wildlife to contend with. But the bears aren't usually out in the day."

Maria pondered this information. "I'll take my chances. I'd like to talk with Wesley. Then I'll be leaving."

"As you wish." Imogene smiled.

* * *

Maggie dozed off in the leather armchair. Emily was on her lap drinking a bottle. Amanda was sprawled out on the couch with Hercules at her feet. Detective Sweeney was talking on the phone, and when he hung up he heaved a sigh, startling both Maggie and Amanda.

"We have some news to report," he said gingerly.

"What is it?" Maggie shifted Emily on her lap.

"This morning they found a car upside down in the river off some backcountry road in the Blue Ridge Mountains. We checked the plates—it's Maria's."

Maggie sat up straight. "Where's Maria?"

"We don't know. The good news is the car was empty. No bodies in the trunk either. I think we can assume that they got out somehow. Our teams are scouring the area right now."

Maggie started to stand. "Jack and I are headed out there now."

"Hold on!" Sweeney put up his hand. "They'll call us when they know something. If you go running off half-cocked every time I give you a piece of information, I'm going to have to keep it to myself. This isn't exactly protocol, you know."

"So what about the flight to Phoenix?" Maggie asked.

"Nothing. Chief Hicks is still at the airport. He thinks it may have been a decoy."

"You mean Wesley got on a different plane?"

"Or no plane at all. We don't know for sure."

"Shouldn't we put out a kidnapping alert now?"

"At this point we've lost the advantage. All we would do is alert the media, and that, as you know, brings in a whole set of new problems. Chief Hicks and I would be court-martialed for not going by the rules, and you'd have to start all over with new investigators. That's not in anyone's best interest."

Maggie nodded. She hadn't thought about the repercussions; it was too late to issue an alert now.

"We also want Imogene to feel safe enough to stay put until we can find her," Sweeney added as he left the room to take a private call.

After he was gone, Amanda said quietly, "Maggie, do you really think they got out of the car?"

"I'm sure they did. They're just hiding out until it's safe. Maybe they weren't even in the car when it crashed."

"Maybe they're injured," Amanda said.

Maggie didn't sugarcoat things. "I don't know, but they might be fine, too. I know that Harrison is a lot more capable than he looks."

"I know. He doesn't look like he can do a lot of things, but he can. Sometimes I wonder if he's really weird or if he's just pretending." Amanda removed Hercules from her lap and fed him a cracker from the box on the coffee table.

"What do you mean, pretending?" Maggie questioned.

"Well, you know how he always wears those really thick glasses, and they're like his security blanket?"

"Yeah, that's the one thing he wouldn't take your mom's advice about." Maggie leaned forward and sat Emily down on the floor.

"Well the other day he left them on our counter for a minute. He never takes them off, and I wanted to see how bad his vision was, so I tried them on."

"You tried his glasses on?"

"Yeah, they were really heavy, but the strange thing is, I could see just fine through them. Maybe they had a little magnification, but they definitely weren't any heavy-duty prescription."

"That is strange." Maggie tried not to show how uneasy she felt at this new information. "Did you say anything to your mom or Harrison?"

"No, I thought my mom might think my eyes were bad too and make me go see the eye doctor. Anyway, I forgot about it. But now that all this stuff is happening and my mom is missing, it makes me think that maybe Harrison has something to do with all this."

Maggie didn't know what to say. The truth was that she had already been thinking similar thoughts, but she didn't want Amanda to be any more worried. "Harrison has been checked and rechecked by the police department, and Wesley's history teacher recommended him to us. I think he's probably just strange, that's all."

"Mr. Hacker knows him?"

"He said he did. He's the one who gave us his name."

"Maybe we should ask him."

Maggie agreed. "I think we should."

* * *

Maria had showered and put on her clean clothes. She was back inside the room she'd woken up in and was trying without success to put Harrison out of her mind and to concentrate on what she had to do. Out of sheer habit she started to make the bed. The coverlet was a red paisley design and didn't look like Imogene's taste. How had Imogene found this remote cabin? How could Harrison have fooled everyone like he had?

She told herself to focus on getting out of there. She scanned the landscape. From the back window she could see that the cabin was nestled inside a thick grove of trees and that there was a footpath that led down a gentle slope to a small clearing about two hundred yards away. Beyond that, she saw the outline of a lake. It wasn't a major body of water, but it could definitely be spotted by a helicopter if she could contact a rescue team. She took a mental note. If she could find out where she was, it would increase her chances of heading in a direction that might get her to a telephone. Maybe she could find a map in the cabin somewhere. She would talk to Wesley, assure him that she would send someone back, and then leave as quickly as possible. The sky was overcast, and it looked like rain was a definite possibility. Not that it mattered. She would forage through whatever elements for however many days it would take her to get away from this place. But then again, she thought as she spied a green jeep partially hidden behind an old woodshed, driving would give her a much better chance of escape. Maybe someone would accidentally leave the keys in it.

Maria cranked open the bedroom window and crawled outside. She scouted around for guards, but she didn't see any. She ducked and ran over to the car and tried the handle. It was locked. She put her hands against the glass and peered inside. It was a mess, the open ashtray full of cigarette butts clearly visible. She heard the sound of crunching pine needles directly behind her. But before she had a chance to turn around, someone grabbed her from behind and clamped a hand over her mouth. She struggled to get free but the attacker pulled her in close and held her tighter.

"Maria, it's me," a familiar voice whispered in her ear. "If you'll let me talk, I can explain." Without removing his hand, he hauled her over into a large woodshed next to the cabin. It was dim and musty and full of spiderwebs. The door was ajar and he pushed her inside without releasing her. "I'm going to let you go if you promise you'll hear me out, okay? Nod your head if you agree."

Maria nodded, and Harrison released his grip.

Maria immediately let out a bloodcurdling scream. Harrison tried to constrain her, but Maria kicked his shin and broke free. "Get me out of here! There are spiders everywhere!" A gray orb spider sprawled out in its web a few feet away. She backed into Harrison and spied a colony of daddy longlegs congregating in the windowsill.

Harrison picked her up, carried her outside, and deposited her under a tree.

"Okay, there are no spiders out here!" he assured her. "Now will you calm down and listen to me?"

Maria turned around and looked contemptuously into his eyes. "You're a liar, a kidnapper, and a spy. What more can you add to that, Peter Jaworsky?"

"I'm not Peter Jaworsky, and I'm not a kidnapper. I won't deny that I'm a spy—I am." Harrison looked around to make sure no one was eavesdropping on their conversation. He lowered his voice. "But not for Imogene. I'm only pretending to work for her so I can get on the inside. I've been tracking her down for almost a year now, and until yesterday I'd never seen her in person."

"Right. Is that what Imogene told you to say? Just tell Maria anything, and she'll believe it. If you're on our side, why don't you just handcuff her and turn her in to the authorities right now?"

"That is exactly what I'm trying to do. I'm trying to get a message to Chief Hicks, but there's no cell service out here. They took my gun away, and I'm outnumbered. There's a bodybuilder and his manic depressive girlfriend with an automatic weapons arsenal, and Imogene's armed too."

"Why did you bring me here?"

"Because after I pulled you out of the river and did some CPR to get you breathing again, I didn't think it would be good manners to leave you soaking wet on the cold riverbank."

"Something about this story doesn't make sense. Just how did you manage to get yourself out of the trunk first, save me, call a cab out in the middle of nowhere, and get us both to the cabin where Imogene is?!" Maria's voice grew louder.

"Keep it down, will you? They'll hear us. I wasn't in the trunk when you drove into the river. I got out of the trunk when you stopped at the airport. You probably didn't notice that undercover police car pull up behind you. Detective Sweeney brought it for me. I got in and followed you at a distance. I couldn't call you—the only way to stop you was to try and pull you over, but you tried to outrun me."

"*You* were in the cop car behind me?"

"I wanted to tell you what was going on then. But I had to get you out of your car first since Imogene had it bugged."

"And how would you know my car was bugged?"

"Because I put the bug there. I had to make her think I was working for her, don't you see?"

"Wonderful!" Maria said sarcastically. "And you set up the kidnapping of Emily and Wesley all to gain her trust, I suppose."

"No. I promise you, we had no idea she was going to take Emily, and I don't know where they took her. Hicks and I knew she might try to get Wesley, but we didn't know when or how. But when she kidnapped Emily, I had to maintain my cover to find out where she was. And it worked. She trusted me enough to let me come to this location. She keeps giving me tests to make sure I'm loyal. She wasn't too pleased that I brought you along. But I think we can convince her that you're with us too. Look at the positives: we found Imogene, and Wesley is here too."

"I must admit that is a clever story, Harrison or Peter or whoever you are. As Jack would say, 'it sounds like a parachute story to me.'"

"Maria, it's the truth. Okay, you want to know the rest of the parachute story? I'll tell you. The double-agent who rigged my parachute was the real Peter Jaworsky. That's who Imogene thinks I am. He was a diamond embezzler who worked with her and was planning to meet up with her for the first time in the Swiss Alps a year ago. But after he tried to kill me, the military took him out, and I took his identity."

Maria was still wary. "And all that super-nerdy, help-me-with-my-wardrobe stuff was just to make it more interesting for you, I suppose?"

"No. The nerd part—that was Imogene's idea. But I am a terrible dresser anyway."

Maria really wanted it to be true, but she felt she couldn't trust him. It was all part of Imogene's plan to keep her off balance. "Forgive me for not believing you." She turned away.

"I know you're skeptical, and I would be too if I were you, but you have to trust that I'm on your side."

Maria whirled around. "I don't have to trust anybody! You certainly didn't trust me and tell me what was going on."

"We couldn't risk letting any of you know. I'm an undercover agent. Even Detective Sweeney doesn't know who I am."

"Who *are* you?"

Harrison sighed. "I can't tell you just yet. It's too dangerous. Until we have Imogene in custody, it's better for us both if you don't know."

"Why is it you and Imogene always seem to know what's best for me? We have nothing more to discuss. Thank you for pulling me out of the car, whoever you are. But I really hope I never have to see you again. I'd better start walking if I want to get anywhere by sundown."

"Maria, you can't just walk out of here."

"Unless you'd like to hand me the car keys, I don't have any other options, do I?"

"I don't have the keys to that jeep, or I'd drive you and Wesley out myself. Another one of her thugs took the car I drove here."

"I would think an international spy like you could figure out how to start a car without the keys."

Harrison placed his hand on her shoulder. "Look, Maria, it's just not that easy. If we try to get Wesley and drive out, she'll hear us leaving. They'll shoot out the tires in one second and then bring us back to the cabin. My cover will be blown. Imogene may have a tender spot for you and Wesley, but from what I've seen so far, she isn't going to take kindly to me crossing her. Which means if they ever do find my body, it will be scattered in four different states. Or suppose we do manage to get away. By the time we give her location to the authorities, she's in her helicopter and finds a way to disappear forever. We throw away a whole year of tracking her down, and we'll never find her. But you can bet she'll find us—and Wesley."

Maria wrenched her shoulder away. "Maybe you're used to pretending you're someone you're not, but I don't have the skills to fool Imogene. I'm leaving—and I will find a way to get Wesley out, too." She started to walk away.

"Wait, Maria," Harrison said as he stood in her way. "Please don't do this. It's too risky."

Maria stopped. "And why would that matter? This is all just a game to you, isn't it? Pretending to care about me and watching me make a fool out of myself that day at the lake. I'll tell you one thing, Harrison. If you didn't already have a career as a traitor, you'd make a very good actor."

Maria saw Harrison's expression soften. "Maybe I'm a better actor than you think. You want me to be totally honest with you? I admit I was acting that day at the lake, because if I could have been myself, I would have done this." He pulled her into an embrace and kissed her.

Maria didn't stop him, even though she knew this was a very bad idea. Imogene was absolutely right about her—she always did go for the wrong kind of men. After a moment she pulled away. "Was that part of the plan, too?" She turned to go.

Harrison blocked her way again. "Maria, I'm begging you not to. Do you have any idea where we are? Do you even know what state we're in? This is rugged country, and there are black bears that roam around here at night. And they aren't friendly to trespassers. The road we came in on is a level one—it has been closed for more than a year, which means there won't be any traffic coming this way. Besides that, the temperature dips into the low thirties at night. You don't have any warm clothes or food, and you won't make it out for at least three days. If there were any way you could, Imogene wouldn't let you go."

"So I should just sit here and wait until my fairy godmother comes to rescue me?"

"I can get all three of us out of here, but I need to wait for the right time. Maria—" Harrison started to speak but stopped when he saw something out of the corner of his eye.

Imogene brazenly walked up to them. "Oh, I do hope I'm not interrupting a lovers' quarrel. But Wesley is awake and would like to see you, Maria."

12

The Encryption

Wesley sized up the four other people in the room. Imogene sat stoically in the wingback chair. Maria was leaning forward on the couch, crushing a tapestry pillow in her arms. She had dark circles under her eyes and was glaring at Harrison. Harrison had a completely unreadable expression. He might have been a hired assassin or a minister stopping by for a friendly chat. Simone sat on the brick fireplace hearth with a machine gun slung over her shoulder, twisting the diamond-studded bar that went through her eyebrow.

Imogene cleared her throat impatiently as if that were the "time's up" buzzer. "See, Wesley, you can witness for yourself that no harm has come to Maria."

"She doesn't look very good to me," Wesley retorted.

"Well, obviously we all look a bit more attractive with makeup and a blow-dryer," Imogene explained.

"He means emotionally," Maria snapped. "Wesley can pick up on these sorts of things. Can't you see that he just wants to get out of here?"

"Don't project your own feelings of betrayal and inadequacy onto Wesley, Maria," Imogene reprimanded. "Wesley and I have already discussed this matter at some length. Would you like to tell her yourself, Wesley?"

Wesley shifted uncomfortably in his chair. He wanted nothing more than to agree with Maria, but he knew he had to convince Imogene that he was softening up to her. There would be no getting away if he tried to fight her right now.

"Mother wants me to come and live with her for a few months. She says it's just a trial period. And if I don't want to stay with her after that, she'll let me come home."

"And just like that," Maria snapped at Imogene, "Wesley wants to go back home, and you'll put him on a plane?"

"That is what I promised him," Imogene answered evenly. "Just like the promise you made to me thirteen years ago, Maria. Do you remember that? The promise that you so easily broke. I wouldn't expect you to know anything about keeping promises. That is a *foreign* concept to you."

Wesley watched Maria's face flash red, and she bit her lip to hold in her anger. "The promise I made to pretend Wesley was your real son was based on wrong information. I didn't know who his father was. You led me to believe he was a drunk, because you knew I left my husband for the very same reason." Maria was fighting to keep her temper under control.

"Maria, if I recall, you called Wesley our miracle baby. You wanted to keep him just as much as I did."

"Why take him?" Maria set the pillow aside. "You have your money—you can just go back underground, and they'll never find you! If you take him, you'll risk everything. They'll keep searching until they find you."

"Let them search. They'll never find us. It's a price I am willing to pay to be with my son again. You really think this is about the money? How much would you be willing to sell Amanda for? There hasn't been a single day in the past two years I haven't missed Wesley. The first time I saved him from his reckless and irresponsible family, he wasn't old enough to appreciate what I did for him. This time he knows the truth. He knows that the people who claim to be his loving parents couldn't wait to trade him for his baby sister."

Wesley flinched and hoped Imogene didn't notice. He kept one eye on Harrison. If his instincts were right, Harrison was on his side. He watched subtly as Harrison put his chin on his hand. To anyone else it was a simple gesture. But to Wesley it was communicating important information. Next, Harrison set two fingers on his cheek. When Wesley gave him an imperceptible nod, Harrison placed his arms to the left and then to the right with one elbow bent and one straight.

That's an A and a G. Wesley took mental note. The next letter was a little modified, since he didn't want to make it too obvious. Right arm bent down, left arm extended up, and then a meaningless scratch on his head to make it look like it was all part of the same motion. Wesley was pretty sure he was signing an E. He knew what Harrison was trying to tell him without deciphering the next two letters, but he followed along just to be sure. As expected, Harrison signed an N and then a T. 2 AGENT. So Harrison was admitting he was a double agent. That much was clear, but whose side was he really on? Wesley signaled Harrison back with an O and a K.

It appeared that Maria was really going to try to hike out. Wesley had to talk her out of leaving. Maria might have many useful domestic skills, but camping and wilderness survival were not among them. She was afraid of the dark, had an extreme fear of spiders, and she had the worst sense of direction of anyone he ever knew. She got lost driving to the grocery store half the time. Imogene knew that too. And he knew that was the only reason Imogene would agree to let her leave.

"Why not let Harrison drive her out of here?" Wesley suggested.

"Because he's coming with us, dear," Imogene patronized.

"One day won't matter," Wesley argued.

"Yes, it will. The matter is closed. Maria has already made it clear that she doesn't want to come with us, and I think that's best. After all, she can't be trusted."

"No, I can't," Maria admitted as she looked at the clock on the wall. "I'd like to go now; it's almost eleven. May I say good-bye to Wesley first?"

"By all means." Imogene made a sweep with her arm.

Maria walked over and gave Wesley a hug. Wesley whispered for her to stay, but she shook her head.

"You'll need a coat." Harrison rushed out of the room. He returned shortly with a heavy canvas hunting jacket that smelled like a campfire.

Wesley wondered what was going on between them. Harrison, who was Wesley's only hope for keeping Maria safe, now seemed eager to push her out the door. The coat's sleeves drooped past her hands, and Harrison helped her roll them up.

"It's a bit warm for a coat today, isn't it?" asked Imogene.

"It will get cold at night," Maria explained. "And I'm still chilled from the river."

"Here, take this water." Harrison pulled a water bottle from the refrigerator and stuffed it in her pocket.

She turned away from him quickly, and nobody stopped her as she walked out the front door of the cabin.

* * *

Maggie hung up the phone after a short conversation with Mr. Hacker, Wesley's former history teacher, and thought about the dialogue once again.

"No, Mrs. Mackey, I'm absolutely positive I never called your home to recommend a tutor for Wesley. I don't know anyone named Harrison Landry. Is there some sort of problem?"

"No," said Maggie, her voice trembling, "there's no problem. We just misunderstood—probably got you mixed up with a different teacher."

"Maybe it was Mr. Hansen, the English teacher."

"Yes, that would explain it. I heard the name wrong—sorry to bother you."

Maggie relayed the conversation to Jack on their way over to scour Harrison's room.

Jack slapped the side of his head. "So if it wasn't Hacker, who was it?"

"It don't know, but Wesley's English teacher is a woman. It was a man's voice, and the caller ID didn't have a name—only a number. I tried to check it, but it was almost a month ago, and it's erased from the log now."

"Maybe it was Hicks."

"Possibly," Maggie agreed. "He sure gets evasive when we ask about Harrison's background."

"And where was Hicks the night Emily was returned?"

"He claims he went to the third address."

"There's way too much that doesn't make sense here, and all I know is I don't trust anyone." Jack opened the cabin door for Maggie. "Not Hicks or Sweeney, and *definitely* not Scary Harry.

Maggie perused the lodging quarters and picked out Harrison's bed immediately. There were thick encyclopedias on the nightstand and several neatly stacked newspapers in different languages placed next to them. The top one looked like it was in Arabic, and another one was in characters that were either Japanese or Chinese.

"Wow. He can really read these? I can't even imagine being that intelligent."

"Yeah, lucky for me you like dumb blonds," Jack quipped as he rifled through the papers and laid them out on the bed. "There's something here—I know it. It's like I'm lookin' right at it, but I don't know what it is."

Maggie nodded as she scavenged around the corner by Harrison's dresser. "I know what you mean. I'm looking at something right now that's really frightening."

"What is it?" Jack asked while checking under the bed on his hands and knees.

"Oh, just a black widow spider the size of my fist," Maggie answered.

"Well, step on it," Jack suggested.

"What? The Snake Stalker is telling me to destroy a living creature?"

"If it's slowin' us down, yes."

"It's in a jar, and it looks very well fed. I'm just going to back away slowly."

"Good idea. Now help me find his laptop."

* * *

The late afternoon sun had burned away the clouds, and the temperature had risen into the seventies. Even though she tried to ration it, Maria had finished her water bottle an hour ago. She had tied her overcoat around her waist, but it was so annoying that she was tempted just to leave it on the ground. Thirst was now the foremost thought in her mind, and maybe that wasn't a bad thing, because thoughts of what had transpired that morning were making her angrier by the minute. She sat down on a fallen log under a tall pine tree and read, for the fifteenth time, the note Harrison had stuffed in her coat sleeve.

> *Dear Maria,*
>
> *I am so sorry if you feel betrayed, but I promise you I'm on your side and will do everything I can to ensure Wesley's safe return. I need you to get to a phone and give this message to Chief Hicks. Do not call the local authorities—they don't have the information or resources to deal with this situation.*
>
> *I saw lights in a cabin off the road about 9 miles from here. Follow the trail east until you get to the tree split by lightning. You'll wind down the side of the mountain for about 3 miles, then head east again until . . .*

Maria stopped reading and crumpled the paper. Why should she believe him? He was probably sending her in a circle right back to that cabin. She was getting more frustrated with every step. *Don't call the local authorities.*

Why not? Because they might find out that Harrison Landry is a traitor to his country and his girlfriend. Girlfriend. Had she really been so stupid to think she was Harrison's girlfriend? That was exactly what Imogene had planned, and Maria had fallen for it just like she had predicted.

"That's me. Good old predictable Maria," she said aloud. "I can be depended upon to support Imogene's team every time." Maria studied the information below Hicks's cell number. She was supposed to trust Harrison, but he couldn't even trust her with a simple message. He had purposely encrypted the information so she wouldn't know what he was trying to tell Hicks. She looked for some sort of clue to unravel the message.

A S A H I

1 2 .5 M
1 6 .2 N
5 .3 K
.2 H
3 .4 K
4 .7 N

Then she read the last part of the note.

> *Do not go into the caves. The bears are not aggressive unless they feel threatened. Be careful. I know we can count on you.*

> *Love, Harrison*

We *can count on you. Is that you and Wesley, or is that you and Imogene?* Maria wondered. But the part that really got her worked up was the word *Love.* How dare he use that term so casually! It was a blatant attempt to make it seem like there was something more between them. Imogene had probably coached him to write that. She would assume Maria would let her emotions take over instead of thinking logically.

Well, not this time. If and when she did get to a phone, she was definitely NOT going to call Hicks. If Harrison was so insistent that she call Hicks and not the local police, then maybe Hicks was working for Imogene, too. She had made the wrong decision thirteen years ago on blind trust, and she had no intention of repeating the error. She would protect Wesley from Imogene, not Imogene and Harrison from getting what they deserved.

Maria was still weak from her car crash and near drowning the night before. She had no idea how to estimate miles on foot. It's not like she was an experienced hiker. She was lost, and she was physically and mentally exhausted. But she was the only one who could help Wesley now. She ignored her thirsty, aching body and willed herself to stand up and start walking again.

13

Dorthea Krebs

Maria shivered under the canvas coat and was thankful she hadn't left it on the trail. It was black outside, and she no longer cared if there was a bear or a wolf or even an alligator waiting to eat her. She was too tired, hungry, and thirsty to be frightened. Harrison didn't know her at all. He said they were counting on her. She couldn't be counted on to rescue anyone, especially if that required navigating a course through an uncharted wilderness.

She wanted to lie down, curl up, and go to sleep, but something propelled her forward. She thought she saw a light. It was dim at first and kept disappearing and reappearing behind the trees. But then it got brighter as she weaved through the thick forest. She tripped over invisible rocks and logs and scratched her face on tree limbs. The moon was three-quarters full, but it wasn't enough to illuminate the path, only the tops of the trees. She stretched her arms out in front of her. It didn't seem like she was on a path at all anymore. After getting gouged in the cheek with a limb, she finally found the source of light. It was a small cabin with light emanating from a curtained window. A satellite dish was perched on the roof. Whether this was the cabin Harrison had led her to or some random place that she had happened to stumble across, she didn't care. She said a prayer of thanks, not knowing who or what she would find inside.

Maria knocked soundly on the door. A windowbox full of lush petunias was evidence that someone must live there. There was no answer for almost a minute. The second time she knocked, she heard a system of bolts and deadlocks being put into motion. The door slowly opened a few centimeters until she could see the face of an old woman, her crepe-paper skin stretched over ancient bones. Her eyes were kind, and Maria felt so relieved she thought she could kiss her.

"Hello. Do I know you?" The woman greeted her cautiously.

"No, my name is Maria Perry, and I'm lost—please, may I use your phone?"

The woman kept her feet planted where she was. "Are you a stranger?"

Maria saw that the woman was a bit confused and maybe a little frightened. "Well yes, but I don't mean you any harm. I'm all alone—"

"Richard says I'm not supposed to let in any strangers." The woman started to close the door.

"No, wait!" Maria stuck her foot in the door. "I'm not a stranger. I'm a friend who has come to visit you."

The woman brightened. "Really? You've come to have some cake and tea with me?"

"Yes, thank you, I would love some cake. May I come in?"

"Well, I suppose, if you're not a stranger. But we have to wait until "Final Jeopardy!" is over."

"Of course," Maria agreed, as the woman allowed her to step inside.

The woman offered her hand. "I'm Dorthea Krebs. Are you my granddaughter?"

"No, I'm not," Maria said carefully. "I'm just a good friend. And I'm very thirsty. Would you mind if I had a glass of water?"

"Why, of course not." Dorthea hobbled slowly to the kitchen while Maria searched the room for a telephone. Surely a woman this old and suffering from dementia couldn't live by herself in a remote area without a phone. But then, she really had no idea how many miles they had driven last night from the place where she crashed her car.

Dorthea came back and handed Maria a glass of water. The water was room temperature and didn't have any ice, but Maria didn't care. She gulped it down.

"Oh my!" Dorthea checked the clock on the wall. "Look at the time. Phoebe and Bernard should be dropping by any time now."

"Phoebe and Bernard are your children?" Maria asked hopefully.

Dorthea pondered for a moment as if she wasn't sure herself. "Yes . . . I suppose they are."

"They come to visit you every night?"

"They do, and sometimes I let them come in, even though Richard tells me I shouldn't."

Maria didn't understand why she shouldn't let her own children come in the house but thought it best not to tax Dorthea with too many questions. If she could contact the police tonight, there might be a chance to get Wesley back before Imogene took him away for good.

"Mrs. Krebs, do you have a telephone I could borrow?"

Dorthea scratched her chin. "No, I don't think so." The theme to *Jeopardy* seemed to alert her senses that she had forgotten something very important. "Excuse me." She turned and walked over to the couch and set herself in front of the television.

Maria knew it wasn't possible to explain her situation to Dorthea, so she slipped down the hallway to check the other rooms in the house. There were only two other rooms. One appeared to be Dorthea's. The other one had a twin bed, a gun safe, and was full of hunting equipment. She found two bowls of cat food and a water dish in the kitchen, a stockpile of videos and TV guides, but no telephone. When she came back, Dorthea was glued to the TV.

"Mrs. Krebs, where is your cat?" Maria was hoping to coax some conversation out of her by talking about something familiar.

"I don't have a cat."

"Oh, a dog then?"

"No."

Maria wasn't surprised that she didn't remember that she had a pet. "So, what time do Phoebe and Bernard usually come?"

"Any time now." Dorthea smiled like a proud parent. "It's a commercial. Would you like your tea and cakes now?"

"Actually, I am pretty hungry. Just the cakes and some more water will be fine."

Dorthea looked out the window when she got up to prepare the treats. "Oh, here they are now!" She rushed as quickly as a woman her age could to the door and started to open it. "Shh," she put a finger to her lips. "You won't tell Richard."

"No, I won't tell Richard." Maria was starting to have a very low opinion of this Richard character. That is, until she saw who the guests were. She watched in disbelief as two large skunks came waddling into the house and headed straight for the food dishes on the kitchen floor. Dorthea was right. She didn't have a cat or a dog. Maria's heart sank when she realized that help wasn't on the way. Someone must come to check on her, bring her groceries and necessities, but when? It might be a week before she could get out of here.

"You can't pet them," Dorthea explained. "You're a stranger to them."

"That's okay." Maria swallowed two tea cakes practically whole. "I'll admire them from here. They're lovely."

"Yes, I think so too. Phoebe is the one with the narrow stripes. Bernard's a bit larger."

Maria pushed her disappointment aside and tried to formulate a new plan. The last thing she wanted was to spend the night outside with the bears and bugs. "Do you think it would be all right if I stayed here tonight?" Maria asked.

"Of course! My granddaughter is always welcome."

"Thank you." Maria didn't try to correct her. "I know it's only nine thirty, but I think I better go to bed—I've had a very long day."

"Yes, you do look tired. You can have Richard's room."

So Richard must be her son, Maria thought as she headed for the bedroom with the shotgun and the elk head. She didn't really think she could sleep yet, but she thought she might hunt for a phone again. She sat down on the patchwork-quilt-covered bed and removed her shoes. She admired the beautiful antique night-stand and then slowly opened the drawer. There was an old phone inside—so old it had a rotary dial, but still, it was a phone, and the cord was wrapped around it. Maria pulled it out and searched for an outlet. She discovered it hidden behind the bed and plugged it in.

Please let there be a dial tone.

It was almost too wonderful to be true. The phone actually worked. Maria poked her head down the hall-way to make sure Dorthea was busy watching *Let's Make a Deal* reruns before she dialed the Mackey's number. Jack picked it up on the first ring.

"Jack, it's me—Maria," she whispered.

"Maria—you don't know how happy I am to hear you, mate. Where are you? Is Wes there, too?"

"No, but I saw him this morning. He's fine, but Imogene has him in a remote cabin. I'm in some cabin out in the middle of nowhere, too. It belongs to a crazy old lady named Dorthea Krebs who has skunks for chil-dren and is addicted to game shows."

"Got an address?"

"Not exactly. All I know is we're somewhere in the middle of a mountainous forest. It's pretty wild out here. Wesley's cabin is several miles from here—Harrison's with them. And I think he's working for Imogene, even though he claims he's working for us. You were right about him, Jack—he's the mole. He gave me a coded message—told me not to take it to anyone but Chief Hicks. But I think Hicks may be in on it, too. I don't know who to trust."

"I don't trust them either. Can you read me the message?"

Maria recited the combination of letters and numbers to Jack. "Does that make any sense at all to you?"

"Can't say that it does, but we'll figure it out—you know they pulled your car out of a lake yesterday?"

"Yes, I thought I was going to crash into a barn. If they found it—" Maria stopped talking and put the phone inside the drawer. The footsteps down the hall came slow and steady.

Dorthea entered with a tall glass of milk. "Here's your warm milk, dear, just like you used to have when you were little, remember?"

"Yes, thank you." Maria didn't really like her milk warm, but she didn't want to start the whole "stranger" business again with Dorthea, so she took a few sips. She was hungry, and the milk eased the ache in her stomach. Plus, it really wasn't that bad, so she drank half the glass. "It's wonderful, just like I remember."

That seemed to satisfy Dorthea, and she padded back down the hallway. Maria picked up the phone again. "Sorry, Jack, the situation here is a little unstable. I'm not supposed to be on the phone. From what I gather, Imogene is planning to take Wesley out tomorrow by helicopter. There are two other—" There was an audible click, and the line went dead. Maria tried to hang up and try again, but the connection was gone. She had forgotten to ask about Amanda and how Emily was doing. She needed to tell him some more details. She had probably left out the most important thing. She checked the wall connection, but the line was still plugged in.

Maria drank the rest of her milk in hopes that it would soothe her unsettled stomach. After trying the phone several more times, she threw her head back on the pillow in frustration. She felt unusually tired all of a sudden. Maybe she would just close her eyes and try the phone again in a few minutes.

14

Code Breakers

Maggie was rubbing her temples and pacing up and down the kitchen. "Jack, we have to tell Hicks." She held out the paper that Jack had scribbled Maria's message on. "I have no idea what this means, but I'm sure it must have something to do with where they've taken Wesley.

"No way. Maria said Harrison and Hicks are in on it."

"She said Harrison. She's not sure about Hicks. So what do we do? We won't be able to find them without explicit directions. Maria didn't even know where she was."

Amanda walked in just then. "Yes, but that's not unusual. My mom never knows where she is."

"Honey, shouldn't you be in bed by now?" Maggie had insisted Amanda sleep at their house again so she wouldn't be alone.

"I was, but I couldn't sleep. I was thinking about how my mom told you Harrison is working with Imogene. Maybe Dylan knows something about what's going on. He and Jamal and Harrison were all roommates."

Maggie looked at her watch. "It's almost midnight. I think the less Dylan is involved in this, the better. If he knew something, he would have told us earlier."

"Not necessarily," Amanda pressed. "Harrison has been teaching Dylan how to break codes. He's actually pretty good at it. If you showed him that, he might be able to figure it out."

"Isn't there someone without a suspicious past who can help us?" Maggie groaned.

"She's right, Mag, we don't have anything at all to go on right now. We could give it a try."

"You're sure there's no 'Dorthea Krebs' listed in the phonebook?"

"Not in Georgia, Alabama, or Tennessee. But then I'm not sure I'm even spellin' it right. Let's pay a visit to Dylan."

* * *

Dylan was watching a portable TV that belonged to Jamal. He had headphones on so he wouldn't wake Jamal, who was sound asleep in his bed across the room. When Maggie and Jack knocked softly and came in to question him, he scrambled to hide the TV and then gave them some made-up excuse about why he was up past curfew.

"We don't care about your curfew," Maggie said. "We just thought you might be able to help us with something. It's a code."

"A code?" Dylan brightened. "Do I look like a CTI or something?"

"A what?" Jack asked.

"You know, a Cryptologic Technician Interpretive," Dylan answered as though it was something Jack should know.

"So Harrison's been teaching you how to break codes?" Maggie asked.

Dylan shrugged. "He showed me some stuff, but I'm not that into it."

"Well this is really important, and it could help us find Wesley," Maggie explained. "We're just wondering if this code means anything at all to you." She showed him the piece of paper on which Jack had scribbled letters and numbers.

Dylan glanced at it and handed it back. "That's not a code."

"What do you mean it's not a code? How would you know?"

"I know it's not a code," Dylan said matter-of-factly. "Because *Asahi* is Japanese."

Jack looked at Maggie and then back at Dylan. "It can't be Japanese. I've been to Japan, and they don't even use our alphabet."

Dylan waited for their full attention to elaborate. "Well, then tell that to the people who write the newspaper." He put his headphones down like he was greatly inconvenienced by helping them. He got up and went over to Harrison's nightstand and pulled out one of the newspapers Jack and Maggie had seen earlier. "Asahi," said Dylan as he pointed to the words *Asahi Shimbun* across the top. The rest of the paper was in Japanese characters. "Harrison had to read his foreign papers every night."

"He's right, Jack!" Maggie marveled. "This is Japanese."

"Whaddaya know . . . but what does it mean?" Jack deferred to Dylan as the current authority.

"I don't know—don't speak that language." Dylan shrugged. "But Harrison has an English–Japanese dictionary around here somewhere. S.B. has one too."

159

Jack and Maggie starting looking for it, and Dylan joined in, dumping out drawers and suitcases. In a few minutes Jack found the dictionary in a bureau. He shuffled through it but was having difficulty finding the word.

Maggie grabbed it from him. "You can't read that without your glasses. Okay, here it is! *Asahi* means 'morning sun.'"

"What about *Shimbun?*" Jack asked.

"Just a minute." Maggie rifled through more pages. "That means 'newspaper.' But it's not written on the information Maria gave us."

"What about the rest of the code?" Jack asked. "It's just a bunch of numbers and letters—not words."

"I'm not even sure what 'morning sun' means," Maggie stated.

Dylan sighed as if the people around him were dense. "It probably doesn't *mean* anything. It's just a location, or a street name. If I were you, I'd look up— here, give me that." He snatched the dictionary from Maggie's hands and started flipping the pages. "Okay, write this down . . . ready?"

Maggie nodded, grabbed a pen, and tore a shred of paper from a German newspaper.

"Okay," Dylan barked. "'North' is *kita.* K-I-T-A. Got that?" He shuffled the pages. "'South' is *minami*— just put an M down." He licked his fingers and turned more pages. "'East' is *higashi* or *H*. And let me guess before I even look it up—'west' starts with an *N*. Oh, here it is: *nishi.*"

Maggie looked at the piece of paper and then at Dylan. "Dylan, you're brilliant! All these letters are on here. The numbers must mean either miles or kilometers. How in the world did you figure that out?"

"It was just logical. Hey, can I come and help you find S.B.? Maybe help you break a few more codes, break some necks . . ."

"We appreciate your help, mate," Jack responded quickly, "but I think you better stay here—"

"To help Penny and Walter protect the kids," Maggie added. "Dylan, thank you—this is huge! Please don't tell Chief Hicks about any of this. We don't know who we can trust at this point."

Dylan smiled. "I don't have a problem keeping secrets from the cops. Just don't tell Grandma Penny I'm watching TV past my curfew. That's rule number sixteen, and if I break it I have to weed the vegetable garden."

Jack patted his shoulder. "Mum's the word, mate."

15

Ranger Rick

Maria was having a very bad dream and couldn't seem to get warm. There was a fan of cool air blowing in her face, and her bed felt very hard. A stabbing pain went up her lower back. She opened her eyes to see that she wasn't dreaming at all. The early morning sun was streaming through the branches of trees, and she was outside on the hard ground wrapped inside the canvas coat Harrison had given her the day before. What had happened to Dorthea Krebs and the warm cabin?

Maria touched her face with her icy fingers for a reality check. Was last night a dream? If not, who had dragged her here, and why hadn't she woken up? Maybe she had been sleepwalking. She had heard that people under a great deal of stress often walk in their sleep. She was certainly a candidate for that experience. It had been dark last night, but still, her surroundings were totally unfamiliar. The cabin was nowhere in sight. In fact, she seemed to be much further down the mountain than she was last night.

Suddenly a horrible thought struck her. What if she'd never found the cabin at all? What if that was all some sort of hallucination brought on by extreme fatigue? Maybe she never even reached Jack and gave him the message. She searched her pockets to find the piece of paper with the coded message.

It was gone.

Maria knew she needed to get some circulation in her limbs before they went numb. She tried to stand, but she felt strangely dizzy, like she was going to be sick. As she steadied herself against a tree trunk, her vision blurred and then came into focus again. This was the second day in a row she'd awakened to a very bad situation.

Several yards from where she stood, a well-worn trail for off-road vehicles appeared, giving Maria a slight ray of hope that she could follow it to civilization.

After fifteen minutes or so of walking, Maria sat down to catch her breath. She heard the sound of a vehicle coming up the road. Without thinking that it might be Imogene or one of her cohorts, she jumped into the road to flag down the driver.

The tan forest ranger truck stopped. Maria was relieved to see that the man who jumped out of the vehicle was very official looking in his sunglasses and park ranger uniform. He was in his fifties, and his pressed shirt sported a badge that read "Ranger Rick."

"Ma'am, are you in some trouble here?"

"Yes, I'm so glad you found me. I'm lost, and there's been a kidnapping. Please, can you take me to a phone?"

"I got a radio on the truck. What's your name, ma'am? And how did you get all the way out here?"

"It's Maria Perry. Wesley Mackey's been taken hostage in a cabin. I escaped and found this old woman's cabin last night and tried to call for help, but this morning I woke up on this trail—"

"Slow down now. No need for panic." Ranger Rick took out a notepad and pen and scribbled something down. "Kidnapping, hostages—this sounds serious."

"Yes, it is. I tried to contact the authorities at the cabin last night, but—"

"Whose cabin? I'm pretty familiar with this area, ma'am, and I don't think there's been anyone living up this way for a very long time."

"Well, there definitely is. She said her name was Dorthea Krebs—"

Ranger Rick pulled his sunglasses down onto his nose and looked Maria squarely in the eye. "Hold on there! Did you say *Dorthea Krebs?*"

"Yes, that's her. Sweet woman, but she's not all there, you know . . ."

"Well, that's an understatement. She's not there at all. Hasn't been for several years."

"So you know her?"

"No, but I *knew* her. She's been dead for about six years now."

"No, you must be mistaken. I talked with her. She has skunks for pets—and a son named Richard."

"Now, ma'am, I'm not sure what you think you saw, but old Dotty Krebs wasn't there unless her ghost is haunting that place."

Maria shuddered. There was something dreamlike about what happened last night, and she didn't like this man's implication that she was some lunatic who was talking to dead people. "I don't believe in ghosts. And I'm not crazy. Please, just let me use your radio to get a message to the police. You do have police here, don't you?"

"No problema, señorita. Sheriff's a good friend of mine. I'm heading back now, so I'll take you myself."

Maria looked at Ranger Rick. He didn't seem too threatening, but he didn't seem to be taking her seriously either. Normally she wouldn't agree to get into some strange man's vehicle, even if he was wearing a uniform. But this was a desperate situation. She was too tired to walk any more, and she had to get to the police before Imogene and Wesley left. She agreed and climbed in the truck.

The truck bounced down the rugged trail while Maria listened to Ranger Rick singing off key to himself. Other than the serenade, he was pretty quiet and didn't seem too interested in her predicament. After several minutes, the ranger stopped the truck and got out. "I just thought you should see something before we chat with the sheriff."

"No, thank you. This really is a very pressing situation." Maria didn't want to see anything. She ate the granola bar he offered her and drank some Gatorade, wondering why he didn't seem to think her story was worth looking into. Time was running out, and she needed to get to a phone and get some help.

Ranger Rick didn't give her a choice. "This won't take long," he said brusquely. He walked around and opened her door, motioning for her to follow. A short path led through a grove of old cypress trees. He pointed to an area with several large statues and headstones sticking out of the ground. Maria walked closer and looked down. Dorthea Krebs's tombstone was clearly marked with her birthdate and death date.

"Still want to tell the police that story you fed me?" Ranger Rick asked accusingly. "Why don't you tell me what you were *really* doing at the cabin?"

Maria sized up Ranger Rick. She wondered if she should turn and run now. He had a vehicle and she was on foot, and he knew the area well. She decided to challenge him. "Listen, I know what I saw. After you take me to a telephone, you can go back and see for yourself. How do *you* know that Dorthea Krebs is really buried there?" She motioned to the gravestone.

"Because I know."

"And why should I believe *you?*"

Ranger Rick looked at the tombstone and heaved a heavy sigh.

"Because she was my mother."

* * *

Wesley's second ride in a helicopter promised to be just as unpleasant as the first ride two years ago. The pilot and three passengers were hiking the short distance to the launch site, which, until today, Wesley didn't even know existed. A helicopter pilot named Wayne led the way. Imogene walked next to Wesley, and Harrison followed them. Imogene, as usual, was wearing the most impractical shoes for hiking that a person could find— sling-back, red leather pumps. Wesley wondered if there were something genetically defective in her brain that made her unable to think like a normal person. At least, whatever her problem was, he couldn't have inherited it.

Wesley tried to signal Harrison to find out what the plan was, but Imogene was getting pretty suspicious of them both. He knew Harrison had slipped Maria a note and that she had gone to find help, but the odds of her being able to find help before they left were pretty slim. Even if she did reach a phone, it would take some time for a helicopter or a vehicle to find them in this dense forest. He hoped that at least she was able to find shelter before it got dark. He thought he'd heard a bear prowling outside the cabin late last night.

The four climbed into the helicopter, and Wesley looked at Harrison for some reassurance. Harrison gave him a thumbs up behind Imogene's back.

The pilot did a thorough check and then started the engine. It took several seconds for the chopper blades to start up, but then they sputtered and slowed again.

"What the . . . ?" The pilot swore and looked at Harrison. "Let's try that again." He tried to restart the engine, but this time it wouldn't start at all.

"What's going on here?" Imogene demanded.

"Maybe you should ask the Boy Scout." The pilot sneered at Harrison. He opened a box underneath the control panel and grabbed a flashlight. He stretched his body sideways and took a look underneath the control board in the cockpit.

"Looks like somebody tampered with the wiring here. Somebody that knows something about choppers."

Imogene looked at Harrison. "Get out now, Peter."

"I don't know anything about helicopters—I'm not a pilot," Harrison defended.

"I said get out." Imogene turned to the pilot. "Can you fix it, Wayne?"

"I think so, but it'll take some time."

Imogene slid her hand over her face. "How much time?"

"Maybe an hour or two. I need to get some new wire—there should be some in my tool kit. I won't take any chances that this will short out while we're in the air."

"Everyone out!" Imogene ordered. "Back to the cabin. And Peter, you and Simone are going to have a talk."

Harrison was silent. Wesley knew he must have pulled the wires to stall for time. It worked, but now Imogene didn't trust him, and his safety net was gone. Imogene always carried a weapon, so Harrison wasn't going to be able to make a break for it. The comment about Simone was understood. As Wesley had discovered, she wasn't much of a talker. He had to think of something to stall for time, to convince Imogene that Harrison was on her side.

"I'm sorry, Mother," he said.

"Whatever for, Wesley?"

"I'm sorry I ripped out the wires."

Imogene stopped walking and spun around in her designer shoes. "*You* disabled the helicopter?"

"I was afraid to fly. Last time I was in a helicopter it really scared me. Two years ago, when they rescued me from the ocean, it was really stormy, and I thought we were going to die. It's like swimming. I get panic attacks now in helicopters. Couldn't we just drive out of here, please?"

Imogene wasn't so easily conned. "Wesley, you really disappoint me. I know you're just covering for Peter because you're very fond of him. I rather like him myself, and I must admit he's the most competent person around here. But I know you wouldn't know how to disable that helicopter even if you had the opportunity to do so, which I'm sure you didn't."

"You don't know me." The words came out of Wesley like razor blades. He fell back a few paces from Imogene. His attempt had failed. It was now or never. He had to make a break before they got back to the cabin. With no time to signal Harrison, he took off running as fast as he could toward the thickest part of the forest, away from the cabin and the helicopter. He had to believe that the only person with a gun wouldn't try to shoot him.

"Wesley, come back here this instant!" Imogene screamed. She started running unsteadily on her high heels.

"I'll go after him." Harrison started to run.

"No you won't." Imogene pulled a gun from her purse and aimed it at him.

Harrison stopped.

"Put your hands up where I can see them."

Harrison complied.

"We'll send Simone and Andy after him. He can't get that far on foot. Keep moving toward the cabin. If you really want to prove your loyalty, Peter, I think I can arrange that."

* * *

The silver Land Rover had turned to dusty brown as it drove on the rugged dirt trail of the deep Georgia backcountry. The windshield was encrusted with mud where Jack had tried to wash the dust off with wiper fluid. It had only made things worse.

"How many miles has it been now?" Maggie asked Jack for the third time in ten minutes.

"Mag, you can look at the odometer just as easy as I can—why do you keep askin' me that?"

"Because it seems like this is taking forever. We must have turned off Morning Sun Road hours ago."

"It's a little slow when you're in four-wheelin' territory. Maria wasn't kiddin' when she said she was in the middle of nowhere."

"Well, we better get somewhere soon before those gas fumes kill us both. It's giving me a headache." Maggie searched her purse for some aspirin.

"You'll be glad we brought those extra cans—I don't think we're going to run into a service station anytime soon."

Maggie rolled down her window for some fresh air.

Jack turned the windshield washers on again, spraying Maggie in the face with washer fluid.

"Didn't appreciate that." Maggie frowned.

"It was an accident. I sure hope this is the right road."

"If you can call this a road. If we find Wesley, we owe Dylan big time." Maggie studied the piece of paper in her hand. "I would never have figured these directions out. Can't we go any faster?"

Jack took his hands off the steering wheel in a gesture of frustration. "You want to drive?"

"Sure, if you want me to."

"No, I don't want you to. Just navigate."

* * *

Maria sat at the desk at the ranger station. The sheriff had given her a soda and some crackers. Harrison had been right about one thing: she shouldn't have gone to the local authorities.

"So let me get this straight." The slight man with a squirrel-like face was attempting to sound authoritative. "Ranger Rick tells me you been trespassing on private property, and you're telling me there's been a kidnapping. I check the police records, and no kidnappings have been reported in the state of Georgia for over a month."

"The kidnapping wasn't reported." Maria wished she could just leave now. "And I wasn't trespassing. I'm the victim of a crime. I escaped but got lost and found an old woman in a cabin."

"And this woman was the ghost of Dottie Krebs?" The sheriff leaned back and put his feet up on the desk. He exchanged looks with Ranger Rick, who was chewing on a piece of beef jerky. "You ever been arrested before, Ms. Perry? For stealing maybe? Drugs?" He leaned forward and clicked the mouse on his computer screen. "For being an illegal immigrant in the United States of America?"

Maria shrunk a few inches. She couldn't deny that she had a previous record. "Please, you've got to let me have one phone call. It's the law."

"It's the *law*. Is that so? Seems like you don't pay much attention to the law yourself, Ms. Perry."

"Arrest me if you want," Maria said angrily. "Just let me make my phone call. There is a fourteen-year-old boy who has been kidnapped by a very dangerous woman, and every minute we spend playing these stupid games gives her a better chance of getting away with it."

"Let her make the call, Quinn." Ranger Rick picked up the receiver and handed it to Maria.

Although Quinn should have had seniority, he quickly cowered to Ranger Rick and allowed Maria her phone call. Maggie's and Jack's cell phones didn't pick up, so Maria called the Mackeys and then her house. When the answering machine picked up, she wanted to leave a message but didn't want Hicks to find it, so she pressed the phone off with her thumb and proceeded to tell the nonexistent person on the other end that she was in the Chattahoochee National Forest. That much she could gather by reading the cover of the local phonebook.

Ranger Rick and Sheriff Quinn exchanged looks and started laughing. Maria knew they weren't buying it.

Quinn left the office to check on an expired hunting license, leaving Maria alone with Ranger Rick. Suddenly the situation became perfectly clear to her. "You were the one who pulled me out of the house last night and left me on the side of the road," Maria accused.

"I don't know what you're talking about. I found you walking on the trail."

"I doubt that very much, *Richard*. Listen, I don't know why you're lying to me or why you're hiding your mother out in the middle of the woods, but let me tell you something. There are people looking for me and a missing boy. When they find out you're keeping me here without charges, you are going to be in very serious trouble."

Ranger Rick checked to see if Quinn was in earshot. "I think you're the one who's in serious trouble. I could have you locked up right now, and no one would believe your cockamamy story for an instant. You have no business snooping around where you shouldn't be."

"Snooping around?" Maria could tell Ranger Rick was covering up something. She tried another approach. "Let's make a deal, shall we? I can tell your mother seems very happy, and that you're taking good care of her. I won't say another word about Dorthea Krebs. Just send someone out here to pick me up—let's say, from the nearest town. I'll pay a fine or whatever and get out of your way, and you can be done with me."

"I'm afraid that's no longer possible." Ranger Rick shook his head. Then he said in a low voice, "Is it so wrong to give her what she wanted? If you could have seen her in that old folks hospital—she was so unhappy, and she kept escaping. The doctors said it was too risky for her to leave, but if I didn't get her out of there, she would have died for sure. All she wanted was to be back in her old home, where everything was familiar. But they wouldn't let me. They said she needed twenty-four-hour care with licensed nurses."

Maria was startled by his sudden confession. "So why not just be honest with me? Was it necessary to drug my milk?"

"I didn't drug you. That was Mom. She puts a sedative in her own milk every night—she might have mixed them up or put it in both. You were already out by the time I got there."

"You disconnected the phone too?"

"It's not supposed to be connected in the first place. You understand why I can't let you go to authorities with this."

"I won't tell anyone! Just help me find Wesley and arrest Imogene, and I'll keep you out of it."

"Too late for that, I'm afraid."

"No, it isn't!" Maria pleaded. "You don't understand. I have such a bad sense of direction, I'd never find that cabin again even if you paid me. I won't tell anyone a thing. All I want is to get help to Wesley now."

Ranger Rick pondered this information for a moment as Quinn came back into the office with a tranquilizer dart gun slung over his shoulder.

"Bears are starting to bother some of the campers," Quinn said. "I better keep this baby in the backseat. Did you force a confession out of the fugitive?"

"I think we better book Ms. Perry on trespassing charges," Ranger Rick said. "She's already had her phone call."

16

Mistaken Identity

It was nearly dusk when Simone and Andy came slog-
ging back to the cabin without Wesley.

"You've been looking for *four* hours, and you still
can't find him?" Imogene bellowed. "Where's Wayne?"

"We don't know. We think he got lost." Andy
looked visibly distressed. "And why is *he* still here?" He
pointed to Harrison.

Imogene waved her gun at Harrison. "He's under
house arrest until he can find a way to lure Wesley
back here. Never dispose of something while it's still
useful to you."

The rumble of a car engine outside startled the
group. "Did Wayne take the jeep?" Imogene asked.

"No, we had it," Simone answered.

"Then either someone is stealing it, or I believe we
have some company." She put her gun down at her
side. "Andy, go see who it is."

"But I don't have a weapon," Andy complained.

"I didn't say 'go shoot them.' I said 'see who it is!'
Shut the blinds," she ordered Harrison. "I want it as
dark as possible in here!"

* * *

When Maggie saw that the narrow road was actually a driveway that led to a cabin, she yelled, "Jack get out of here! Put the Rover in reverse! If this is the right cabin, we can't let them see us!"

Jack slammed on the brakes. "Well how else are we going to get inside?" he asked.

"We can't just go up and knock on the door."

"Why not? We have a gun."

"Yeah, but I'm sure they do, too. And I'm betting Harrison is a better shot than both of us."

Jack threw the car in reverse and backed down the trail about fifty yards. One of the tires got caught on a rut and started to spin. Maggie threw the gear shift forward. "Great! Now we're stuck!"

"Well if you'd quit tryin' to drive from the passenger seat . . ." Jack scowled as he tried to rock the SUV out of the ditch. "We're makin' too much noise." He shut the engine off. "We might as well announce our arrival on a bullhorn. We better try and sneak up on foot."

"That would have been a great idea to start with." She handed him the gun as they exited the vehicle and shut the doors as quietly as possible. Together they hiked through the tangle of trees toward the cabin, avoiding the open driveway.

"Why are you giving me the gun?" Jack asked. "You're the one who's a better shot."

"It's dark. You know I have night blindness."

"That's all in your head. Nobody can see in the dark."

"Okay, then give me the gun." Maggie stuck out her hand.

"Never mind, I'll keep it. So how do we get in undetected?"

"You go around back and see if there's some other way in. I'll try the side window. This is reconnaissance only. We'll check things out, meet back here, and then figure out what to do."

"Roger that, mate. I'm right behind you." The red streaks of sun had all disappeared, and the dark shadows of night moved in. Maggie heard Jack's feet crunching in the leaves behind her. "Shh, walk softer." She turned around and saw that whoever was behind her definitely wasn't Jack. A shadowy figure grabbed her around the neck. Maggie flew around and karate chopped the assailant on the shoulder blade. He doubled over, and she kicked him in the chest. Her attacker seemed shocked by her skilled response. She clubbed him on the shoulder with the back of her hand, and he fell motionless to the ground. Maggie rolled him over in the leaves but couldn't identify who he was. *One of Imogene's people, most likely*, she thought. Their noisy entrance had cost them the element of surprise. At least Maggie knew that they would be waiting for her. She shook out her hand and jogged stealthily toward the cabin. She didn't call out for Jack. She didn't want to give herself away in case he had already been taken hostage.

Maggie snuck up to the side window and discovered that it was slightly ajar. Whether this was a stroke of luck or a deliberate trap didn't really matter. She took the bait, opened the window, and climbed in.

Inside the bedroom it was dark, but she could sense that people had been living here recently. The room was warm, and she guessed if she hit the light switch the light would turn on. The bedroom door creaked as she opened it, and she stopped and held her breath. Every sense was alerted, and even though she could barely see, she could feel the vibration of footsteps in what appeared to be the living room. She had tiptoed softly into the main room and crouched behind the coffee table when she caught the outline of what appeared to be a man holding a gun with his back toward her. She guessed he was waiting here for them if the first line of defense failed. Catching him by surprise would make this unpleasant task a lot easier. Buoyed by the fact that she had so easily defeated her first attacker, she took a deep breath and hurled herself out into the open room, sprung off the coffee table, and knocked the gun away. Without hesitating, she kicked him in the ribs, leaned in and grabbed him by the arm, and heaved him over her shoulder, slamming him onto the hardwood floor. That was easy. He didn't move. She dusted off her hands and was going to try and find the gun when suddenly the lights turned on and illuminated the subject of her attack.

Jack was lying unconscious on the floor.

"Bravo! Bravo!" Applause and the heinous voice of Imogene oozed from the corner of the room.

"Jack!" Maggie dropped to her knees and cradled his head in her hands. "I'm so sorry."

"What a loving family!" Imogene praised. "That was pure entertainment. Peter, you didn't tell me how sweet they are together!" She walked over and picked up Jack's gun and handed it to Harrison. "Why don't you show us where your loyalty really lies? Would you like to do the honors, or shall I let Simone?"

Jack's eyes fluttered, and Maggie stroked his face with her hand.

"Are you crazy?" Harrison said evenly. Meanwhile, Simone hoisted her automatic weapon on her shoulder and moved in closer. "Why kill them now when we can use them as bait to find Wesley?"

Maggie reached for a sofa cushion and put it under Jack's head. She thought she heard Harrison just say they needed to find Wesley. He must have managed to escape somehow. She looked around and took in the sight of a hard-looking woman with a machine gun, a muscleman with a crew cut, Harrison Landry, and Imogene. She wondered how, in a dark room with five possible targets, she had managed to take out the one person on her team.

"Mag, I don't think this was a very good plan." Jack tried to sit up, but he clutched his side and groaned in pain.

"How do you plan on getting Wesley back, Peter?" Imogene asked.

Maggie diverted her attention from Jack and turned her wrath on Harrison. "You've been in on this the whole time, haven't you?" She let Jack roll off the pillow as she sprung to her feet and ran straight for Harrison, kicking him in the chest. He grabbed her leg and threw her down, but the gun flew out of his hands.

"Maggie, don't do this," Harrison warned. "I don't want to fight you."

"Why not?" Maggie pulled herself to her feet. "You're going to shoot me anyway." She ran at him again, spun around, and tried to hit him in the face with the side of her hand. He blocked the hit and tripped her, but she twirled and kneed him in the thigh.

Jack was trying to edge over to his gun while Imogene watched the karate performance with a smug smile. She motioned for Simone and Andy to let them be. Jack watched the fight, trying nonchalantly to retrieve the loose weapon.

Maggie picked up a nearby chair and tried to whack Harrison over the head. He ducked, and she smashed it against the wall.

"I'm impressed," Harrison said approvingly as he wiped his forehead with the back of his hand. Maggie connected with a kick to his ribs and then went for his throat. Harrison grabbed her arm and twisted it behind her back, pinning her to the wall. "I'm really sorry to have to do this to you, Maggie. You're quite the worthy opponent. Andy, hand me that rope."

Maggie tried to head butt Harrison, but he knew all the countermoves. He forced her over by Jack and wrapped her hands behind her back with the rope, tying it securely.

"Tie them both to the banister," Imogene ordered.

"I was planning to," Harrison agreed.

"I'll tie up the Snake Stalker," Andy volunteered as he came over with another rope.

"No, you won't," Harrison barked. "I'm the Eagle Scout, remember?"

Imogene walked over to Maggie, Jack, and Harrison. "Make sure those knots are secure."

Harrison handed her the ends of the rope. "You still don't trust me?"

Imogene stared at Harrison and yanked the rope. "I make it a habit not to trust anyone."

"What are we tying them up for?" Simone asked. "Just put a few bullets in them and we won't have to worry about it."

"Great idea!" Harrison yelled sarcastically. "This is precisely why you are not in charge here," he said patronizingly. "Do you have any idea how easy it is to trace a bullet to a gun? There are people in forensics who are very good at this sort of thing, and it might take them a few days or weeks, but when they find the bodies here, they will see that they've been shot and will be able to find out exactly what type of gun the bullet came from, where that gun may have been purchased, and when. Then they'll follow that paper trail right up to your new vacation house in the Cayman Islands."

Simone and Andy looked at each other.

"We can kill two birds with one stone here—without bullets. We'll make it look like an accident *and* get Wesley to come back," Harrison explained. "Simone, would you like to fetch me a gas can from the back of your jeep?"

Simone glared at Harrison, handed her automatic weapon to Andy, and went to carry out the order. Imogene watched Harrison guardedly.

"So the helicopter is all ready to go?" Harrison asked.

"Yes, we're just waiting for the pilot," Imogene reminded him.

"If that's the guy I met on the trail," Maggie snarled, "I think your flight is going to be delayed!"

"You took out the pilot, too?" Jack asked with admiration.

"Harrison, can't you see she doesn't even trust you?" Maggie squirmed against the ropes on her hands. "She's not going to let you get out of here alive. She'll kill you after you've done her dirty work. You're too much of a liability."

"I'm not doing her dirty work," Harrison explained. "You are."

"What are you talking about?" Maggie demanded.

Simone came in with the gas can. "Where do you want me to dump this?"

"Hold on a minute, Simone." Harrison stuck his arm out. "We need to wait for the right time. If I'm not mistaken, they parked their Land Rover just up the road. I'm sure Wesley will shortly find out they're here, if he hasn't already."

"But he escaped hours ago," Andy argued. "We looked everywhere. He's miles away by now."

"I don't think so." Harrison directed his comments to Jack and Maggie on the floor. "Wesley trusts me, and the fact that he tried to cover for me because he thought I disabled the helicopter is proof of that." He looked at Imogene, who nodded her head approvingly. "He's a clever boy and is very good at hiding. He doesn't have a blanket or any water, and he's smart enough to know he can't hike out of here on his own. When he finds out that Jack and Maggie are in trouble, he'll come running back."

"But how will he know they're in trouble?" Simone asked.

"Because we're going to make it really obvious," Harrison explained.

"Oh, I get it. We torch the place!" Andy impressed himself with his brilliant deduction. "Here, I'll throw some gas on them." He started to unscrew the top of the can.

Harrison looked at Imogene with total exasperation. "Honestly, where do you find these people?" He grabbed the gas can away. "Step back, you misanthrope. I'm not a fan of torture. There's no reason to burn them alive. The smoke will get them before the flames do."

"I quite agree." Imogene nodded.

"Thanks for the favor," Jack snarled at Imogene. "I suppose this is how you reward people who save your life?"

Harrison pulled off the lid and started pouring gasoline in a trail along the outside wall. "All of you need to get out of here before I light this. Spread out around the perimeter. Imogene, wait for me by the helicopter, and I'll get Wesley when he comes back."

"You heard him. OUT!" Imogene bellowed.

"You too, Imogene," Harrison ordered. "Get out now—it's not safe."

"And you'll be coming out with me." Imogene picked up Jack's gun and aimed it at Harrison. "Right now." She pulled the trigger and a bullet sailed past Harrison and into the gasoline-saturated floor. The bullet exploded on impact, and like a trail of dominoes, the fire spread in a thin line around the room. A flame jumped to the gas can in Harrison's hand and he threw it down and dove out the front door behind Imogene.

17

Smoke Screen

The flames hit the gas can and exploded onto the front door, blocking the front exit. The fire climbed up the walls in the small cabin while Maggie and Jack, tethered back to back with the banister between them, struggled to get loose. Maggie twisted her wrists, and Jack rubbed the ropes on his hands against the wooden post. They could already feel the searing heat.

"Okay, Mag, I admit it!"

"Admit what?" Maggie coughed as smoke entered her lungs.

"You were right. You *can* take me down."

"Jack, we're trying to figure out a way to stay alive. That's really not important now."

"I think you busted one of my ribs . . . maybe my back, too."

"I said I was sorry. Will you focus on getting us out of here, please!"

"I knew there was something funny about Harrison from the get-go. But nooo—nobody every listens to me. Like I haven't been around enough to spot a scoundrel when I—"

"Will you stop already? I think Harrison was trying to save our lives."

"By burning us alive? I don't think so."

"No, his karate skills are way better than mine. He could have really taken me out—but he was fighting defensively."

"We're dyin' here, and you still think he's a good guy."

"Maybe he is . . . here, pull the end of this rope. I can't reach it!" Maggie fought to hand him one of the loose ends, and he felt around until he grasped it between two fingers. "Pull harder!"

"Why?" Jack challenged her. "You're just making the knots tighter."

"Don't argue," Maggie ordered. "Just do it!"

Jack worked the rope from Maggie's wrists into his fist and yanked it as hard as he could by twisting his hand. The knot securing Maggie's hands pulled through, and she yanked her arms free.

"I knew it! He used the bowline escape knot!" Once her hands were free, she quickly removed the ropes that secured her to Jack and the banister. Then she turned around and, in one quick motion, pulled the knot from Jack's wrists. He coughed, and she helped him stand up. "Can you walk?"

"Yeah." He scanned the room quickly. "But I don't exactly see a way out of here."

Maggie threw up her hands in a panic. "There's no way to get out without running through the fire." She ran over to the kitchen nook window and checked the frame. "This window doesn't open. Every exit is blocked by flames. We'll have to run through the fire."

Without responding, Jack picked up a chair and threw it through the window.

The extra oxygen fed the fire, and it instantly doubled in size. Maggie felt the intense heat singe her face. Sharp glass stuck out of the rim, but before she could process what was happening, Jack lifted her up and heaved her through the broken window frame. She sailed through the air momentarily, landed hard on a dirt slope, and then tumbled down the hill until her motion was halted by a small sapling. She sat up just in time to see Jack jump off the kitchen table and ricochet off the window ledge. He rolled down the dirt and landed next to her.

The window they had just flown through now spouted flames that reached the roof.

"What was that?" Maggie asked in disbelief.

"That was me rescuing you from a burning building."

Maggie suddenly felt woozy. "Jack, there's a piece of glass sticking out of your arm. She pointed to his right arm, where a three-inch window shard stuck out of a bloody hole just below his bicep.

Jack examined it as if it were a ding in his car door. "Well, that's not good."

The fire had reached the gas appliances, and large thundering explosions sprayed Jack and Maggie with hot embers.

"Move away from the cabin!" Maggie screamed as she wrenched Jack up with his good arm and ushered him away from the burning house. They dove into a thicket by a locust tree, where they were shielded from the hot flames.

"Jack, I need to take that glass out now, but I can't see very well in the dark. I'll go get the first aid kit and a flashlight out of the truck. Wait here for me."

"No, we're not splittin' up again, and there's no time. How about this?" Jack pulled a small penlight out of his back pocket.

"Okay, that'll do, but you have to hold it—I need both hands." She hesitated and examined the wound more closely. Jack gritted his teeth in anticipation.

"This will hurt," she warned.

"Would you just yank it out already?"

"Okay, brace yourself." Maggie grasped the piece of glass with one hand, steadied Jack's arm with the other, and pulled slowly but forcefully. Jack winced in pain as she threw the glass down and studied the hole in his arm that was steadily oozing blood. "I don't think it severed your brachial artery."

"And if it did?" Jack was breathing heavily.

"It would be bad."

"How bad?"

"You'd could lose your arm—and your life—if we couldn't stop the bleeding."

"Thanks for breakin' it to me gently."

Maggie ripped Jack's shirt with her teeth, then bandaged the wound. "It's not pretty, but it'll have to do. And by the way, thanks for throwing me out the window. In another few seconds that explosion would have killed us."

"Well, it's the least I could do after you beat me up."

"I didn't know it was you! I told you I can't see in the dark." Maggie kissed his cheek. "We have to find Wesley before Imogene does. We can assume Harrison is on our side now, so that gives us better odds. You really need to keep calm for the bleeding to stay under control. You'll have to wait for us here."

"Negative on that idea. I'm comin' with you." Jack stood up and pretended to be fine.

"You can't—you're bleeding!" Maggie protested.

"Exactly. If it bleeds, it leads." Jack pushed her aside with his good arm and started walking toward the front of the cabin.

"And what about your cracked rib and broken back?"

"I'm a fast healer."

* * *

Wesley didn't know which he spotted first, the flames ripping out of the cabin window or his family's Land Rover parked on the trail. He was glad to see that his dad had found him but was worried about the possibility that he might be inside the cabin. Smoke poured out from under the front door, but he couldn't tell if the fire had reached the door or not. He knew the rules of fire safety—never run into a burning building. But he also knew that the fire department wasn't going to be pulling up anytime soon. He took a large gulp of air and sprinted for the front door. The door handle was hot, so he wrapped his hand in the tail of his shirt and tried to open it anyway. Before he knew what had happened, he heard someone bounding out of the shrubs.

"Wesley, no!" A man tackled him to the ground, momentarily knocking the wind out of him.

When Wesley recovered, he saw that Harrison had pinned him to the ground, and Imogene was following him closely. From his vantage point all he could see were the spiked heels of her impractical shoes digging into the dirt.

"They got away," Harrison said close to Wesley's ear. "Listen to me. Head back down the trail the way we came in. Stay by the trees but don't come out unless you hear me, your dad, or Maggie call you. Got that?"

Wesley nodded. Imogene was standing only a few feet away, her hands on her hips. "Wesley, that was a very irresponsible thing to do," she reprimanded. And then she addressed Harrison. "Don't you think you're being unnecessarily rough?"

Harrison slowly helped Wesley up. "I had to do what was necessary." Without warning, he kicked Imogene's gun out of her hand and struck her sharply on the shoulder blade. "Run, Wesley!" he shouted as Imogene folded in half and collapsed onto the ground. Harrison let her fall and pounced on her gun. He holstered it in the back of his jeans. Wesley stopped running to see what had happened.

"Keep going!" Harrison ordered as he scooped Imogene's rag-doll body up and dragged her across the rocky dirt.

Wesley ducked behind a large pine when he saw the green jeep's headlights illuminate the scene of Harrison pulling Imogene's body away from the fire. He remained undetected as the jeep roared past him. Simone was in the driver's seat—he could tell from the cigarette dangling out the window. Wesley heard her shout to Andy, "He's with them. Shoot him!"

Andy stuck his gun out the passenger seat window and aimed it at Harrison.

Harrison hoisted Imogene's flaccid body in front of him to use as a shield. But at close range, Andy still had a clear shot at his head. Wesley had to think fast, or Harrison didn't have a chance.

"I'm over here!" He stepped out from behind the tree and waved his arms.

The jeep turned sharply until the headlights were shining directly on Wesley. It was too late to regret his decision. He hoped he could run fast enough to lose them a second time. He headed down the path where he knew his dad's SUV was straddling the road. There was only enough room for a person to pass on foot. He darted around the vehicle and continued down the trail. The darkness would definitely assist his retreat, but dodging the headlights was going to take some dexterity. At least he had bought Harrison some time.

From behind the tree, Wesley heard the sound of metal crunching on metal as Simone swerved and rammed the side of the Land Rover with her jeep. He peeked around the tree to see the stranded vehicle rock back and forth before it settled down. He had sprinted for another tree when he heard the gears grind. Simone must have thrown the jeep into reverse without stopping first. He watched her back up twenty yards, shift forward, and then floor it. She rammed the jeep directly into the side of the Land Rover. The tire in the deep rut prevented it from sliding, and when two tires came completely off the ground, Wesley could predict what was going to happen. The Rover teetered, and then, like a slow-motion video, it rolled over and landed on its side, clearing enough of the trail that Simone could plow through with the jeep.

Wesley didn't have time to ponder the fact that Simone had just destroyed their only means of escape. He jumped into the thick darkness of the woods, scrambled behind an old rotten log, and hoped that the headlights wouldn't land on him. The jeep rumbled past him on the trail. They didn't stop to look for him, and he wondered if they thought he was further ahead or if they'd just decided he wasn't worth the effort and should get away while they could.

He waited at least five minutes for the sound of a friendly voice. He could hear the fire growing closer and could see the smoke getting thicker. He figured he'd better leave now before he got trapped. By then the wind had shifted and was blowing smoke and ash in his direction. He looked toward the cabin to see how high the flames were, but all he could see was a brown, smoky glow. He prayed that Harrison was right and that Jack and Maggie weren't still inside. Embers blew into a nearby tree and ignited the top branches. The fire was burning out of control. He wouldn't be going back to the cabin.

18

Wildfire

By the time Jack and Maggie got back to the Land Rover, the smoke was so thick that they could barely see their vehicle. They had heard the jeep slamming into something but didn't expect to see their truck lying on its side in the road like a dead animal.

"Jack, we have to find a way to get this right side up— it's the only way out of here." Maggie searched around for something to use as leverage, but all she found was her backpack, which had been thrown out in the crash.

"Uh, Mag, even if I could lift a thousand-pound truck, I don't think that's a very good idea."

"Why not?"

"Gas cans, remember?"

"Oh great!" Maggie threw her arms up. She looked up to see that a nearby tree had caught fire and was spraying embers all around them. It wasn't necessary to expound on the situation. She and Jack started running full speed away from the car and down the dirt trail. In less than thirty seconds, a loud blast followed by a gust of hot wind engulfed the two of them. Maggie and Jack ducked for cover behind the same log Wesley had hidden behind earlier. Sparks rained down around them.

Jack looked at Maggie, her disconcerted expression illuminated by multiple fires.

"What?" he asked.

"I'm so glad we brought that extra gas along."

"We'll find another way out," Jack insisted.

"Another way?" Maggie said angrily. "That was our *only* way out!"

A voice that sounded like it came from above startled them. "Not necessarily. Actually, we do have access to another mode of transportation." Harrison climbed down from a nearby tree and walked over to Maggie and Jack.

"Well, if it isn't Houdini himself!" Jack snarled. "Where's your buddy Imogene?"

"She's unconscious. We have to get to the helicopter before the pilot does. When is Hicks coming?"

Jack walked closer to Harrison and saw that his face was covered with dirt and soot. "Hicks isn't coming."

"What do you mean he isn't coming? How did you get here without him? Didn't Maria give him the message?"

"Maria didn't call Hicks. She called us."

"But he's the only one who knew the code."

"Evidently Dylan is a lot smarter than he looks," Maggie explained.

"You gave *Dylan* that code?" Harrison asked.

Maggie nodded. "It took him about two minutes."

"So, you're telling me Hicks isn't here, and he doesn't even know you're here?" Harrison started pulling nervously on his hair.

"That's right," Jack confirmed.

Harrison shook his head. "We have a very big problem."

Jack clutched his bleeding arm. "A *problem?* Well, maybe I have a problem with you kidnapping my children, manhandling my wife, and trying to burn us alive!"

"Jack, if you haven't figured it out by now, I had to play along with Imogene, or she would have killed all three of us. I tried to make it look real without hurting Maggie—"

"You didn't hurt me," Maggie interjected. "I could tell you were just being defensive."

"And you're very good, by the way," Harrison commended. "I was planning to knock Imogene out before I lit the fire. I didn't want to block your exit, but she fired the gun before I could stop her."

"Fortunately, we were able to figure out the knots," Maggie added, while Jack threw up his hands in disbelief that this conversation was taking place.

"Where's Wesley?" Harrison looked around as if he might be standing there, unnoticed.

"We haven't seen him," Maggie answered.

"I told him to wait for us down here."

"And if I were him, I'd do the exact opposite," Jack growled. "Why do you think he would trust you?" Jack stepped right up into Harrison's face.

"He knows I'm a double agent, Jack."

"You mean double-crossing agent!"

"Enough already!" Maggie separated the two men. "We don't have time to argue. The fire's getting closer."

"If no one's coming for us, we really have to get to the chopper," Harrison explained. "It's back behind the cabin, so we don't have a lot of time before we'll be cut off by the fire. Let's go!"

"But what about Wesley?" Maggie cried.

"He had at least a fifteen-minute head start," Harrison shouted without turning around. "He could be too far away for us to catch up to him on foot now. We can't risk taking time to hunt for him in the dark. And he can't hear us over the noise of the fire. What we need right now is transportation, or we won't be able to outrun this fire."

Jack and Maggie followed Harrison half a mile back the way they had just come through the forest.

"Is he going to be all right with that arm?" Harrison stopped to wait for them to catch up.

"*He'll* be fine, mate," Jack answered with obvious annoyance.

"What about Maria? Did she make it back all right?" Harrison asked hopefully.

"No," Maggie answered. "We haven't heard from her since last night, and we have no idea where she is."

Harrison was visibly disturbed by this piece of news but said nothing. As they rounded the back of the burning cabin, he seemed perplexed by the scene in front of him. "I left her here. She was tied up," he stammered.

"Good job, secret agent man!" Jack said accusingly. "After all this, you let her escape again!"

"I couldn't exactly haul her around on my shoulders while I looked for Wesley, Jack!" Harrison shot back. "Someone had to have untied her. Well, at least she doesn't have a gun."

Harrison ran further down to the helicopter, and Maggie and Jack followed. He opened the door. "It looks like the pilot isn't the one who moved her, or the chopper wouldn't still be here."

Harrison reached under the control panel and pulled out some wires. "I think I can get this thing started, but unfortunately I've never actually flown one of these before."

"What? You mean you don't know how to fly?" Maggie asked.

"No. I know a little bit about helicopters, but I'm not a pilot. I was hoping I could lift it off the ground and at least get us on the other side of the lake." The chopper blades whirred into action, and the cabin control panel lit up.

Jack sighed. "Great, is there any more information you'd like to share? Move over!" Jack pushed Harrison roughly over the center console and into the passenger side as he climbed into the cockpit. Jack fished around and pulled a manual out of the same console and thumbed through several pages.

"Can you fly this?" Harrison asked.

Maggie had climbed into the seat behind him. "No, he can't."

"Sure I can. Hey, my brother Tommy does this for a living. How hard can it be?"

"Very hard!" Maggie contradicted. "I know you've ridden in a lot of helicopters, and you might think you can do this, but you've never flown one! This is crazy! We can still walk out of here!"

Harrison turned around and tried to calm Maggie down. "No, we can't. We've lost too much time already. We'll never find Wesley before morning unless we can get up high and turn on the searchlight. Jack, if you're at least familiar with this, give it a try. I can work the throttle, and you can work the rest of the controls with your left hand."

Jack threw down the manual and started pushing levers and buttons. "Where's the horizontal stabilizer? I know that's an important one."

"Try that," Harrison suggested.

"This is really not okay with me!" Maggie said to herself while Jack fumbled with the buttons and levers on the console.

The fire was starting to spread onto the grassy area that led to the helicopter. A small pine tree that had been engulfed in flames tipped over and landed a few feet from them. The wind whipped the flames into a fury.

"There's a lake right here." Maggie was practically in tears. "We can just jump in and wait until the fire goes around us."

"Less talking please," Jack said in a schoolteacher voice. He studied several computer screens and dials and pretended to make sense of them. "Okay, Harry, let's pull her up."

The helicopter lifted several feet above the ground, and Jack randomly tested several switches. "If I'm not mistaken, this one moves us forward." The copter lurched backwards. "I meant this one." The helicopter moved forward out over the lake but quickly lost altitude and skimmed the water.

"Up!" Jack shouted at Harrison. "We need some elevation now!"

Harrison was trying to work the gear while the helicopter started sinking in the water.

"I think you've got that control!" Harrison hollered.

"Wait, here's the altimeter."

"That doesn't give you altitude. It only measures it." Harrison reached over Jack and punched a lever that did absolutely nothing.

Jack pressed something that moved the tail rotor and swung the helicopter sharply left. Water lapped up the side of the helicopter.

Maggie covered her eyes with her hands. "We survived a fire only to drown in a helicopter."

"C'mon, this has to be it!" Jack tried another button at the same time as Harrison adjusted the throttle. The helicopter pulled up out of the lake, but nobody heaved a sigh of relief because they were headed straight for the trees. "Hang on, mates, this is going to be a close one!" They gained elevation and cleared the trees, but the bottom of the chopper clipped the tops of several trees.

Maggie stopped breathing.

"Yes! I knew this couldn't be that hard," Jack said.

Maggie spread her fingers to form shutters over her eyes. "We still have to land."

"No problem," Jack quipped, "we'll just do what we did in reverse."

Harrison was flipping switches haphazardly in the copilot chair. "Not bad, Jack. I haven't been in one of these for almost a year. When I find the searchlight, we'll try to locate Wesley, and then we'll put it down in the nearest clearing. My guess is that he went southeast." As he pointed out the direction with one hand, he flipped a small, red switch with the other and the searchlight suddenly came on.

"Are you sure he didn't get trapped in the fire?" Jack asked.

"He's too smart," Harrison assured Jack. "I saw him run in this direction when he was trying to divert Simone and Andy away from me. And I'm sure they didn't catch him." Harrison stopped. "Wesley saved my life."

Jack looked out the window now that the ground was illuminated somewhat. "He's an amazing kid." He remembered the spitting viper and how Wesley had given himself up to Imogene's thugs to save his life. It wasn't the time to get emotional so he turned the conversation. "That's some fire you started, Harry. I wonder how many years you can get for arson?"

"This wasn't supposed to be the plan," Harrison defended. "If you recall, Hicks and his team were supposed to be here for the sting operation, but somehow the message was intercepted."

"Well, mate," Jack said unsympathetically, "maybe you should have shared the plan with the people who have dealt with Imogene before."

"Jack, we're not exactly amateurs here. If we had told you the plan, you would have just botched it sooner."

"There's a door on your side," Jack said bitterly. "Feel free to leave at any time."

Maggie leaned forward in her seat. "Excuse me, could we find Wesley first? We can let the male egos battle it out later. Right now let's concentrate on keeping this helicopter from crashing and on looking for our son, who's trying to hide and run from a forest fire at the same time! Isn't this enough to deal with at the moment?"

"He started it," Jack said. "And you left out that he let Imogene escape, and my arm is severed."

"That too. But your arm isn't severed—it's punctured."

"Might as well be severed, for as well as it's workin' right now," Jack grumbled.

Harrison leaned closer to the window. "Hey, I see something!"

"Is it Wesley?" Maggie asked.

"I can't tell. Whoever or whatever it is seems to be running pretty fast."

"What do you mean, *whatever* it is?"

"I mean, it might not be human. There's a lot of wildlife around here."

"Just say it, Harrison." Maggie shook her head. "It's a bear."

"Okay, it could be a bear."

"Or a fat deer with black fur and short legs," Jack said. "Let's see if we can get a closer look."

"No, Jack—don't go down until we have to land," Maggie pleaded. "There's not much of a clearing here."

"Trust me, Mag. I can do this."

Maggie shook her head in frustration. "Do I have another choice?"

* * *

Maria sipped at the soup Sheriff Quinn's wife had sent with him to the ranger station. At least she wasn't still locked up in the holding cell they had kept her in earlier. The day was gone, and she wondered if Imogene and Wesley were on their way out of the country by now. She couldn't believe she'd had such bad luck with every person she had run into so far. Even Dorthea Krebs, as kind as she was, couldn't offer her any help. And now the sheriff himself was proving to be the worst impediment so far.

"I normally go home, but tonight I get to guard a genuine felon," Sheriff Quinn said gleefully.

"But you said I could go home earlier." Maria just wanted to whack him over the head and get out of there. She felt like she was becoming the criminal that he was accusing her of being.

"I said you could go home if Ranger Rick dropped the charges. I think he's making sure everything checks out before we escort you off the premises."

"What do you mean by 'checks out'?" Maria asked.

"Exactly what I said. He wants to make sure nothing's missing on his property."

"So you've been out to the cabin on his property?" Maria asked.

"Once or twice. Most of us try to steer clear of Area 51."

"Area 51? Isn't that the name of the place in Nevada where people saw all those UFOs?"

"Hey, you're pretty smart for being an alien yourself."

Maria tried not to show her anger. "So I guess I'm not the first person who has reported strange things going on there. Why do you call it Area 51?"

Quinn sidestepped a response. "You want some butter on that roll?"

"No, thank you, these rolls are very good plain." Maria wanted to be as polite as possible to avoid getting locked up again.

"Yeah, Darlene's a good cook. How about you? Got a husband?"

"N-no." Maria started to answer and then thought better of it. If Quinn knew nobody would be missing her, he might try to keep her here longer. "Well, actually I am engaged. I'm sure my fiancé is wondering where I am right now."

"Really?" Quinn seemed skeptical. "A fiancé. What's his name?"

Maria had no time to think. She blurted out the first name that came into her head. "Har—aldo. His name is Geraldo."

"And what does this Geraldo do?" Quinn prodded.

"He's in the military. A Navy SEAL, actually."

"Impressive. Not too many of those around." Quinn seemed to buy her story. Probably, Maria thought, because there was some element of truth to it.

"So what else has happened in this Area 51?" Maria tried to sound like she was making small talk.

Just then static came over the two-way radio. Quinn nearly jumped out of his chair. The crackling voice proceeded with the message. "We got a forest fire out of control over near Bear Canyon, headed due southeast at about ten miles per hour. Do you copy that?"

Quinn compressed the speaker with his thumb. "Ten-four. That's a 904 at Bear Canyon. Does Rick know? Over."

"Affirmative. He called us. We need all available forestry on alert now. Can't bring helicopters in till morning. Over."

"I'll issue a code 33. Over."

"We've already done it. We need you to evacuate now."

"Can you give me a 10-20?"

"We're en route, by Sawtooth Creek."

"Copy that, over and out."

Quinn put on his jacket and ignored Maria's pleading stare.

"That forest fire is in Area 51, isn't it?" she demanded.

Quinn walked over to the window to take a look. Maria shot up next to him and followed his gaze up the mountain. She had no trouble spotting the orange glow against the black sky.

"You'd be right about that," Quinn answered.

Maria grabbed his arm to get his attention. "Then there are a whole bunch of people who need help! There's Dorthea Krebs and Wesley—he might still be there. Imogene and others—they probably started the fire. You have to believe me. I'm telling you the truth!" Maria was frantic.

"Listen, Ms. Perry. First of all, Ranger Rick is already up there, okay? If there's anyone who needs evacuating, he'll see to it. Second, we got to get ourselves out of here in case the wind picks up. We could be in the path of the fire."

"But Ranger Rick is in danger too—these people have guns!"

"Well who doesn't around here? I don't know anyone who would go out in these parts in the dead of night without a weapon. You just need to settle down. We see this type of thing all the time in the summer. It's nature's way of cleaning out the forest."

"So you're just going to run away from the fire?"

"That's usually the best course of action when you're dealing with a forest fire."

"You're just a big coward!" Maria shouted. She was through trying to be amicable. "You're supposed to uphold the law and protect citizens, but you won't even check into something when you have evidence staring you in the face!"

"I didn't say I was going to run. You didn't let me finish. Maybe I will head up and check things out. But if I do, I better start seeing a little more cooperation from you." Quinn pointed a finger at Maria. "Because I'm going to have to take you with me."

19

Next of Kin

Wesley slid into the opening of a cave in the side of the mountain. That was a close call. When a helicopter swooped overhead and the searchlight landed on him for a split second, he dove into a tangle of brush for cover. He knew nobody up here knew how to fly a helicopter except Imogene's pilot, so he must have found a way to repair it, and now they were after him again. He'd crawled over to the side of the mountain, where he'd discovered a cave and would have gladly just huddled there for the night if he hadn't heard noises inside. Harrison had told him about the bears, and it gave him goosebumps on his already chilly flesh. He was wearing a short-sleeved shirt and was getting pretty cold. He didn't have any food or water, and it didn't look like he was going to get any for some time.

He thought of Maria and wondered if she'd had to spend the night in the forest before she found safety. If she ever did make it to safety. He had been through frightening things before, but even when he'd been caught in an ocean storm, he'd always been with someone. Being all alone was a different sort of fear. Crickets chirped around him, and the smoke partially obscured the stars. He had never known just how dark it could be without any form of artificial light. His skin felt itchy all over. He'd probably just crawled through a patch of poison ivy—he would have had no way of avoiding it. He knew it wasn't safe in this cave, but it was useless to just walk around in the pitch dark tripping over things. He didn't know how long he'd been running, but he was far enough away from the fire that it no longer illuminated his way.

When he saw headlights coming up the trail, he didn't know if it was help or Simone and Andy in their jeep. He kept hidden in the brush until it passed, and he could see that it wasn't the jeep at all but a truck. He couldn't tell for sure, but he thought he saw an insignia on the side. A forest ranger had probably come up to check on the fire. He acted fast and jumped out onto the trail, yelling as loud as he could and trying to flag down the truck. It went about thirty more yards, and he thought it had missed him, but then the vehicle came to a stop. It backed down the trail until it was even with Wesley. The man in uniform rolled down his window and studied Wesley. He didn't seem at all surprised to meet a lone teenage boy on the trail.

"Are you Wesley?"

"Yes, I am."

"Son, we've been looking all over for you. Hop inside."

Wesley was so relieved that he'd been rescued, he didn't hesitate to climb into the front seat of the four-door truck. But as soon as he shut the door, he heard the locks engage. He sensed the presence of another person in the backseat and hoped it was another forest ranger. He turned to see who it was.

Suddenly, being alone in the dark wasn't the most terrifying thing he could think of. Being confined in the same space as *her* again was worse.

* * *

"Nice landing," Harrison said in a voice that might have been praiseworthy or sarcastic.

"I would have liked to see you do any better," Jack retorted. "Those trees needed pruning anyway.

Armed with their flashlights, Jack, Maggie, and Harrison ventured out onto the trail where they thought they had seen movement a few minutes earlier.

Maggie was shaking as she observed the tree branches that the helicopter blades had sheared off strewn about the ground. The chopper was leaning at an angle because it had landed on a small boulder. "I just hope we don't have to leave the same way we came in."

"Are you cold, Mag?" Jack asked.

"Not as cold as you. At least I have a whole shirt on. I'm fine."

"Look at this." Harrison pointed his flashlight onto the ground. I see some footprints in the dirt." He ran ahead several yards. "Someone was here, that's for sure."

"He's right, Jack. I think Wesley came this way!"

Jack seemed to gain energy from the prospect that Wesley might be close by. He ran along the trail, calling Wesley and aiming his flashlight at everything but the moon.

"Jack," Harrison reprimanded, "I don't think it's a good idea to draw so much attention to ourselves."

"Why not? If Wesley's here, he's not going to see us unless we make ourselves known. If anyone else is

here, tough luck for them. You have the gun, don't
you?"

"Yes, but I'm not too eager to use it in the dark, especially while I'm holding a flashlight in the other hand."

"Well, the other guys have the same disadvantage," Jack reasoned.

Harrison asked Maggie, "Is he always this cavalier?"

"Only after he's lost a pint or two of blood," said
Maggie.

"Why should I be worried?" Jack asked. "I've got
the two best karate experts in this half of the hemi-
sphere to take care of me."

Harrison shook his head to show that he was going
to let the comment slide. "Well, Jack, if we run into
any wildlife, we'll let you handle it."

* * *

Wesley was relieved to be sitting in a warm kitchen with
a cup of hot chocolate, but it was about the only thing
he was content with at the moment. He expected
Simone and Andy to be at the new hiding place, but he
got the impression that they had ditched Imogene, and
that she wasn't too happy about it. This guy named
Ranger Rick seemed to know Imogene, but Wesley had
no idea what the connection was. If he sat quietly in
the corner, they might forget he was there altogether,
and he'd find some way to slip out of the cabin. But
where would he go? He'd seen the glow of the fire
before they'd gone inside the cabin, and he wondered if
it would eventually overtake their new hideout.

Evidently Ranger Rick shared the same concern.
He was pacing around in front of the refrigerator, while
Imogene calmly sat sipping tea at the kitchen table.

"She won't evacuate without them!" Ranger Rick said angrily.

"You'll have to make her, Richard," Imogene said, pulling her teabag out and setting it on the coaster. We need to get out now with Wesley—he's in very great danger!"

"Well, maybe you should have thought about that before you let those hoodlums set your cabin on fire."

"Richard, in case you didn't notice, I'm as much a victim of this arson as you are."

"You can tell your really sad story to the police."

"Just as soon as you tell them how you faked your own mother's death to get her insurance money."

"It wasn't about the money, and you know it. But you do know a lot about faking death, don't you, Genie?"

Imogene stirred her tea. "We have a lot in common, don't we Richard? We are both fiercely loyal. And we'll do what we have to in order to protect the ones we love."

"I wouldn't call starting a forest fire protecting—"

Richard stopped talking when an old woman padded into the kitchen. "Richard," she said accusingly, "who are these people?"

"Mother, you know Imogene. Genie Kovacs."

"You remember me, Aunt Dottie," Imogene gushed, "your favorite niece."

Aunt Dottie looked skeptical. "You're my relative?"

"Of course I am. I'm Lucille's daughter!"

Aunt Dottie's brow furrowed. "My sister Lucille moved away. She never liked it here."

"That's right, Mother." Richard coaxed her over to the hall closet. "We're going for a drive, so I need you to put your coat on."

"I don't want to go for a drive."

"I know, but we need to go now."

Aunt Dottie pulled away from Richard and folded her arms across her chest. "I won't go, Richard. Phoebe and Bernard are expecting me."

"You can see them tomorrow." Richard sighed and looked at Imogene. "See? This is the thanks I get for helping you out. You burn my cabin and upset Mother."

"I don't believe it was ever *your* cabin, Richard. It belonged to my family. In any event, you've been more than compensated for any inconvenience. You can buy your mother a new cabin in Tahiti, where it's much more comfortable."

Aunt Dottie perked up as if someone turned the light on. "Tahiti? Richard, tell this woman we aren't going to Tahiti."

"Mother, I believe *The Price Is Right* is on. Why don't you go watch it?" Richard abandoned the coat idea and nudged his mother into the family room.

Wesley watched silently, soaking in as much information as possible. It was obvious this old woman couldn't be much help to him, but he wondered about Phoebe and Bernard. Was Imogene really her niece, or was she just pretending? He tried to remember whether he'd ever heard her mention Richard or Aunt Dottie before. He hadn't, but the name Kovacs sounded familiar. He tried to think of where he'd heard that name before.

After coaxing his brain for a few minutes, he remembered where he'd seen it. Imogene's maiden name was Kovacs, and it used to be written on his birth certificate—or rather the fake birth certificate Imogene had framed in the hall.

But whether this was Imogene's real family or not didn't really make any difference at the moment. Wesley was stuck in this cabin, well hidden in the woods on some obscure trail, and unless he stole the truck keys and drove out of here on his own, he didn't see how this bit of information would assist him.

Imogene and Ranger Rick were taking turns insulting each other.

"I remember when we were kids," Ranger Rick said. "You were the smart one, and Delphina was the good-looking one."

"And you, Richard," Imogene said snidely, "were neither." She cast a look at the photo on the refrigerator. "You were always a mama's boy, and I see things haven't changed."

"Excuse me for taking care of my elderly mother."

"It looks more like she's the one taking care of you."

Wesley was getting very tired of the banter, and they weren't going to let him go outside, so he requested permission to lie down on the couch. Imogene could see into the family room from where she was, so she agreed, with the stipulation that they might have to evacuate at a moment's notice.

Aunt Dottie didn't seem too aware of her surroundings, but Wesley thought maybe she could help him without even knowing it. If he could just find out when Phoebe and Bernard were going to show up, maybe he could sneak outside and explain what was going on before Imogene and Richard got to them. Imogene seemed pretty sure that Wesley wouldn't run off again. There were only two doors in this house. One was in the kitchen and would be impossible to get through without being seen, and the other one was locked on the outside by a padlock. The bedroom

windows were boarded up and nailed shut on the outside, making the cabin look like it was abandoned long
ago. Wesley knew he would only get one chance. After
that, Imogene would find some way to restrain him or
lock him in the cellar. He definitely didn't want to do
anything rash.

Wesley strolled over to the boarded window in the
family room wishing he could see an escape route. It
was obvious that Richard wanted to keep his mother
from wandering off. Two things struck him at once:
there was an emergency flashlight plugged into the
wall, and he could hear a light rain starting outside.
The flashlight was too big to conceal, but at least he
knew where it was. The rain was both good and bad.
Good news for the forest fire. Bad news for a forced
evacuation.

He jumped when someone touched his arm. He
whirled around and saw that it was Aunt Dottie.

"Dear me, but I didn't mean to scare you," she said.
"I think Phoebe and Bernard are here early tonight.
Richard won't let them in, so you'll have to visit
through the door."

"Do they always listen to Richard?" Wesley asked
cautiously.

"He doesn't talk to them," Aunt Dottie said bitterly.

Wesley studied the woman's eyes. Somehow he got
the impression she was more alert than she let on. "I
would really like to meet them."

"Yes, and they would like to meet you, too."

20

 Bear Tracks

Jack was covering up the fact that he was getting light-headed, and he was ignoring Maggie's pleas to sit and elevate his arm. He had a feeling Wesley had come this way, and he couldn't afford to waste time tending to what he believed was a minor flesh wound. He was leading Maggie and Harrison through the forest in fifty-degree weather with half of his shirt tied around his bicep. Even though he insisted he wasn't in any pain, he was starting to stagger.

Harrison noticed Jack's condition. "Maggie, you need to take Jack back to the helicopter now. He's in shock, and you both need to get warm." He chipped another notch in one of the trees with his pocket knife.

"Nothin' doin', mate. I'm just fine," Jack said weakly.

"Jack, he's right. If you don't go back, we're going to have to carry you out."

"I said I'm fine!" Jack reiterated. "We know Wes came this way because we can see that the tracks lead right through this brush. If we stop now, the rain will wash it all away. Plus, if Maggie and I are cold, then Wesley is too."

Harrison illuminated the mouth of a cave with his flashlight. "Please don't tell me you went in there, Wesley," he said quietly.

"If he didn't have a flashlight, there's no telling where he might have gone," Maggie said as she put her arm around Jack to let him lean on her.

"Okay, I'll compromise," Jack said. "Why don't you two just leave me here in front of this cave a minute while I catch my breath." He sat down and leaned up against the wall, his breathing shallow. "At least it isn't rainin' inside."

"But it's something much worse." Harrison squatted down and aimed his flashlight at the soft ground.

"Are those what I think they are?" Maggie gasped.

Jack was already close to the ground and nodded his head. "They're bear tracks. But that's not all. Look at this." He pointed out the sneaker tread with the Nike insignia pressed into the dirt. "Wes is in here, and I'm going after him." He pulled his feet up underneath him and stood. Without further explanation, he headed into the cave.

"Jack, wait!" Maggie tried to stop him. "We can't be sure he went in there—we need to think about this first!"

"She's right, Jack. This isn't one of your TV shows," said Harrison.

"Why thank you, Harry. How about this? Black bears can weigh up to seven hundred pounds. They don't hibernate, and they're nocturnal. They'll usually leave you alone unless provoked, but if they are, you're in a boatload of trouble. And unless you get a perfect shot, a small gun like the one you're holding is useless.

I told Wes I would find him, and I will. Wait here if you like."

Maggie shifted the backpack on her shoulder. "I'm going with you, Jack."

"You people have no common sense!" Harrison argued. He pulled out the gun to hand it over and then reconsidered. "Never mind, I'm coming too."

The trio traveled through the cave in silence. It had a rather high ceiling and was large enough to allow them to walk side by side."

"This isn't just a den," Jack noted. "It's like a condo in here."

"Shh!" Maggie nudged him.

After twenty yards or so, the cave narrowed, turned sharply, and then ended abruptly. Jack illuminated the floor and clicked his tongue to indicate he had something to tell them. "You were right, Harry. There are bears in here," he said calmly.

"And they're adorable," Maggie said. "They can't be more than a few weeks old." One of the two sleepy bear cubs yawned and shifted its nose in its sibling's fur.

"Sure, they're cute," Harrison ranted. "But Wesley isn't here, and neither is their mother, so I suggest we leave immediately."

"That's the first time I've agreed with you all night, mate," Jack concurred.

They turned single file and headed for the opening of the cave. This time Jack was at the back of the line. When they reached the entrance, they heard a rustling of leaves and what sounded like footsteps.

"Wes, is that you?" Jack stopped and shined his light toward the opening of the cave. Maggie and Harrison had just slipped through the cave's entrance when Jack's light caught the outline of a large, furry beast. The massive black figure reared up on two legs and let out a low, rumbling growl. The bear couldn't have been more than six feet away from Jack.

Jack froze and Maggie clamped her hand over her mouth to stifle a scream. Harrison scooped her up and pushed her toward the nearest tree. "Climb up!" he ordered. Maggie needed both hands to climb, so she tossed her flashlight to the ground and nimbly hoisted herself into the branches of a large pine tree.

Meanwhile, Harrison turned his gun toward the bear. The bear was barely illuminated by Jack's flashlight, but Jack wasn't. If Harrison took a shot, there was a good chance he would hit Jack.

Maggie wasn't far enough up the tree to distract the bear in her direction. The bear eased back down onto four legs and walked even closer to Jack, growling menacingly.

"Jack," Harrison said softly and evenly. "You're blocking the entrance to her cave. You have to try and let her pass without looking threatening."

"Got that," said Jack. He backed up several feet until he was plastered against the cave wall. Two feet directly above his head, a tangle of shrub roots stuck out of the wall. Jack could barely see in the dark, and even with two good arms it would be a stretch to jump up and pull himself to higher ground. *Only as a last resort,* he said to himself.

Harrison bent over slowly and picked up a dirt clod. He tried not to let his flashlight waver, but he didn't dare move it from the bear. He threw the dirt clod against the opposite side of the cave, and it made a splattering noise as it broke into tiny pieces and trickled down the wall. The bear turned her head momentarily but then returned to the person who seemed to be threatening her domain.

Without warning, the bear charged Jack like a bull to a red cape.

Jack was still weak from the loss of blood. *If I miss this, I'm dead,* he thought as he jumped up and grabbed the root with both hands. Searing pain ripped through his right arm as he pulled his body up, and the bear ran under him and straight into the wall. Jack's leg brushed the bear's shoulder. He swung his body around and tried to find a foothold on the side of the crumbling cave wall, but his injured right arm gave way, and he was left hanging by one arm with his feet dangling a few feet from the ground.

"Harry!" Jack yelled. "You have to shoot. I can't hang on!"

"No!" Maggie screamed at Harrison. "You might hit Jack!" Maggie dislodged the backpack from around her shoulder and tossed it at the bear. It fell short a few feet. "Over here!" she yelled to distract it.

The bear paid no attention. She was locked onto her prey. Now that Jack had dropped his own flashlight, Harrison couldn't see to shoot at all.

Jack was close enough to smell the bear's breath. She swiped at him, and he hit the top of the bear's head with his foot. The bear reached up and caught him on the ankle, pulling him to the ground with a thump. Jack saw huge teeth and prepared himself for the inevitable.

All of a sudden the bear stopped. She growled with annoyance and then paced in front of Jack, shaking her head like a dog trying to rid itself of its collar. Jack's heart was pounding so loud that he didn't hear the voice at first.

"Get away! Shoo!"

It sounded like Wesley, and it was coming from outside the cave. "Wes? Stay back!"

"I said go away!"

For some reason the bear seemed frightened by the sound of Wesley's voice and promptly turned and ran past Jack into the cave.

Jack lay crumpled in the dirt and didn't know which was more annoying, the pain in his arm, the stinging gouge on his leg, or the strong offensive odor of skunk that assaulted him. Wesley walked right up to him and tried to help him up off the ground.

"Wes, it's good to see you." Jack hobbled to his feet and tried to embrace his son. "But it's not good to smell you!"

"I know." Wesley pulled his dad away from the cave. "That bear thought so, too."

Harrison ran toward Wesley and Jack. "Brilliant defense! You skunked that bear! How did you think of it?"

"I learned it from one of my dad's old shows."

Harrison maintained a comfortable distance from Wesley.

"Whew! That is potent stuff." Jack hobbled over to find Maggie as he winced in pain.

Maggie half climbed and half jumped out of the tree. "Wesley, you saved all of us! I don't care what you smell like!" She backed up and fanned her nose with her hand. "But that's strong enough to knock us all out!"

"I pretty much took a direct hit. I'm not sure if it was Phoebe or Bernard—but Imogene and Richard both took off. Is Emily okay?"

"She's home, and she's fine," Maggie filled in as they hurried away from the cave. "Who are Phoebe and Bernard?"

"Skunks! But we need to get back to the cabin right now," Wesley urged them.

"Wes, the cabin burned down," Jack tried to explain.

"No, it's a different cabin—the ranger took me there, and Imogene, too. Ranger Rick is Imogene's cousin—they're working together."

"Okay, okay, slow down," Jack said. "Ranger who?"

"Ranger Rick."

"How did you find us?" Harrison asked.

"I just headed back the way I came, and as I got closer, I could hear you and see your flashlights—and this marking on the tree." He pointed out one of Harrison's tree markings and then stopped when he got a good look at his dad. "Dad, is that blood? Your arm is . . . pretty messed up."

"It'll be fine, Wes." Jack held up his blood-stained right arm. "It's a good thing I'm left-handed."

"But you're *not* left-handed," said Wesley.

"Well, I was thinkin' it's time for a change, then."

"Wesley," Harrison said, getting back on task. "Do you think you could tell me how to find this cabin in the dark?"

"Yeah, it's about twenty minutes up the trail—but I was running. You have to stop and pull a log back over the trail if you're in a car, but I just jumped over it. Where's our car?"

"It sort of blew up," Maggie explained.

"Do they have a vehicle?" Harrison asked Wesley.

"The ranger truck."

"And it's just Imogene and this Ranger Rick person?"

"No, there's an old lady too—Aunt Dottie. She has Alzheimer's, I think."

"This is the one who has skunks for pets?" Jack asked.

"That's her. How do you know?"

"Because that's where Maria told me she was when she called."

"Is Maria there now?" Harrison asked.

219

"No," said Wesley, sounding troubled. "I haven't seen her since yesterday morning."

"I think we should all stay together," Maggie suggested. "Some people have a way of disappearing when we separate."

"And some people attack their husbands," Jack added.

"Let me take care of this," said Harrison. "I'm going to the cabin to find Imogene and some transportation. Wesley, I want you to go with your dad and Maggie back to the helicopter. DO NOT try to fly it again; just wait for me to come and get you. If I'm not back in one hour and Jack is okay, start hiking out without me." He handed Maggie the gun.

"But you need this more than we do," Maggie protested.

"No, you take it. I'm not going to confront them if I don't have to. I'm just going to steal the truck. We still don't know where Simone and Andy or the pilot are."

Harrison shined a flashlight on his watch. "It's five past 0100 hours. Everyone clear on the plan?" Harrison didn't wait for them to agree or disagree. He took off running up the path where Wesley had directed him.

"I don't like this," Jack said, after watching Harrison disappear into the night.

"You still don't trust him?" Maggie asked.

"No, I just have a feeling . . ." Jack stopped in mid-sentence, "like I'm going to lose . . ." He stumbled a few steps and then swayed forward. Maggie stepped in front of him and broke his fall just as he lost consciousness. Wesley grabbed him too and helped her set him gently on the ground.

Maggie forced open an eyelid and shined the flashlight in his eye. "It's okay Wesley, he's just fainted," she said.

"Is he going to be okay?" Wesley asked.

"I think so. His pulse is rapid, but he's had a pretty rough night. I had a first aid kit in my backpack, but I threw it at the bear. You stay with him and elevate his feet while I run back to the cave entrance to get it."

"No, let me. I'm the one wearing bear repellant, remember?"

"But you won't know where to look. At least I have an idea."

"Here." Wesley ripped a large piece of his shirt off and draped it around Maggie's neck. "Hurry back." Maggie took the larger flashlight and the gun and ran back toward the cave.

21

Showdown

Harrison jogged the distance to the cabin in about twenty minutes. The path was fairly easy to follow, and his direction was aided by the increasing odor of skunk, although he was getting used to the smell by now. When he saw the cabin, it was dark, and the front door was ajar. He leaned forward and rested his hands on his thighs. Either Wesley was in really good physical condition to run that far, or this Navy SEAL was losing some of his stamina.

From the look of things, he was too late. Wesley's skunk scheme had been very successful in forcing everyone to evacuate. If the smell was strong enough to scare away a bear, he was fairly certain there would be no one waiting inside to meet him. He approached the front door, where he could tell the actual skunk spraying must have occurred. The odor was so strong it burned his nostrils, but he pushed on inside to check things out. He didn't dare turn on the lights as he scouted around for clues about where they might have gone. The back door was padlocked, and the windows were all boarded, so there was only one entrance. If Maria had called Jack from this cabin, there had to be a phone here. He searched each of the rooms. As he entered what looked like an old woman's bedroom, he heard the rumble of a car engine outside. He wondered if Imogene had returned to get something. He crouched in the dark hallway where he could listen. The front door was still ajar.

He heard two car doors slam and then voices approaching the cabin. "The windows are boarded!"

"Phew! I told you this place here is abandoned," a man's voice said. "Only thing been living here is a skunk."

"She may be gone, but I know she was here, and I'll prove it to you." The light came on.

Harrison recognized Maria's voice immediately. He dove for cover behind the family room couch, where he had a limited view of the kitchen area.

"Stay close to me!" the man's voice growled. "As far as I'm concerned you're still under arrest!"

Harrison heard the refrigerator door open. "Look, there's food in here. And how about this?" Maria was producing some sort of evidence to the man. "Why would Richard keep a picture of *himself* on the refrigerator?"

"He's a bit vain, really," the man answered.

Harrison slid over to the edge of the couch and pressed his back tightly against the wall. He could see that the man had a sheriff's uniform on, and Maria's back was to him. The sheriff had a gun in his holster, but Harrison figured he could take him as long as he had the advantage of surprise.

"You're in on this too, aren't you?" Maria said accusingly. "You two small-town cops are just covering for each other."

"You call it what you want. But when my friend finds a trespasser trying to steal stuff on his private property, and that trespasser is an illegal alien with a record—you're darn right I'm gonna uphold the law." The sheriff was only a few feet away from discovering that someone was watching him, and Harrison wouldn't be able to change his position without giving himself away.

There wasn't time to find out what the sheriff's motives were. Harrison leaped out of his hiding place, threw his body weight into him, and tackled him to the floor.

"What the—?" The sheriff threw a punch at Harrison, but Harrison rolled over and his fist connected with the floor instead. Harrison and the sheriff wrestled around the kitchen floor, but Harrison quickly gained the upper hand. Maria took the opportunity to make a run for the front door.

"Maria, wait, it's me!" Harrison struggled with the sheriff in a headlock.

"Who *are* you?" the sheriff grunted through clenched teeth.

"Someone who doesn't appreciate the way you treat a lady."

"Hey, you got this all wrong, Geraldo. It's not what you think."

Harrison tightened his grip around the sheriff's neck until he lost consciousness. He laid him down carelessly on the floor and reached over to his holster to remove his gun.

"Don't move!" Maria shouted from the doorway.

Harrison raised his hand in the air and turned around slowly, rising up from a squatting position to standing. Maria edged closer until she was only few feet away. She had a loaded tranquilizer dart gun in her hand and was aiming it at his chest. "Drop the gun *now!*" she ordered.

Harrison let the gun fall out of his hand. "Maria, I'm so glad to see you. Please—I can explain everything later, but we've got to drive back and get Wesley, Jack, and Maggie. They're waiting for me on the trail."

"All three of them are waiting for you?"

"Yes, I came alone to find Imogene."

"That's interesting. Too bad I don't believe you." Harrison could see that Maria's nerves were frayed, and there was no telling what she'd been through the past two days.

"Maria, put that down before you hurt someone."

"Hurt someone?" Maria's eyes were full of fury.

Harrison realized it was an extremely poor choice of words. He wanted to tell her how sorry he was and how much he really cared about her, but it was clear that anything he said would not be well received at the moment.

They were running out of time. Imogene was making her escape, Jack needed medical attention, and a forest fire was headed in their direction. Harrison knew there was nothing more he could say to make Maria believe him. He dove for the tranquilizer gun, trying to knock it out of her hands. He was hoping Maria either didn't know how to use it or would be afraid to.

He was wrong on both counts. He heard the sound right before the dart sliced into his right leg. The dart went all the way through the muscle in his thigh, just barely missing the bone. For a split second he couldn't believe she'd really done it. He reached down and pulled the dart out with his right hand. It seemed like everything was moving in slow motion. He looked at the dart in his hand and then at Maria, who had lowered the gun and looked every bit as stunned as he felt.

"Maria . . . I really wish you wouldn't have done that," was all he could say before he crumpled to the floor.

* * *

Maria studied the two men lying in a heap on the kitchen floor for a full thirty seconds before she ran over to Quinn and grabbed the sheriff's car keys out of his pocket. She had to pull herself together fast, or she wouldn't be able to get away. She wasn't going to trust anyone or listen to anyone this time. Imogene and Wesley were probably long gone by now. She would drive back down the trail until she found something— anything. She examined Harrison. Was there any possibility he was telling the truth?

I did what I had to, Harrison. You gave me no choice. She scrutinized his face. How could someone so unassuming be so corrupt? He really didn't look like a criminal. But then, those were the best at their craft. The ones with no conscience, who could act and deceive— and pretend to care about someone they were really just playing games with. She needed to drive away now. Quinn was starting to stir. She looked at Harrison once more and heaved a sigh.

What exactly propelled her to action, she didn't know, but she grabbed Harrison by the arms and lugged him over to the front door. He was a lot heavier than she expected. She took a deep breath and strained to heave him as upright as she could so she could hoist his limp body into the backseat of the SUV. She threw him in, not so delicately, smashing his face into the seat. She moved his head so he could breathe and then checked his pulse. All she could tell was that he had one. For a moment she thought about picking up the radio to call for help, but then she remembered that Ranger Rick was also connected to this line.

She needed to hurry. She climbed into the driver's seat and noticed with dismay that it had a stick shift. Could anything else go wrong? She had never driven anything but an automatic. There was nothing for her to do but learn fast. She started the engine and ground the gears. The car stalled when she popped the clutch too fast. She started it again. To add to her panic, Quinn was at the front door and heading straight for her. She tried to put the gearshift in reverse, but nothing happened. Quinn was at the car window. She hit the door locks as he banged on the window with his fist.

Once again she started the car and jammed the gear forward and right. She headed backward for about twenty yards. Quinn was still chasing after her. She couldn't risk turning around and stalling the car again, so she backed up another bumpy hundred yards, scraping foliage along the way, before finding an area wide enough to turn around. Quinn was still screaming and threatening her. After a six-point turn with at least as many stalls, she lurched forward and headed down the trail.

Harrison had rolled onto the floor, but Maria couldn't stop to check on him. She felt a sick feeling in the pit of her stomach, like she had made the wrong decision once again.

22

Road Rage

Wesley was holding his dad's head in his lap when Maggie came running back with the first aid kit.

"What took you so long?" Wesley challenged.

"I had a hard time finding the cave again," Maggie admitted. "I have night blindness. Is he conscious?"

"He comes in and out," Wesley answered. "Shouldn't we be putting pressure on his arm?"

"Normally yes, but there might still be some pieces of glass in there, and that would do more damage. I can't tell what the situation is in this light, so we'll have to play it safe."

"Do you think Harrison will come back in time?" Wesley looked at Maggie's watch. "It's been an hour."

"I know. Let's give him a few more minutes. You and I will have to carry your dad out."

Wesley had been praying for their safety since the fire started. When he saw headlights coming down the road, he felt his prayers had been answered. "I really hope that's Harrison," Wesley said.

He left Maggie and his dad under the cover of darkness as he ran to the trail. If it was Imogene and Richard again, he would recognize the truck, but this time it was a different vehicle altogether. It looked like a police SUV, and if it was someone hostile, he was out of luck, because his flashlight had already given him away. The brakes slammed, and the SUV died rather than stopped. The door opened, and Wesley did a double take.

"Maria?"

"Wesley! I can't believe I found you! Are you alone?"

Before he could answer, Maggie sprinted up behind him. "Maria! You don't know how happy we are to see you. And especially to see you driving a car. Have you seen Harrison?"

Maria's delighted face suddenly turned into an expression of anguish. "Maggie," she said. "I think I've just done something really bad."

Maggie had already opened the back door. She took a step back and gasped. Harrison's lifeless body was illuminated by the overhead light.

Wesley shined his flashlight on the floor. It took a moment for the scene to register, and then he put his hand over his mouth. "Is he dead?"

Maria's hands were shaking on the steering wheel. "I don't know—I shot him with a tranquilizer dart," she admitted as if she had just spent her last morsel of emotion.

Maggie quickly crawled over and pressed a finger to his neck. "He's not dead, but his pulse is weak. We need to get him to a doctor along with Jack. Wesley, help me move him and pull your dad into the car. Let's put this seat down."

"What happened to Jack?" Maria asked mechanically.

"He was attacked by me, a broken window, and a bear," Maggie answered, not offering any more details.

Maggie didn't ask Maria why she'd shot Harrison. Wesley didn't either because he could see that anything might push Maria over the edge right now. He didn't want to ruin the odds and make it three out of five people incapacitated.

The three of them lifted a semiconscious Jack into the vehicle and laid him next to Harrison. Wesley couldn't help feeling it looked like two bodies in a hearse.

"Maggie," Maria quickly interjected. "You have to drive—I can't drive a stick shift."

"Maria." Maggie grabbed her by the shoulders. "I need you to drive while I sit in back—just in case I need to do CPR. Do you understand me? You can do it. You got here, didn't you?"

"Just barely. And I don't even know where I'm going. I already drove off a bridge once . . ." Maria added.

Wesley could see that Maria was about ready for a breakdown. It was more than the driving; she was worried about Harrison.

"I'll drive," Wesley said.

"You can't drive, Wesley," Maggie stated.

"Yes I can. And I can drive a stick."

"Where did you learn that?" Maggie asked skeptically.

"Grandpa taught me. I drive his old truck all the time," Wesley admitted. He didn't want to break his promise to keep it a secret, but this was an emergency. "Plus, I think I know the way. Harrison showed me how to memorize things so I wouldn't get lost. I paid close attention on the way up."

Maggie looked at Maria, then back at Wesley. "No, you're still too young and inexperienced."

"I'm really good, I promise!"

Maggie sighed and looked at Jack and Harrison. "Fine. Get in. But don't go too fast."

Wesley tried not to look too nervous as he hopped in the driver's seat. Maria seemed relieved to be in the passenger seat. He started the engine with no problem and eased the clutch into first gear. Though they were soon rolling down the rugged trail without incident, Wesley had never felt so much pressure in his life.

It looked like everything was finally under control until the sheriff's radio buzzed on. Wesley recognized the voice, and it looked like Maria did too.

"Quinn, I need you to copy on a 940-J. We have an emergency situation—fugitive on the loose. The fourteen-year-old juvenile is an arson suspect. Please detain the fugitive if you find him—oh yeah, he's identifiable by a skunk odor."

"So he's telling the sheriff I set the fire!" Wesley hooted.

"Who set the fire?" Maria asked.

"Harrison and Imogene," Maggie answered and tried to condense what had happened into a few sentences. "Well, Harrison was trying to prevent Imogene from shooting us."

"So he helped you escape?" Maria clarified.

"He did." Maggie picked up Harrison's wrist and checked his pulse. "It looks like he really is a double agent—and he's on our side. Where have you been this whole time?"

"They kept me at the ranger station."

"Who did?"

"Ranger Rick and Sheriff Quinn."

"What for?"

"They said I was trespassing, and they didn't believe my story since I had a past criminal record."

"Maybe we should get on the radio and tell the police where we are," Maggie said.

"We can't," Wesley explained. "Ranger Rick will hear us and know we've stolen this car."

"He's right," Maria agreed. "Ranger Rick and Sheriff Quinn can't be trusted. They'll find us before anyone else does."

"Which one is Imogene's cousin?" Maggie asked.

"Ranger Rick is," Wesley answered. "Aunt Dottie—the old lady—and Imogene's mother are sisters."

"Really?" Maria asked.

"So where's Imogene?" Maggie asked.

"She took off in the truck with Ranger Rick and the old lady," Wesley explained.

Jack was stirring in the backseat, trying to sit up. "Mag?"

"How do you feel?" Maggie asked.

"Like I'm half dead."

"That's good, because it means you're still half alive."

Jack looked at the pallid body next to him. "Mag?"

"What?"

"If he's there," he pointed to Harrison, "and you're here and Maria's there—who's driving?"

Maggie didn't have time explain. "Wesley is. Lie back down."

"Oh. I didn't know Wes could drive."

"Well, I didn't know you could fly a helicopter either."

Wesley perked up. "That was you in the helicopter? Awesome!"

The radio crackled again, and this time Ranger Rick sounded annoyed. "Quinn, I just spotted your vehicle about a quarter mile past Devil's Creek. If you don't answer me, I'll assume this is a 503."

"He knows it's us!" Maria panicked.

"But he won't catch us," Wesley assured them as he stepped on the gas. It was starting to rain again, and the SUV slid as he cornered.

"Wesley, pull over. You better let me drive now," Maggie ordered.

"We can't stop—they're probably behind us now!" Wesley didn't slow down. "I can lose them!" He knew it was crazy to try and outrun someone who knew these roads like the back of his hand and who had about forty more years' driving experience. But right now there wasn't another choice.

Maria buckled her seat belt and checked to make sure Wesley's was secure. Wesley thought she was probably regretting her decision to let him drive. He wouldn't let them down. The people he cared most about in the world were in this car. He tried to focus on the scenery so he wouldn't get lost. He remembered there was a dead cypress tree in the place where he would have to turn, but it was hard to see any landmarks until he was right next to them. He drove as fast as he could without sliding off the bumpy road. Several minutes passed, and truck headlights appeared behind him. Wesley didn't dare adjust his rearview mirror, so he shouted at Maggie.

"Is it them?"

"I don't know who 'them' is, but it's a truck. I can see two people inside."

Maria twisted around in her seat. "It's Ranger Rick. Can you shoot out their tires?"

"No! This isn't some detective show—I don't even want to try." Maggie rustled around in the back, climbing over Jack and Harrison. "There's a toolbox back here . . . Maria, try to find the button to roll down the back window."

Maria fumbled around and unlocked the doors before finding the rear window control.

Maggie promptly chucked a wrench outside, but it missed the truck completely. She emptied a bag of screws into the dirt, trying to puncture their tires and then got ready to use a hammer. "Wesley, slow down a little. Maybe I can hit the windshield."

"Don't slow down!" Maria counter-ordered. "If we can hit them, they can hit us!"

Wesley wasn't listening to either of them. Was he supposed to turn left or right at the upcoming fork in the road?

"Maggie, which way should I go?" There wasn't time for her to make an assessment, so Wesley veered right. The road was a little rougher here, and it made him think he'd gone the wrong way. The car splashed in several puddles of mud where the rain had pooled. The tires skidded, and Wesley corrected the car and geared down without hitting the brakes. Walter had taught him well.

The area was a little less densely forested, and Wesley cautiously added more speed. But Ranger Rick didn't let the gap widen.

Maria was chewing on her fingernails when she suddenly started to panic. "Wesley, you have to turn around. The fire is burning across the road!"

"I can't turn around!" Wesley stated the obvious.

"Roll the window back up!" Maggie ordered.

Wesley had to fight to keep his composure. He could see the trees burning along the road up ahead. Where was this car chase going to end? Should he keep going until he drove into the fire? Wesley checked his gas gauge. It was half full.

"We have to stop. We can't drive into the fire!" Maggie cried.

Ranger Rick was still tailgating him, and Wesley was determined not to let him catch them. The little maneuver he was thinking of would be risky, but so was stopping or driving into the fire. He slowed down slightly and cranked the steering wheel sharply to the left. Maria screamed as he drove the SUV down an embankment, suspending them in midair for several seconds before the tires came back into contact with the ground. The vehicle skimmed small trees on either side. Shrubs scraped the underside of the car, and the front axle hit a small boulder, causing a landslide of dirt and rocks. When the terrain was level enough, Wesley turned back the way they had come. "Don't worry," he said. "I can get back onto the road."

The car was quiet. "Is everybody okay?" Wesley asked.

Maria didn't answer. Wesley figured she'd probably passed out.

"We're fine," Maggie said weakly. "I'm just having a moment of déjà vu."

Wesley had no idea what she was referring to, and he was too busy completing his U-turn and trying to find a place where he could get back onto the road to figure it out. Ranger Rick wasn't giving up. He had stopped and turned around in the road and was behind them once again.

"Oh, no you don't!" Wesley pressed the gas pedal to the floor.

"Slow down!" Maggie ordered. "If we hit a tree at this speed, we're dead! But other than that, you're driving very well."

"Thanks," Wesley murmured. "I think the road forks up there. Which way do I go now?"

Before Maggie could answer, a new set of headlights appeared, and an unidentified car facing them head-on flashed its bright lights.

"Never mind, that answers my question." Wesley veered and took the right fork to avoid hitting the car. "Did you see who it was?" he asked Maggie.

"I couldn't tell. It's too dark." Maggie turned and strained to see out the back window. "Whoever it is just pulled out behind the ranger truck."

"So they're both after us," Wesley stated. He didn't take Maggie's advice to slow down. He was starting to get used to the speed. "Look, there's a lake up there." Wesley pointed. "I think I recognize this!" He distinctly remembered a large clearing around a small lake on the way up. Ranger Rick must have known this would be an opportunity for him to lose them because he moved in even closer. The other vehicle was so close behind Ranger Rick that if Wesley even tapped his brakes, they would all be in a pileup. The situation was extremely precarious, and Wesley saw that it was going to get even worse as they entered the clearing.

"Look, it's a police car!" Maria appeared to still be with them. There was another SUV with police lights parked in the road directly ahead. Wesley had to make another split-second decision. He was going so fast that his only choices were to steer the car into a cluster of trees or into the lake. He slammed on the brakes,

K.L. Fogg

knowing that he might not have enough time to stop before all three cars crashed into the cop car or went flying into the lake. The tires locked, and the SUV power-skidded into a three-sixty.

Wesley thought for a few slow-motion mirco-seconds as they were spinning that he had just success-fully killed every person in the car. There was nothing to do but hang onto the steering wheel and keep his foot on the brake. He heard a crash but didn't feel the impact. They were still moving, traveling through space and time, and he waited for his life to flash before him. Some small trees slowed them down, and the vehicle finally came to a stop right at the edge of the lake. A plume of water showered the side window.

For a minute it was absolutely quiet, and the fact that he felt no pain made him think that he really was dead after all. He saw a bright light and wondered if he were having a near-death experience.

The light got brighter, and then there was sound.

"Get out of the car right now with your hands in the air!"

He knew one thing. This wasn't a heavenly greeter. He saw that Maggie and Maria were speechless.

Ranger Rick had tried another option and had slammed his truck into the branches of two trees. The other car had plowed into Ranger Rick's fender.

"I think we better get out of the car," Wesley prod-ded. "It's the cops."

"It's a whole SWAT team," Maggie said in awe.

Wesley pressed the door handle and carefully got out, raising his hands above his head. Maria and Maggie followed him.

He looked over at Ranger Rick, who was out of his car and showing the police his park ranger badge as if

238

it exonerated him from all wrongdoing. A burly FBI officer threw him up against the truck and handcuffed him. Two officers were helping a frightened Aunt Dottie out of the passenger seat.

"Richard," his mother scolded. "You're going to be grounded for this!"

Wesley counted. There were six patrol trucks surrounding them, including the one behind Ranger Rick.

One of the officers looked familiar to Wesley. Chief Hicks sauntered up and holstered his gun. "May I ask which one of you was driving this vehicle?"

Wesley looked around. Surely he would be arrested for driving without a license. "I was, sir."

"You're the driver of this car?" Hicks's penetrating stare was uncomfortable.

"Yes, sir," Wesley answered unequivocally.

Hicks motioned for Sweeney to come over. "Let's make this perfectly clear for the record. You're fourteen years old, you have no license, and you were driving a stolen vehicle at dangerously high speeds in the backcountry at night."

"It was an emergency—my dad and Harrison are injured."

"It's okay, kid. I just wanted to make sure." Hicks patted him on the shoulder. "I think you deserve a commendation. Excellent work."

Hicks took out his radio and spoke into it. "Suspect Imogene Vandergrift is not in the vehicle. We have apprehended a male suspect with ranger ID named Richard Krebs. We need a paramedic helicopter at Lake Chatagwa pronto."

Two paramedics were already attending to Jack and Harrison. Maggie ran over to see if Jack was still okay. Chief Hicks grabbed her arm and held her back.

"Hold on there, Maggie. I have a few questions for you first."

"What, are you going to arrest me?" she asked angrily. "I demand to know why you didn't tell us about this from the beginning!"

"You'll be briefed when you get back to the station."

"It's a little late for a briefing! We should have been told about this a month ago!"

"I want to know how you found out about this location."

"We cracked a code Harrison gave to Maria."

"Why didn't you give it to us?"

"Because we thought you and Harrison were working for Imogene. We could have saved a lot of time if we had known who we could trust. So how did you find us?"

"Between Maria's car, the fire, and police scanners, we narrowed things down. Do you still have the code written down?"

"No, it's incinerated, along with our Land Rover, but Wesley knows where both cabins are—or were, anyway. I'm sorry, but can we do this later? My husband is getting airlifted to the hospital, and I would really like to get there as soon as possible."

Hicks ran over to Detective Sweeney, who was questioning Maria.

Wesley was standing all alone, wondering where he was supposed to go. Everyone seemed to have something urgent to do except him.

"What?" he heard Hicks roar. "She shot him with a tranquilizer gun? What in blazes would she do that for?"

The conversation faded into the whir of chopper blades as Wesley moved away from all the stress and confusion. He had thought he was driving away from

Imogene the whole time, and she wasn't even in the car. He was bitterly disappointed that he didn't get to witness the police locking her in handcuffs and hauling her off in a patrol car. She had to be close by, but he knew from experience that it was a lot easier to hide in the dark woods than it was to find someone there.

"Everybody move out!" Hicks hollered. "We got a forest fire that could block our exit any minute now."

"Wesley," Detective Sweeney said. "Are you okay?" He was the first person to inquire about his condition.

Wesley didn't know the answer. "Are my dad and Harrison going to be all right?"

"We've got paramedics working on them right now."

Wesley was suddenly very tired and wanted nothing more than to curl up in his own bed and go to sleep with Hercules at his feet. "I'll be fine," he answered.

23

The Safety-Deposit Box

The nurse came in and brought Jack a cup of ice water and then threatened to take the hospital bed remote away if he didn't stop adjusting his bed.

"The constant noise is bothering the other patients."

"But I can't get comfortable. My legs are restless."

"Your family's here to see you—I'll send them in two at a time."

"Do I look like an invalid?" Jack asked. "Send in the whole gang before I figure out how to launch this rig." He pressed the button down until his torso was nearly vertical.

The nurse shook her head and sighed. "It's against the rules, but I'll see what I can do." She walked out as Maggie came in with C.J. and Wesley came in with Emily.

"There's Daddy!" Maggie said as Emily reached her arms out to Jack. Wesley restrained her.

"You look good," Maggie said as she kissed him, letting C.J. slobber on his cheek.

"You all look good—and you smell good too." Jack sniffed his approval as Emily gave him a kiss too.

"It only took three tomato juice baths," Wesley explained. "Teddy got one whiff of me, and I think he ran away from home."

"Good work, mate. That'll cut our food bill in half," Jack said. "So when do I get out on parole?"

"Probably tomorrow. They need to watch that for infection." Maggie pointed to the sutures in his arm. "I've heard you're the most annoying patient up here."

"You heard right. I've got a reputation to uphold."

Maggie checked the monitor connected to Jack's IV. "Your oxygen's a little low," she noted. "Take a couple of deep breaths for me."

Jack winced. "Do I have to?"

"If you want to come home, you do."

Jack complied. "How about Harry? What happened to the secret agent man?"

"Well, that's a long story."

"I'm not going anywhere soon."

"We found out his real name is Alex Harris. He isn't a tutor at all. He is a genuine government spy."

"See, I told you! He *was* hiding somethin'!"

"Yes, you were right about that, but he's not a sociopath. Anyway, he was out cold for a couple of hours after Maria shot him in the leg with a tranquilizer dart. But he's awake now and, other than a sore leg, he's doing fine."

"So Maria shot him, eh?" Jack smiled.

"Yes, well just like you, she didn't trust him. But it turns out he's been working on the Vandergrift case for more than a year. They started suspecting Imogene might be alive several months ago. Alex Harris has been pretending to be an agent named Peter Jaworsky—the guy who rigged his parachute and tried to kill him. So it turns out the parachute story is true after all. Anyway, we can give you the details later. He's getting released today and should make a full recovery. But I'm not so sure about Maria."

"What's wrong with Maria?"

"Your basic broken heart, I think."

"So he dumped her?" Jack asked in disgust.

"No, he's been asking to see her, but she doesn't want to talk to him. I mean, she's really confused about everything. She's been worked around so much, she doesn't trust anyone anymore—not even herself."

Wesley pushed a pacifier back into Emily's mouth. "I hope she changes her mind. They make a great couple. And Alex isn't even mad at Maria for shooting him with the dart gun."

Jack nodded. "Well Wes, that's what real men do in situations like this. They have to forgive and forget. I mean, when the woman you love takes you out, you just have to deal with it and move on. That's why you won't hear me complainin' about my cracked rib." Jack looked at Maggie with a pitiful expression.

"Not more than once every five minutes anyway. Why do I get the blame?" Maggie defended. "You jumped out a window, crashed a helicopter, and got yourself attacked by a bear!"

"Don't listen to her, Wes. It was a perfect landing— I had to thread the needle in the middle of a forest. And my rib was cracked before all that." Jack stuck his hand up with his palm forward. "Not that it matters—I wouldn't even mention it, but you brought up what's-his-face, and I just wanted you to know that I forgive you."

"That's nice, because we do have to live together." Maggie adjusted the back of his hospital bed. "Oh, and get this—Alex Harris used to play football in college.

He was a quarterback. Remember how Jamal noticed he could really throw?"

"A smart football player," Jack mused. "That's an oxymoron, isn't it? Is there anything this guy doesn't do?"

Maggie thought for a moment. "Yes, he can't fly a helicopter."

Jack smiled smugly.

"So, is Harris—I mean Alex—going to leave now?" Wesley asked.

"I don't know what his plans are." Maggie started to explain, but C.J.'s five minutes of good behavior suddenly expired, and she started to get fussy. "I'll take her out to Grandma." She met Hicks as she was leaving.

"How's the patient?" Hicks asked Jack.

"More like the *im*patient," Jack answered sullenly. "I'm just dandy, and you?"

Hicks ignored Jack's grumpiness. "Maggie, I need to have a word with you and Jack, if I could."

"Can it wait, Chief?" Jack said, annoyed. "I'm tryin' to visit with my family here."

"I'm afraid this information is extremely important. You might not want me to wait on it." The look on Hicks's face was very unsettling. "I need to talk with just you and Maggie." He motioned to Wesley with his eyes as if Wesley were too young to understand he was being asked to leave.

"Did they find Imogene?" Wesley asked.

"Not yet, Wesley, but we've got some very good leads, and I'm sure it won't be much longer," Hicks stated. "Could I ask you to wait outside for a minute?"

Wesley was visibly disappointed that he wasn't considered mature enough to be included in the conversation. "I'll take both girls to Grandma." Wesley scooped C.J. in his free arm and exited without arguing.

"What is it?" Maggie suddenly looked worried.

"I have two pieces of information for you." Hicks motioned to the large manila envelope he was carrying. "Before I show you what I have in this envelope, I need to give you a little background on what we already know."

"Are we going to like this?" Jack asked.

Hicks's face was expressionless, and he didn't answer. "You know that Alex Harris has been following this case since last April. We have evidence that suggests Imogene Vandergrift is involved in the embezzlement of some diamonds. Well, until a few months ago, we weren't sure how much she was involved. And until a few days ago, Alex had never met Imogene in person or been able to find out where her headquarters are. But there is actually another person working with Imogene whom we've known about for almost a decade. She's the mastermind of this whole operation. She goes by the name Colette, and she has ties to terrorists in Europe and South Africa. Imogene is her biggest client. Nobody knows what this Colette person looks like or how old she is—she seems to change her look and float below the radar all the time. All anyone knows is that she's very beautiful, which is part of the reason why she's able to get away with things. She's probably in her early or mid-thirties because she's been doing this for twelve years now. Imogene and Colette have formed a partnership, and Alex was hoping to trap them both."

"So are you any closer to finding Colette?" Maggie asked.

"Maybe. We have some evidence that leads us to believe Colette may be responsible for taking Emily— and returning her."

"Okay, you got our attention. Who is it?" Jack asked.

"I'm getting to it, Jack. Let me finish. We searched Richard Krebs's cabin and vehicle. We didn't turn up anything of value except a key from his glove box. We traced the key to a safety-deposit box in an Atlanta bank. They just opened it a while ago."

"What was in it?" Jack asked.

"Several things. Some expensive jewelry, a necklace, and these." Hicks pulled two 8x10 photos from the envelope. He set the two pictures side by side on the white hospital sheet so that Jack and Maggie could both see them, and then he waited.

Maggie gasped and put her hand over her mouth. She looked as though she might faint.

Jack picked up the photos one at a time and put them down. "So what? These are pictures of Maggie— they just doctored them up."

Maggie stared at the woman in the photos. There were only two people in the world it could be. Either it was her or her identical twin. Her hair was longer than she usually wore it, and straighter. She was wearing clothes she had never seen and would never have picked out—a peasant blouse, flowing skirt, and beaded sandals. It definitely wasn't her style. The woman in the photos had a large handbag slung over her shoulder, and she was in mid-stride. In one picture she was looking straight ahead. In the other she was looking off to one side.

Maggie involuntarily shuddered. "Could it be Nicole? Where were these supposedly taken?" Maggie asked in a much calmer voice than she was feeling.

Hicks was ready with the answer. "We can tell from the buildings in the background that this is Johannesburg, South Africa."

"Can't you tell if this is a forgery?" Jack asked.

"Not always. Of course, this isn't the original—it's a copy of the one we found in the safety-deposit box. With today's digital technology, even an amateur can do a lot of layering and then can print it like an original. They could have taken Maggie's head and attached it to someone else's body—people do it all the time. With close examination we can detect differences in skin tone, but then there are ways to get around that too. They could have left the body and changed the clothing."

"So in other words, you don't know if this is real or fake?" Maggie asked.

"That's true. But because Nicole's body was never found, we can't ignore a piece of evidence like this. Colette also started working right around the time your sister disappeared. And that's another tip—the name *Colette* is a derivative of *Nicole*. There's too much here to be a coincidence. That's why I'm showing this to the both of you." Hicks said to Maggie. "I'd like your parents to see it too. Are there any distinguishing features between you and your sister?"

"Sure, there are a lot, but you can't see them in these pictures. Nicole had a small mole on her left cheek, but there's a shadow there."

Jack looked more closely. "They had different eyes. This looks more like Maggie to me."

"Nicole would never have abandoned her child," Maggie said.

"And what about her husband?" Jack frowned. "She wouldn't have left either one of us. She was happy."

Maggie felt a catch in her throat and wanted to run out of the room. She didn't like this turn of events, this conversation, or these bizarre pictures that were making her heart race.

"Let's have Penny take a look," Jack suggested.

"No!" Maggie grabbed the pictures away. "It would devastate her! We need more information first. This whole thing is absurd!"

"Mag, calm down," Jack said.

Maggie waved the pictures in Jack's face. "Don't you get it? Nicole's been missing for thirteen years! If she's alive, that means she either abandoned her family or has some sort of memory loss and doesn't know who she is. Either case is tragic. A mother never really heals from losing a child, and these pictures will only open old wounds that have taken Mom a long time to heal."

"There is one other thing to consider," Hicks said hesitantly. "Someone was able to just walk into your home in broad daylight, pick up Emily, and walk out without being detected. If this person looked exactly like Maggie, it would explain why no one noticed anything unusual."

"It wasn't my sister. Even if she were alive and brainwashed, she wouldn't kidnap her own niece—it's not possible!"

Hicks cleared his throat. "I can't tell you how many times I've heard someone claim that something isn't possible. Jack, you found out your son was alive after eleven years. A lot of people thought Imogene was dead too, and she turned up after eighteen months. I think we've already established that anything is possible."

Maggie was shaking her head to show that she didn't agree.

"Don't you have any other leads on this Colette person?" Jack prodded.

Hicks looked inside the envelope. "I told you, we also found this." He produced another photo of a silver chain with a heart-shaped locket.

Jack studied it carefully. "I gave this to Nicki when our son was born."

"That was also in the safety-deposit box," Hicks noted.

Maggie grabbed it from Hicks. "It still doesn't prove anything!" She was near tears. "Maybe this was with Wesley. We know Imogene rescued him from the ocean."

"Or she claims she rescued him," Hicks hinted. "Imogene may have actually *bought* him."

"Hold on!" Jack jumped in. "I don't like what you're suggesting."

"This is ridiculous!" Maggie turned her back on Hicks and paced around the room. "You are insinuating that my sister sold her baby and became an international diamond thief."

"There has to be some other explanation," Jack asserted.

Maggie picked up the envelope and stuffed the pictures inside. "You didn't know my sister," she said to Hicks accusingly. "I don't know where these pictures came from, but I can tell you I'll figure it out, even if I have to hunt down Imogene and get it from her myself."

"Maggie," Hicks said. "I'm sorry to have upset you—"

"Upset me? You have no idea. And you leave my mother and father out of this." She held the envelope up and waved it at him. "This is a lie!"

"Maggie," Hicks said sternly. "Promise me you won't go try and find Imogene again. Leave that part to us."

"I'm not promising you anything." Maggie tucked the envelope under her arm and hurried out of the room, leaving Hicks and Jack with nothing to say.

24

True Confessions

Maria folded the last piece of laundry and started looking for other chores to keep her occupied. She really should go over and talk to Maggie, but the chance that *he* might be there was too great a risk. Why she was avoiding Alex Harris was difficult for her to understand, let alone explain to anyone else. It was some combination of pride, anger, and guilt—all those self-indulgent sins that a good person shouldn't allow. All she knew was that she couldn't see him right then.

He was probably mad at her, too—and, granted, he had good reason to be, but how could he have expected her to trust him? Just because he was some international undercover spy didn't give him the right to play on her emotions like that. To think that those ridiculous glasses had just been a device to allow Imogene to listen in on all their private conversations made her secretly glad that she'd shot him with that dart gun. Whatever pain he was feeling in his leg was going to go away a lot faster than the pain he had inflicted on her.

Amanda came running into the house flushed and out of breath. "Mom, Harrison—I mean Alex—is here and wants to talk to you!"

Maria's heart started pounding. He wasn't supposed to come over. She was going to wait for him to leave, and then there wouldn't be anything to deal with or sort out. No choice was an easy choice. What did he want from her? An apology? She hadn't prepared anything to say.

"Tell him I'm not home," Maria said as Amanda rolled her eyes and tilted her head toward the open door.

"You can tell me that in person," Alex answered from the doorway, where he stood with a bouquet of flowers in one hand.

"Look, he brought your favorite flowers!" Amanda gushed.

Maria took in the sight of an armful of pink Gerbera daisies. "I didn't know you could get that kind of information in a background check," she said icily. Why was she being rude? She didn't move toward him but stayed firmly planted several yards away.

Amanda shot her mother a disappointed look and then suddenly remembered that she had something important to do outside and quickly disappeared.

"Maria," Alex started, "I want to tell you I'm sorry . . ."

"For what?" Maria tried to act casual. "I'm the one who should apologize—for shooting you." *Was that really an apology?* she thought.

"Under the circumstances, I don't blame you. I would have done the same thing." He took a step forward and then stopped. "It wasn't fair for me to put you in that situation."

You're absolutely right about that, Maria silently agreed. "Well, then." The air in the room grew heavy, and Maria didn't have any idea what to say. She wanted him to leave and stay at the same time. "Will you be moving on as someone else's tutor then?"

"Actually, Hicks has a special assignment for me."

"Oh, right." Maria blushed at her stupidity. "You aren't really a tutor."

"No. But I've always wanted to be a college professor."

"Look, Alex," Maria said, "I really am sorry about shooting you. I know that probably messed up the whole operation."

"We all made it back safely. That's the important thing. I heard Wesley did some pretty impressive driving."

"Yes, I would have liked to have been sedated for that experience," Maria admitted.

Alex fidgeted with the flowers, not knowing what to do with them. "Would you like to take a walk?"

Maria opened her mouth to refuse him, but nothing came out, so she just shook her head.

Alex set the flowers on the table in the entryway. "It's okay. I understand." He started to go and then changed his mind. "I just want you to know that it wasn't all an act—how I feel about you. I'm leaving. My flight leaves this afternoon. So, I guess this is good-bye then?"

"I guess it is." Maria could think of nothing else to say. "Good-bye, Alex."

Alex looked disappointed, like he had expected that she would try to ask him to stay. "Before I go, can I ask you just one question?"

Maria nodded. "All right."

"Who is Geraldo?"

* * *

Wesley could see that whatever Hicks had told Maggie was not good news. She shuffled around the house like she was trying to figure out the answer to some unsolvable puzzle in her head. She snapped at the girls, and when Wesley tried to pry information from her, she just shrugged and said everything was fine; she was just recovering from all the recent stress. But something was very wrong, and all kinds of scenarios kept playing in Wesley's head. Maybe his dad was having some serious complications at the hospital and they didn't want him to worry about it. It was possible that Imogene was plotting to take him away again with a new plan to ruin his life.

Wesley went outside to the tire swing, his usual place for pondering life's problems. His solitude was interrupted by an unsolicited visit from Dylan.

"Hey S.B., I was wondering when you were going to thank me for saving your life." Dylan sauntered up to the tire swing and pushed it in a circle.

"Thanks, Dylan, for saving my life," Wesley intoned as he spiraled past Dylan.

"You're welcome. This one's for free. Next time you'll have to give me your horse."

"According to you, Grandma Penny already gave you my horse."

Dylan grabbed the tire and brought it to a halt. "That's right, she did. You can pay me in cash then."

"Where's Jamal?"

"My prison guard has been released from his duties. So I came over to look after you."

"Gee, thanks."

"No problem. I figured you might need some help now that your life is *really* messed up."

Wesley was accustomed to this type of conversation from Dylan, but for some reason he thought he detected something under the surface.

"What do you mean *really* messed up?"

"I mean, those photos of that lady, or your mom or whoever it is. That is so freaky that she's still alive."

"I know she's alive. I just spent the last few days with her."

"You did?" Dylan stepped back like someone had kicked him in the face.

Wesley was getting frustrated with Dylan. "You mean that you didn't know that Imogene had kidnapped Emily and taken me as a hostage?"

"I knew *that!*" Dylan threw his arms down. "I'm not talking about Imogene. I mean your *real* mom."

"Who, Maggie?"

"No, Maggie's sister."

"Dylan, you're confused. My real mom died thirteen years ago."

"You mean you don't know?"

"Know what?" Wesley studied Dylan's face. "If you know something Dylan, just tell me what's going on," he demanded.

"Maybe I shouldn't say anything, but Maggie was talking to the man formerly known as Harrison about some pictures they found in Imogene's safety-deposit box. They look like Maggie—but they're not. It might be your real mom."

"Wait—they were talking about this in front of *you?*"

"Sure, I can keep my mouth shut."

Wesley didn't bring up that Dylan's telling him this was proof that he couldn't keep his mouth shut.

"Well, maybe they didn't exactly see that I was in the room when they were there. I was sort of in the corner . . . behind the bed."

"What did you hear?" Wesley said, pumping Dylan for all the information he was worth. "They really think my mother is still alive?"

"They don't know, but Maggie was pretty freaked out about it. She won't even tell your grandparents." Dylan shook his head as if trying to show his sympathy. "And I thought *my* family had problems."

Wesley pondered the shocking new development for a moment. If his mother was alive, who was his dad married to? His life *was* really messed up. "Welcome to my world." He didn't know if this piece of news was supposed to make him feel good or bad, but right now he didn't feel much of anything. At least now he knew why Maggie was acting so strange.

"So what are you going to do?" Dylan had a knack for being insensitive in most situations.

"I'm not going to do anything," Wesley replied. "Grandpa Walter says life is just like the weather. Sometimes it's good and sometimes it's bad. You can't control it, but if you wait around a few minutes, it usually changes."

Wesley thought he saw Dylan's expression change very slightly.

"Rule number 21," Dylan said.

"I didn't know there was a rule number 21," Wesley noted.

"It was recently added," Dylan noted. "Rule number 21: Grandpa Walter is right ninety percent of the time."

"Why only ninety percent of the time?" Wesley asked. "Why not all the time?"

"He had to make an allowance for the ten percent of the time he disagrees with Grandma Penny."

* * *

Maria wiped her wet cheeks with the shoulder of her shirt. The pathway up to the oak tree seemed longer than the time she remembered walking it with Harrison. Harrison Landry—he didn't even exist. It was as if he really had been in the trunk of her car when she'd driven off the bridge. He was gone, and he wasn't coming back. The sooner she could deal with this reality, the sooner she would be able to put the past behind her and go on with life as usual.

She could have been a little nicer to him, though. What was wrong with her anyway? If anyone was guilty of committing a terrible sin, it was her. She had been an accessory to kidnapping, and the Mackeys had forgiven her and had even taken her and Amanda into their family. Who was she to let her pride get in the way of forgiving someone else? Besides, it wasn't up to Alex to let her in on some top-secret operation. What kind of top-secret agent went around telling everyone who he was?

She reached the initial-carved oak tree and told herself she would turn around then, but for some reason she had to walk over to it. And for some reason she needed to touch it, too. Then she could go back home. Her eyes went straight to the spot where it said, "Jason loves Maria." The "Jason" had been scratched out and replaced with a fresh carving that read "Alex." Maria traced it with her fingers as tears streamed down her face.

"I think people who deface nature ought to be shot," she heard a voice say behind her.

Maria didn't turn around. "Yes, and the person who did this did get shot." She turned around and avoided eye contact. "I thought you left already."

"I missed my plane," Alex said without remorse.

"That was a pretty dumb thing to do."

"Not as dumb as walking away without telling you how I really feel."

Maria connected her gaze to Alex. "Don't do this."

"I haven't done anything yet." His hair was blowing forward into his face, and it reminded Maria of what he used to look like.

"I really miss Harrison."

"You know, Harrison and I are a lot alike."

"Look Alex, I'll admit there might have been something between us, but everything's changed now. You're not the person I thought you were."

"Who did you think I was?"

"I thought you were a shy, intelligent Navy SEAL."

"And who do you think I am?"

"You're an undercover agent."

"I never kept that from you. Why does that cancel everything else out?"

"Because it does. This whole time I thought it was just me and you, and it was really Imogene, too. That makes everything different. Why couldn't you have just been yourself from the start? Why did you have to put on the act?"

"The act was to protect you—and me too, I guess. Imogene wanted you to fall in love with me so she'd have some leverage to bring you back to her side. She wanted you to come with us. I didn't plan on getting involved. I just wanted to make her think I was doing what she'd asked. And I thought if I was weird enough, there wouldn't be any chance of you liking me."

"Well guess what? That's one part of the operation that failed. Do you have any idea how horrible I felt when I woke up and thought you were still trapped in the trunk of my car?"

"Yes. Probably the same way I felt when I watched you drive your car off that bridge."

"Then when Imogene called you Peter, I wished you'd really been in the trunk."

Alex sighed. "I'm sorry for all that." He started to say something and then stopped. He started again. "Peter Jaworsky used to be my best friend."

"The same guy who tried to kill you?"

"The same. We played football together in college. I know this may be hard to believe, but I was first-string quarterback at Navy for a while. Peter was a defensive lineman, and he was always razzing me that the only reason I was even on the team was because my dad had some influence at the university. We spent a lot of time together on and off the field. He had a girl-friend named Allison, and she decided to break up with him and date me instead. We sort of got engaged."

"Sort of? How can you be sort of engaged?" Maria questioned.

"Okay, we were engaged. Peter got jealous, and then one week in practice he tackled me and broke my wrist. He swore it was an accident, and I believed him. I was out for the rest of the season, and when I finally healed, guess who was the new first-string quarter-back."

"Peter?" Maria answered.

Alex nodded.

"So what happened to Allison?"

"She decided she wanted to marry someone else, which was actually a good thing, but she didn't go back to Peter. I decided to graduate early and go through the SEAL program in California. Believe it or not, I actually talked Peter into coming with me. We went through the program together. He was always competitive, but I never even suspected that he might be a double agent until the day he tried to kill me. I didn't see that he was bad until it was too late."

"What happened to him? Did he get arrested?"

"I don't know. No one has seen or heard from him since the parachute incident, and he's presumed dead. The reason I took his identity is because he already had a connection to Imogene and—" Alex caught himself. "Someone else."

"That must have been really hard for you—the fact that he was your friend."

Alex nodded. "Imogene was your friend too. I guess we both know what it feels like to have a close friend betray us." He looked at his hands and then cleared his throat. "You probably feel that I betrayed you, too, but I promise you that I didn't. I understand if you don't want to see me anymore. I just want you to know that I never expected to fall in love with you."

Maria was surprised by his candor. She figured as long as they were being honest, she might as well confess something to him. "You want to know who Geraldo is? When Sheriff Quinn—the guy you took out at the cabin—asked me if I was married, I told him I had a fiancé named Geraldo. I said he was in the military—a Navy SEAL with a black belt in karate."

"Really?" Alex smiled. "He sounds like a great guy."

"Yeah, well, he's pretty much out of my league."

"I highly doubt that . . ." Alex leaned over and kissed her.

Maria embraced him and decided she was through trying to talk herself out of this relationship.

"So did you come out here to torture me before you left me?" Maria asked.

"Well, truthfully I wasn't planning on leaving just yet."

"What?" Maria furrowed her brow. "You just said you missed your plane!"

"And that's true. But I missed it on purpose. Hicks wanted to send me to Johannesburg, but I told him I was done."

"With this assignment or for good?"

"For good. There's an opening for a language professor at the University of Georgia. I thought I might apply for that."

"You're giving up your career as an undercover agent to become a schoolteacher?"

"Why not? I've been thinking about it for some time."

"So that whole line about 'this is good-bye' and everything was just a trick so you could spy on me and follow me up here," Maria accused.

"Actually, I was here first. I could accuse you of following me."

"But I didn't."

"Well, if there aren't any witnesses, then it's your word against mine."

"Except for this incriminating piece of evidence." Maria pointed to the "Alex loves Maria" engraving. Do you deny carving this on the tree?"

Alex looked at her and smirked. "Only if you deny that you wanted me to."

"You are so frustrating!"

"And you, Maria, are a quixotic enigma." Alex pushed a piece of hair off her face.

"That better be a compliment."

Night Shift

"Is it your job to make sure I don't get more than five minutes of peace and quiet?" Jack barked at the nurse who entered his room for the third time in less than a half hour. "Because if it is, you're doing a fabulous job. Doesn't this place have a curfew or something?" He noticed that the night shift nurse was new, and he regretted starting off badly with her, especially since she was packing a loaded syringe and was headed straight for his arm.

"Actually, I don't need that. I just got my pain meds a while ago."

"This isn't for the pain. It's an antibiotic for the infection." The nurse unceremoniously stabbed him in the arm.

"Ouch! On second thought, I'll take the extra pain meds." Jack looked at the nurse and did a double take. "Hey, don't I know you?" He suddenly felt strange, and his vision started to blur.

The nurse walked over to the foot of his bed. "How do you feel, Jack?"

Jack squinted his eyes. "Fuzzy."

"That's good. That means the medicine is working. Now, you and I are going to have a little chat, and then you can go to sleep, okay?"

* * *

Maria looked at the photos Maggie had set on her kitchen table. "So Alex knows about this?"

"As of today he does. But I just can't show my parents until we have some answers."

"I wish I could give them to you, but all I know is that Imogene told me she'd found a baby in a life jacket floating alone in a life raft and that she swam into the ocean to save him before the raft sank. She said there were snakes in the water, and that the locals called it the serpent tide."

"I know. I heard her tell Jack about it that day on the ocean. But she never answered me when I asked about Nicole."

"She never said anything to me about his parents except that his mother was dead, and his dad was in a coma. Imogene told me to go put the life jacket back in the ocean, but obviously I never did that."

Maggie was sitting with her elbows on the table, clutching her forehead with both hands. She shook her head.

"She'll make up anything to get what she wants." Maria tried to comfort Maggie.

"I know, but the question is why?" Maggie picked up the pictures and gestured with them. "Why would she have some doctored pictures of me or pictures of Nicole and an actual necklace that belonged to my sister locked in a safety-deposit box?"

"I don't know. She always has things planned out way in advance. She's an evil genius. Wesley and Amanda had that figured out a long time ago. That's why they called her 'Evil Gene.'"

Maggie started to respond when her cell phone rang. "It's the hospital," she said. "I better get it." She flipped it open and answered it. "No, he doesn't have any allergies that I know of." Her face grew cloudy, and then she grabbed a handful of hair and ran her fingers nervously through it. "Okay, I'll be there in twenty minutes." She slammed the phone shut. "Jack's acting crazy—he's had some sort of reaction to the medication."

"Is it serious?" Maria asked.

"I don't know. Everything right now is serious." Maggie grabbed her purse and flew out the door.

* * *

Maggie stepped into Jack's hospital room and took several deep breaths before she got close enough for Jack to see her. He had the remote in one hand and was surfing through channels so fast the TV looked like a strobe light. The doctor followed Maggie in.

"Hey, Mag! How's it goin'?" Jack sounded like he'd had one too many beers. "Hey there, Dr. Dolittle." He waved his hand.

"What drugs have you been giving him?" Maggie turned and grabbed the penlight from the doctor's pocket without asking and examined Jack's eyes.

"Nothing strong," the doctor defended. "Five milligrams of Lortab. He hasn't been in that much pain."

"That low of a dose shouldn't cause slurred speech and dilated pupils," Maggie stated. "He's obviously been given something else. I want to talk with the nurse on duty immediately."

The doctor summoned the nurse while Maggie tried to get information from Jack.

"She gave me a shot." Jack pointed to his arm.

Maggie examined Jack's arm and could see a small dot of blood. "Who gave you a shot?" she prodded.

"There's no injection listed on his chart," the doctor said as he checked his clipboard.

"The nurse did," Jack answered. "She said it was penithillon, no pneshillon." Jack laughed at himself.

"Penicillin?"

Jack stabbed his finger into the air. "That's it! That's a funny word, *penespillon*."

"Jack, listen to me." Maggie took a hold of both his shoulders. "This is very important."

"*Muy importante!*" Jack giggled. "That's 'very important' in Spanish."

"Yes, I know. Try to focus, Jack. What did the nurse who gave you the shot look like?"

A plump nurse with frizzy brown hair walked in the room. "Honey, I didn't give him anything. I just heard him talking to himself and reported it to Dr. Doyle."

"Not her." Jack steered his finger over to the nurse. "She wasalot prettier than her."

"I'm so sorry," Maggie apologized. "He's not himself."

"It's all right." The nurse waved her hand. "At least we know his vision is okay."

"Jack, what did she look like?"

"She looked like you, Mag."

Maggie blanched. "Do you mean exactly like me?"

"Not *exactly*."

"Was it Nicole?" Maggie asked hesitantly.

"It couldn't be . . ." Jack scratched his head. "Because she died, right?"

"Yes, she did." Maggie turned and ordered the nurse to check the trash for hypodermic needles. "Get security in here. And get someone from the lab to get a blood sample so we can figure out what that phony nurse gave him."

"I think you're jumping to conclusions," Dr. Doyle stammered. "We don't just let anyone in here. He might have had a reaction to the anesthesia from surgery. Some patients—"

"That was hours ago! He was completely coherent when we saw him earlier. Listen, doctor." Maggie was obviously angry. "Someone committed a crime here, and the longer we sit around in denial, the longer it's going to take to catch the perpetrator."

"Catch the purple traitor," Jack echoed.

"We need to lock down this hospital right away," Maggie said sternly.

"That's not a good idea," Dr. Doyle responded. "It's been more than forty minutes. That's plenty of time for this so-called perpetrator to leave the building. Besides, it would create an unnecessary panic."

"So you plan to do nothing? I don't believe this!"

While Maggie and Dr. Doyle disagreed on how to handle the situation, Jack continued a conversation with himself. "You want to know the password? The password is *Halloween*."

Maggie stopped in the middle of her sentence. "What password?"

"The password."

Maggie leaned down to speak directly into Jack's face. "The lady who gave you a shot gave you a password?"

"Nope. I wouldn't tell her." Jack zipped his lip with his fingers and pantomimed throwing away the key.

"The password to what?"

Jack closed his eyes.

Maggie shook him awake. "Have you seen her before?"

"Who? What?"

"The lady who came in here." It was obvious to Maggie they were losing him.

Jack's eyes began to droop. "Sure."

"Where?"

"Sailboats . . ." His head listed to one side.

"You're not going to get anything more out of him. He needs to sleep it off," Dr. Doyle said.

"Jack, don't go to sleep." Maggie shook him again. "If we let him sleep, he'll never remember when he wakes up."

"He's not making any sense now," Dr. Doyle stated.

"Where have you seen her, Jack?" Maggie demanded.

"There was water . . ." Jack was losing the fight to stay awake. "I trusssted her. She lied to me, Mag." He was out cold.

"Who lied to you, Jack?" Maggie jostled him. He didn't stir. "Wake him up! We need to know this now!"

Dr. Doyle pushed Maggie aside and checked Jack's pulse. "I think we need you to leave now, Maggie. His heart rate is fine. He's just having a rebound from being sedated. We'll hook him up to the monitor and call you when he wakes up."

"You'll call me?" Maggie roared. "That's reassuring," she added with sarcasm. She stepped forward, but the nurse firmly grabbed her arm.

"Let the doctor do his job, Mrs. Mackey."

"Mrs. Mackey," Maggie repeated in a detached voice. Her eyes filled up and a single tear rolled down her face. She quickly wiped it away with the back of her hand. "Mrs. Mackey . . ."

The nurse reassured her. "You better get some rest, honey. It sounds like you had a rough couple of days."

"I need to go now." Maggie exited the room so fast the people in the hallway probably thought the building was on fire.

* * *

Chief Hicks looked at his watch. It was past midnight and he wished he was at home watching a movie with his wife instead of coming all the way out here—out of his jurisdiction—and trying to oversee things himself. But the fact was that this was too important of an operation to leave to the rookies, and now that he no longer had Alex Harris working with him, he knew no one else had the experience to make quick decisions on the battlefield. Crouched down behind a boulder in the dirt next to Detective Sweeney, he felt like he was witnessing a real-life horror movie. What could be more cliché than watching two criminals dig up a coffin in the dead of night?

The cemetery plot belonged to Dorthea Krebs, who they had determined was still very much alive, and the gravediggers were none other than Imogene's cohorts, Simone and Andy.

Earlier that day, the forestry had gotten the fire under control and had given the forensics team the go-ahead to comb around the Krebs cabin to dust for fingerprints and look for evidence. One of the detectives spotted a vehicle parked inside a thick grove of trees not far down the road from the cabin. When he radioed back with the description and license plate, it checked out as the jeep that Simone and Andy had used to kidnap Wesley. Hicks told his team to find the duo and keep them under surveillance. He ordered them to hold off on any arrest until he could get there, in the hope that Simone and Andy might lead them to Imogene. He grabbed Sweeney away from his poker buddies, and several hours later they were hiding in a thicket, watching the felons exhume a coffin.

Rocks and pine needles stuck in Chief Hicks's elbows as he inched forward to get a better view with his night-vision binoculars. He couldn't hear the conversation, but it was obvious from her body language that Simone was forcing Andy to do most of the hard labor.

"Hey Chief, you think they're planning to bury someone or dig someone up?" Sweeney asked.

"I don't know. For all we know they could be digging to China. It feels like we've been here all night."

"We have been here all night," Sweeney noted. "It's one in the morning."

"Well, Imogene isn't here, and I've got a feeling she isn't going to show up. I think we better grab them while we've got the chance." Hicks adjusted his headset and spoke into the attached microphone. "Hey Goulais, you guys still awake over there?"

"Copy that, Chief. Ready and waiting."

"Can you tell if the suspects are armed?"

"Only with shovels, sir."

"Okay, they're both out of the hole now. On three we move in. One, two, three." Four FBI detectives darted to the place where Simone and Andy were digging.

"Police! You're under arrest! Put your hands in the air!" Hicks shouted as four loaded weapons were aimed directly at Simone and Andy.

Simone was so startled that she dropped her shovel. For a moment Hicks thought she might try to jump in the hole, but she didn't. She put two muddy hands on her head and let loose a string of swear words. Andy kept his shovel and raised it.

"Drop it!" Sweeney ordered.

Andy threw it down. "I told you we should have waited," he said to Simone.

"Cuff them," Hicks ordered the two officers. "Then escort them back to the patrol car."

While two agents handcuffed Simone and Andy, Hicks shined his flashlight into the hole. The top of a smooth surface showed through the dirt. "I guess we better check out what's in there."

"Can't it wait until daylight, Chief?" Sweeney begged. "This is already creepy enough. Plus, we'll have to dig out the rest of it ourselves."

"What a stroke of luck." Hicks bent down a picked up a shovel. "Look what we have right here."

Sweeney looked visibly fatigued but took the shovel and started throwing dirt out of the hole. After thirty minutes or so, the casket lid was uncovered enough to try to lift it. Goulais had returned and brought them a crowbar.

"You sure you don't want a team to lift this out first?" Sweeney said, stalling for time.

"If you can't handle this, Sweeney," Hicks said disparagingly, "just say so."

"Anybody in there?" Sweeney knocked on the coffin before he shoved the crowbar under the lid and jimmied it up. He opened the casket lid slowly, with a creak, and turned his head away in anticipation of finding some ghoulish decaying corpse.

Hicks illuminated the interior of the casket with his flashlight. He let out a loud, shrill whistle. "Sweeney, it's a good thing you didn't look, because I can guarantee you this would have shocked your socks off." He shook his head. "If this doesn't give you the chills, boys—nothing will."

Sweeney still had his head turned and his eyes shut.

"Keep 'em shut, Sweeney. You won't be able to handle it." Hicks pulled out his phone and made a call. "Alex," he said. "Call me as soon as you get this. I think I found something that will convince you to come back. We just dug up Dorthea Krebs's coffin, and it's definitely not empty."

26

Breakdown

The sound of a crying baby isn't usually a pleasant thing to wake up to, but when Wesley woke up to two crying babies, it was like music to his ears. The fact that both of his sisters were still in the house made him sigh with relief.

"Mom," Amanda called from the adjoining bedroom. "I changed my mind; I don't want a little brother or sister."

"That's good," Maria answered. "Because you're not getting one."

Wesley checked the clock at 5:45 and met Maria shuffling into the nursery. "I'll get C.J." Wesley was used to the early morning routine. "If you take them back to bed with you, they'll sleep a little longer."

"Good idea, because I'm not awake yet." Maria lugged Emily out of her crib when the phone rang. "Is this what it's always like in the morning here?"

Assuming it was Maggie, Wesley answered the phone with his free hand. "Hello?"

"May I speak with Maggie Mackey, please?"

"She's not here. May I take a message?"

"This is Cynthia Selnick, a nurse at Muir Hospital. Who am I speaking to?"

"Wesley Mackey."

"Well, then, when your mother returns, you can tell her that your father is awake now."

"But she spent the night at the hospital. You can tell her yourself," Wesley responded.

"No, she didn't," the nurse assured him. "We sent her home last night and told her we'd call her."

Wesley started to argue the point, but then he realized that alerting the hospital staff or Maria that Maggie was missing might not be such a good idea. "She must have come home late last night, then. I'll give her the message."

* * *

Maggie sat on the broken pieces of wood that jutted out of the white alder, the only remnants left from a fort that had been constructed more than twenty years ago. The tree had grown around the fort like it was cradling a baby in its branches, and the remaining pieces of the fort were permanently imbedded in the tree. She had wrapped herself in a blanket, but the sun was warm enough, so she shrugged it off, letting it fall down about fifteen feet to the ground. Her vision was blurred from lack of sleep, and it took her a while to recognize that the person riding up on a palomino horse was her mother. It was too late to hide—she and her black horse were plainly visible.

Penny parked her horse, dismounted, and looked up into the tree with her hands on her hips. "So now you're running away from home?"

"Maybe I am. How did you find me?"

"You haven't changed much, Maggie Sue. This is the first place I looked. Everyone at the house was fixin' to call the cops when they found out you were missing. I told them to hold off a few minutes—I'd be able to find you." Penny began climbing the tree, and Maggie knew it was useless to try and stop her spry mother from clambering onto the creaking boards.

"I think this place is due for a renovation," Penny said as if there were nothing strange about Maggie being here.

Maggie shook her head, and fresh tears came gushing out. "My life is due for a renovation."

"You've been through a lot the past few days. We all have."

"I can't do this anymore." Maggie broke into tears.

"I know, but the worst part is over now."

"No." Maggie sniffed. "You don't know what I'm talking about."

"Then why don't you clue me in?"

"I can't keep putting up a front, pretending to be someone I'm not."

"And just who are you pretending to be?"

"A good person. A good wife, mother, and daughter."

"And you're not?"

"No, I'm not. Underneath the phony exterior, I'm really a bad person. I'm selfish and rotten, and I always have been."

"You are not a bad person."

"Oh, yes I am. You don't know the half of it. Remember when we built this fort? We were twelve. Nicole and I couldn't agree which way the window should face. I thought sunsets were prettier than sunrises, so it should look out west. Nicole said sunrises were prettier than sunsets and wanted it to look out east. We only had one piece of glass for the window, and I was determined that we do it my way. So I got Jeffrey Scoggins to help me put in the window when Nicole was at dance lessons. When she found out later, it was all done. We couldn't change it without breaking the window. She wasn't even mad really, just hurt that I had to be so sneaky about it."

"So you're feeling guilty about that now?"

Maggie nodded. "Don't you get it? It's not just about the window. I've taken her whole life!" She flung her arms out in a half circle. "She died and I stole her husband, and I'm raising her son. I kept telling myself it's what Nicole would have wanted. But how do I know that? We never agreed on anything. The truth is, it's what *I* wanted. Me. It's all about me."

"You *stole* her husband?" Penny laughed. "You act like Jack had nothing to say about that."

"Maybe he didn't. Maybe he just missed her so much that I was the closest thing to replacing her. She was sweet and kind to Jack. What do I do? I beat him up!"

"That was an accident."

"But it's just not right that I'm here and she's not."

"It's not your fault she died, Maggie."

"Maybe not, but it is my fault that I don't want her to come back. Yesterday Hicks showed us these pictures—he said Nicole might be alive. When I saw them, the only thought I had was that my life is ruined. I didn't want her to come back and take Jack and Wesley away from me. The truth is, Mom, I don't want her to be alive, and if she is alive, I don't want to find her. That's what kind of person I am."

A breeze picked up and rustled the leaves in the tree. "You think that not wanting her to come back and ruin your life makes you a bad person?" Penny asked.

"Yes." Maggie wiped her face, and Penny handed her a tissue. "Well it does, doesn't it?"

"If it does, then I guess we're both bad people, because I wouldn't want her to come back either."

"You wouldn't?" Maggie was shocked. "But she's your daughter!"

"And so are you—what a fix we'd all be in if Nicole were roaming around somewhere, still alive. Maggie, I can assure you, Nicole's spirit is alive, but her physical body is dead."

"How do you know that?"

"Because I saw those pictures, and it's not Nicole."

"You saw the pictures?" Maggie turned. "How?"

"Never you mind how I found out. Just know that you should have come straight to me, because I could have saved you a lot of grief."

"But how can you tell? You haven't seen Nicole for thirteen years. She might look different now."

"Well she might look older, but I'm certain she wouldn't switch from being left-handed to right. Whoever it was, she was wearing her purse on the right shoulder. Nicole always wore hers on the left. The face is yours, Maggie, but the body and clothes belong to someone else. You don't carry yourself that way—it's obvious."

"Jack said it was me too." Maggie hung her head. "I honestly can't tell."

"Well, you don't see yourself as much as we do— and when you do, it's usually in reverse—in the mirror. And besides, I told you. I know Nicole is dead."

"How?"

"Because thirteen years ago I did a lot of praying. I didn't want to believe she was gone. I cried for months until I got my answer."

"What kind of answer?"

"I felt an inner peace. I was able to deal with it after that."

"Did you tell anyone?"

"I told Dad, and that's all."

Maggie was quiet for a moment as she pondered this new information. Penny was pragmatic and didn't have an overactive imagination. She always had a deep spirituality, and Maggie was only beginning to see the depth of her wisdom.

Maggie pulled a careworn photo out of her pocket. In the picture, the twelve-year-old twins were both striking a dramatic pose. "I always felt like she was the better one—the favorite. Like everyone was thinking it should have been me instead of her."

Penny seemed disturbed by this comment but gathered her thoughts before she proposed a question. "So, when Emily was kidnapped, were you thinking they should have taken C.J. instead?"

Maggie looked at her mother. "Of course not. That never entered my mind. I wished they wouldn't have taken either of them."

"But you admit Emily is the better-tempered child," Penny insisted.

"So, it doesn't mean I love C.J. any less."

"Exactly. Your dad and I wished we could bring Nicole back, but we never wished it was you instead. We love you both."

"Mom, quit trying to use common sense when I'm having an emotional breakdown here."

"I'm sorry dear, but you just don't have that luxury right now. Your husband and children need you."

"Why does life have to be so hard?"

"I don't know that answer." Penny sighed.

"Imogene is trying to get us to believe Nicole is alive, but why?"

"I think that's pretty clear."

"Why?"

"She wants revenge. We took Wesley—and Maria too. Now she wants to break up your family. Look at you—you're a mess! She planned to get Maria involved with someone she thought was an assassin. And then those tabloid photos of Jack—we know now that she had to be behind all that. She knows how to work people around, but we have to be smarter than her."

"But even though I know that, it doesn't make it any better. Why do I still feel lousy?"

"Because you need to quit being so hard on yourself."

"I don't know how to do that."

"For starters, we could change locations. This piece of wood we're sitting on is like a rock, and I've got splinters in my backside. Think we could finish this conversation on nice soft chairs?"

"I think I'll be okay now," Maggie assured Penny. "You go home, and I'll try to pull myself together."

* * *

Alex stood at the Mackeys' doorstep, wondering if he should knock or ring the doorbell. He was still trying to think of how he was going to break the news to Maria. Since things were starting to go better with her, he really didn't want to ruin all his progress. Wesley opened the door and seemed overjoyed to see him.

"Hi, Alex," Wesley said as though Alex and Harrison were one and the same to him and nothing had ever changed between them. "You're just in time for lunch."

"Oh, that's not necessary. I already ate."

"Lucky for you, because I think we're having strained peas and carrots."

Alex laughed. "You seem to be doing pretty well, under the circumstances."

"I'm used to it by now. If you think this is crazy, you should have seen my other life."

"I guess it's all relative." Alex forged past Wesley into the kitchen, where Maria was wiping the remains of C.J.'s and Emily's lunch off the floor.

"Any good leftovers?" Alex asked.

Maria jumped at the sound of his voice. "It depends on how hungry you are." She handed him the remains left in the baby food jar.

Alex took it and grimaced. "And have we located the missing mother of these two?"

"Penny found her. She just left for the hospital to pick up Jack. Do they have any idea who might have drugged him or why?"

"I don't know. Hicks doesn't brief me anymore—remember?"

Maria stood up and rinsed the sponge in the kitchen sink. "That's right, you're just one of us now."

Alex fidgeted with one of the buttons on his shirt.

"Is there something you wanted?" Maria asked.

"Yes, well I was thinking about yesterday, and remember how I told you I wanted to take that teaching job and quit the undercover stuff?"

"You've changed your mind," Maria said accusingly.

"Not so much *changed* my mind . . . more like I never really made it up completely."

"I knew it," Maria said matter-of-factly as she turned and opened the dishwasher.

"How could you know? I just got a call from Hicks this morning!"

"Because someone like you would never be happy settling down into a routine teaching career."

"I think I could."

"Sure you *could,* but you don't want to, right?"

"Well . . . No, I don't want to."

"So are you asking me what to do?"

"Yes. What you think carries a whole lot of weight with me. I want to know if you would approve of me going back to finish this case."

Maria turned around. Alex felt like he was talking to a seasoned interrogator. "Alex, what you do is your business. I don't think you should be planning your life around what I think. It's not like we're married or something."

Alex was stunned, and his face turned pink. It was true—asking her to help him make important career decisions was pretty presumptuous of him. But he hadn't expected her to call him on it. "So, hypothetically speaking, if I were planning on . . . asking you to marry me, what would your answer be?"

Maria thought for a moment. "Well first of all, you're younger than me—that's a problem."

"Only one year." Alex was surprised this would bother her.

"And second, you're smarter than me. You'd get bored of me after a while."

Alex looked into Maria's eyes and realized that she was flirting with him. "Actually, I'm not as smart as you think. I failed out of calculus in the sixth grade."

"Right. Who takes calculus in the sixth grade?"

"So, you're saying you would never marry someone who's slightly younger than you and better at math?"

"I didn't say that. It's possible that we could work it out. But hypothetically speaking, if you asked me to marry you, and I was to ignore our obvious differences and say yes, I wouldn't be opposed to you returning to work as an undercover agent."

"You wouldn't?"

"In fact, I'd agree that we have to find Imogene now, while we still have some leads. You're the best person for the job, and Hicks still needs you."

"So, now you're trying to get rid of me?"

"Maybe," Maria teased. "But there are still a lot of things we don't know, like how those pictures got in the safety-deposit box, and who Colette is."

"Wait—how do you know about all that?"

"Everyone knows. With Dylan around, nothing is a secret."

"Yeah, I'm thinking about hiring the kid myself. So let me summarize here. What you are saying is that you would approve of me going back to my job as an undercover agent."

"Yes, I think you should."

"Really . . ." Alex mulled it over. "And if I have to travel to, let's say, South America; would that mean that you would be dating other men while I'm gone?"

"Hmmm," Maria pretended to consider. "I don't think Geraldo would approve of that."

Alex grinned. "No, he wouldn't."

27

Interrogation

Chief Hicks ushered Alex into his office and sat him down in a chair. He locked the door, checked to make sure it was secure, and then placed a briefcase on his desk.

"If only you could have been there when Sweeney opened that coffin lid," Hicks said with a gleam in his eye. He pinched his thumb and forefinger together. "I was this close to leaving my job and disappearing forever."

"I know. You told me that already," Alex said impatiently. "Are you going to tell me what was in there?"

Hicks rubbed his palms together. "I don't think I could describe it adequately, so I'm going to show you instead. Picture this." He set the combination and spun the briefcase around so that it faced Alex. "A satin-lined coffin sprinkled with hundreds . . ." He popped the case open to reveal an ocean of sparkling white diamonds. ". . . of these."

Alex watched as Hicks plunged his hand in and grabbed a fistful of the precious gems. He opened his hand and let them cascade back into the briefcase. Some of the stones were as large as buttons.

"Okay, I'll admit it." Alex was duly impressed. "I've never seen anything like it in my life."

"They were just spilled all over inside the casket." The gleam in Hicks's eye almost matched the stolen gems. He held one that looked to be about four carats up to the light. "I could have pocketed just one or two of these babies and been set for life. Who would ever know?"

"Nobody." Alex shrugged. "Just you and your conscience."

"Yeah. Darn that conscience anyway. I couldn't do it. We gotta get these out of my stewardship and into a vault before I change my mind."

"Where are they going?"

"An armored truck is going to take them to Atlanta and then probably D.C. until someone can figure out what to do with them. The transfer is going to be pretty risky. That's why I need you, Harris."

"There's nobody else you can trust?"

"Well, that too. But no. Do you have any idea how many *billions* of dollars we're looking at here?"

"Enough to finance a small country."

"Try a medium-sized country. You know Imogene is not going to just let that go. You can bet she knows we've got her life's work right here and that at some point they're going to be moved."

"So you think we can use the diamonds as bait to catch her?"

Hicks smiled. "Hey, for a military guy, you're pretty smart."

"I'm in. Let's do it." Alex picked up one of the diamonds and examined it. He closed his palm around it, and when he opened it, the diamond was gone.

"All right, enough of that!" Hicks scolded.

Alex waved his hand over his palm and the diamond reappeared. "You're absolutely right, Chief. The more I look at these, the more I think I need one."

* * *

Jack was in the kitchen trying to loosen the Velcro on his right-arm sling with his left hand. "Forget this!" He impatiently ripped off his sling and threw it on the floor.

"Shouldn't you leave that on?" Maggie asked as she brought Jack a sandwich and set it down on the table.

"No. Aren't you going to eat too?"

"I'm not hungry."

"Mag, you're pushin' a hundred pounds here. I think you better eat."

Maggie said nothing and poured Jack a soda.

"This is killin' me, Mag. Could we just talk about it?"

"About what?"

"The pictures, last night—everything."

"What do you want me to say?" Maggie asked.

"Whatever's on your mind."

"Why don't you say what's on your mind?" Maggie turned the water on and started rinsing some already clean dishes. "I mean, your former wife could still be alive. And you don't have any feelings on that?"

Jack sighed and put his sandwich down. "Okay, I think we're talkin' now." He motioned for her to sit down. "First of all, I never thought those pictures were of Nicole."

"But if they were?"

"Then it would have made me mad."

"Why?"

"Because she wouldn't be the person I thought she was. She would have fooled us all."

"Just tell me one thing, Jack," Maggie said. "Why did you marry me?"

"Is this a trick question?"

"Just answer me."

"Because I love you."

"Is that it?"

"Well, no. You also look great in a swimsuit."

Maggie blew out her breath. "Men just aren't deep thinkers. You're not following me."

"Listen, Mag," Jack said, suddenly becoming serious. "I didn't marry you as a replacement for Nicki."

"You're sure?"

"Of course I'm sure. The two of you are nothing alike. Nicki has been gone for a long time. My life revolves around us now. You, Wesley, C.J., and Emily. That's not going to change."

Maggie didn't answer.

"What else can I say, Mag? Look at it this way. We are the only couple on earth who both loved my first wife."

"I know. When you put it that way . . . that is unusual."

"Yeah, we could go on the Jerry Springer show."

Maggie laughed.

Jack pulled her in and kissed her.

Wesley walked into the kitchen and cleared his throat to announce his presence. He was busily text messaging on a cell phone. "If anyone is interested, I have a news flash."

"Good news, I hope," Jack said.

"Alex is on his way back. He said they arrested Simone and Andy, and they found a ton of diamonds buried in that old lady's coffin."

"What old lady?" Jack asked.

"Dorthea Krebs—but it isn't actually her coffin because she's not really dead."

"Hey . . ." Jack said. "Why are Alex and Hicks giving *you* all this information before us?"

Wesley shrugged. "They aren't. I have your phone. Don't you ever delete your phone messages? There's like sixty old ones in here!"

"I've been busy," Jack said. "And why are you using my phone? Where's yours?"

"I don't know," Wesley explained. "Maggie took it."

"As long as you're gettin' the scoop from Alex," Jack said. "Ask him if they have any clues about the lady who drugged me last night."

"But you talked with her, right?" Wesley said. "Why can't you just give her description to the police?"

"He can't remember anything," Maggie explained. "The lab tests showed she gave him a mixture of drugs with Verced. It makes you forget everything."

"Why did she need to drug me?" Jack asked. "I can't remember anything when I'm *not* on drugs."

"She probably wanted some information from you," Maggie said. "That's what we're all trying to figure out."

"So I told you the nurse looked like you?"

"Yes, but not exactly. That was after you started speaking Spanish, and after you insulted the nurse by saying she wasn't pretty."

"No wonder she gave me a cold sponge bath. Speaking in Spanish, eh? Was I good?"

"Okay, Dad, I'm deleting all your old messages," Wesley announced.

"You do that, Wes." Jack went back to his conversation with Maggie.

"I need your password," Wesley mentioned.

"It's one, zero, three, one," Jack answered.

"What?" Maggie stopped them.

"I was talking to Wes."

"I know, what's your phone's password?"

"One, oh, three, one."

"That's ten thirty-one."

"That is correct," Jack confirmed.

"Wait a minute! When you were acting weird last night, you said that the password was Halloween. Halloween is ten thirty-one. We thought you weren't making any sense, but she must have been trying to get your phone password."

"That's strange. Why would she need my password? You don't even need a password to get contact numbers out of the phone."

"But you need it to get phone messages," Maggie reasoned.

"Or erase them," said Wesley.

"Then she probably already erased them." Jack sighed.

"No, she didn't," Maggie said. "I took your phone home because the battery was dead and left you Wesley's phone on the table in the hospital—in case I needed to call you—but then I forgot about it until Wesley asked me for his phone this morning."

"So, you're the one who lost his phone!" Jack accused.

"I didn't lose it. Obviously, that woman must have taken it."

"Well that's a lucky turn of events," Jack noted. "Because it looks like she stole the wrong phone."

Maggie took Jack's phone away from Wesley. "Well, we'd better start listening to your messages and figure out what she was after. Don't delete *any* of them."

"Give me some credit, Mag." Jack put his phone up to his ear.

After listening to a long lineup of old messages from his family and Zeke, Jack heard the message he was looking for.

"Hello, Jack. You don't know me, but my name is Whitney. I have some very important information concerning Wesley and the safety of your family. Imogene Vandergrift may be alive. Call me back at this number as soon as you can. I'll be waiting."

"Bingo!" Jack replayed the message on speaker for Maggie and Wesley. "I have a feeling my tabloid girl-friend is connected to all this. Wes, do you have any idea how old Whitney is?"

"I think she's six or seven years older than me. She can't be more than twenty-one."

"It doesn't fit with what Hicks told us they know about Colette," Maggie said.

"Hicks doesn't *know* anything. It's all conjecture." Jack scratched the stitches on his arm. "She may be too young to be Colette, but she's not too young to stab me in the arm with a needle."

Maggie shook her head. "But you said she looked like me. Whitney is a blonde."

"If she had on a dark wig, she might have looked like you," Wesley ventured. "Especially when Dad doesn't wear his glasses."

"All I know is that we need to find Whitney Ray," Jack said. "Whether she's tied to this Colette or just Imogene's niece, we need to have a chat with her."

* * *

Alex put Jack's cell phone in his pocket. "Good detective work, Jack. We'll take this recording to the station and have it analyzed."

"So do you have any leads on Imogene?" Jack asked.

"We have several, yes."

"And?"

"I can't go into it just yet. We have to keep some of this classified for the time being."

Jack huffed as if Alex's comment was a direct insult. "So after you find Imogene, what are you going to do?"

"We'll let you know."

Jack leaned forward and studied Alex. "You're just full of information, aren't you? Anything else you'd like to volunteer? Like what your intentions with Maria are? Or is that classified, too?"

"Jack!" Maggie looked at him reproachfully.

"Jack," Alex said evenly. "Why do you dislike me so much?"

"I don't dislike you, Al. I actually think you're quite the charmer. I just don't trust someone like you to stick around."

"Someone like me?"

"You know, a secret agent man."

"What he's trying to say, Alex, is that Maria is like part of our family, and she obviously cares for you . . ." Maggie said, trying to smooth things over. "And Jack doesn't want Maria to get hurt, that's all."

"Don't tell him Maria likes him," Jack said to Maggie. "It'll only encourage him."

Alex looked so uncomfortable with the line of questioning that he almost slipped into his shy "Harrison personality" again. He shoved his hands into his pockets and started to explain but was interrupted by a frantic knock on the door.

Penny didn't wait for someone to answer but stepped inside, followed by Walter and their dog, Teddy. "You've got to talk with her. Tell her it's absolutely the wrong thing to do!"

For a moment it wasn't clear who Penny was referring to.

"Talk to who?" Maggie asked.

"Dylan's aunt Jonelle. She says she needs Dylan to come back home. She claims she can't afford a baby-sitter and that she needs him to tend the kids while she takes some night classes so she can get a job."

"The timing couldn't be worse," Walter added. "The kid is finally getting his act together."

"This will just set back all the progress he's made!" Penny was near tears.

"Does Dylan know about this?" Maggie asked.

"He does, and he's devastated, of course," said Penny. "He said he won't go back, and I don't blame him. He'll end up on the street again, back to his old ways. She can't do this!"

"Legally, she can," Walter argued. "We just have to convince her to change her mind."

"Is it because of the news of the kidnappings?" Alex asked.

"I don't know, but I'm sure that's part of it." Penny shook her head.

Jack walked over to Penny and put an arm around her shoulders. "Don't worry, Mum. We'll fix it. Isn't there a way we can take this before a judge or something?"

"It's not a custody case," Alex stated. "This was just an informal agreement, so you can't do anything unless you bring some sort of charges against her."

Penny patted Jack's hand. "I don't want to do that. I just want Dylan to be able to stay a while longer—at least through the summer."

"And then what?" Maggie asked. "Are you planning to adopt him, Mom?"

"I haven't thought that far ahead. But I know he isn't ready to go back yet."

"Does she always get this attached to people?" Alex questioned.

"Sometimes," Jack answered. "But I'm still her favorite."

"I'll help in any way that I can." Alex seemed almost as concerned as Penny. "Maybe we could get child services involved."

Penny sighed. "I don't know how much time we have. Jonelle says she's coming out tomorrow to pick him up."

"Why the rush?" Maggie scrubbed Teddy's fur with her fingers.

"Yeah, where's the fire?" Jack added and then looked sheepish.

Penny looked at her watch. "Well, we've got about eighteen hours to figure out how to put this one out."

* * *

The young blonde didn't seem to belong in the sterile interrogation room. She certainly didn't look the part. Alex kept asking himself if anyone could really be this stupid, or if she was just pretending to throw them off. So far the only thing they had learned from talking to Whitney Ray was that she was an aspiring model and an actress. She was certainly pretty enough to be a model, but her IQ was definitely on the low end of normal.

Imogene would never tolerate someone this incompetent.

Whitney picked at her impeccably manicured nails while Hicks attempted to get a straight answer from her.

"You can't keep me here," she said stoically. "There's no law against paying cash for a new car."

"That's not why you've been brought in," Hicks told her for the second time. "You have a cell phone in your purse that belongs to Wesley."

"I'll sue you for searching me without a warrant."

"We don't need a warrant, Miss Ray. We already have evidence that you stole the phone from Jack Mackey's hospital room and that you posed as a nurse and injected him with drugs."

"What kind of evidence?" Whitney looked as guilty as a kid caught raiding the cookie jar.

Hicks gave Alex a furtive glance. "Several employees from the hospital have positively IDed you." Alex knew that much was true, but then Hicks embellished a little. "And we have a positive match of your fingerprints on a syringe we found in the trash."

"That's impossible!" Whitney protested.

"Why is that impossible?" Hicks asked.

"Because—I was wearing gloves."

Hicks shook his head and laughed.

"I don't believe it," Alex joined in. "Up until now, I thought all the dumb blonde jokes were so unfair."

"Wait." Whitney suddenly realized why they were laughing at her. "You don't really have my fingerprints, do you?"

"No," Hicks admitted. "But we have a confession, and that's even better."

"I'm not talking until my lawyer gets here!" She pouted.

"Suit yourself." Hicks threw his pad of paper on the table. "We can wait until he flies out from California. I'm sure you'll enjoy the lovely accommodations here in cell number nine."

"Whitney, my advice is that you take this deal," Alex suggested. "Tell us what we need to know, and we'll drop the charges against you. Otherwise, we can't help you."

Whitney threaded her fingers through her long, golden hair. "I already told you what I know. I don't know who Colette is. Aunt Genie gave me an assignment, and then she fired me because I failed the first test."

"And the first test was . . . ?" Hicks asked.

"Making it look like Jack and I were having an affair."

"You made the cover of all the tabloids. Why did Imogene think you failed?"

"Because I left a message on Jack's phone. She said that was *unprofessional*." Whitney wagged her head back and forth.

"So you went into Jack's hospital room and injected him with drugs to try and get his password so you could erase the evidence. Then when you tried it and realized it didn't work, you took the phone and left. Isn't that right?"

"I don't have to answer that. I'm taking the fifth commandment."

Hicks threw up his hands in exasperation.

"This isn't a courtroom, Whitney. You're not on trial. If you'll just answer the questions, we promise to let you go."

"Today?"

"Yes, as soon as you cooperate." Hicks picked up the brunette wig. He laid several photos of the mystery woman who looked like Maggie on the table where the wig had been. "Is this you?"

"Of course not. You can tell that doesn't even look like me."

"Do you know who it is?"

Whitney shrugged. "It looks like Jack Mackey's wife to me, but I don't know her personally."

"Have you ever been to Johannesburg?"

"Maybe. I travel around a lot."

"What about your mother? Delphina Lockhart."

"I don't know. She doesn't check in with me all the time."

"Miss Ray, you aren't giving us anything of value." Hicks sighed and clicked the top of his pen. "Let's lock her back up," he said to Alex. "We'll give her another chance to talk in a few days."

Whitney suddenly became more talkative. "Wait a minute. I think I've heard Aunt Genie talking about getting someone new to be Colette. I mean, I'm not sure Colette even really exists, other than in Aunt Genie's head. But maybe it's like she's a whole bunch of people."

"That doesn't make any sense," Hicks said with obvious impatience. "Stop playing games with us."

"I'm not. It's just like *Remington Steele*."

"Who?" Hicks asked.

"Don't you ever watch old TV shows?" Whitney asked. "Pierce Brosnan played this detective, Remington Steele—only he was really just the face for Laura Holt, the real brains behind the operation."

"We already know Imogene is the brains behind Colette," said Hicks.

"I think Colette *could* be more than one person," Alex stated. "Maybe it all started with Imogene or

Delphina, and it could have been several women over the past thirteen years. Whitney might be the most current protégé. Is that what you're trying to say?"

Whitney strummed the tabletop. "Sure, if it gets me out of here. You're wasting your time anyway. Aunt Genie will just leave the country as soon as she gets her diamonds back."

"How do you know about the diamonds?" Alex asked, alarmed.

"I watch the news." Whitney said. "Are you going to accuse me of burying them in that coffin too?"

"No, I'm not. But Imogene's not going to get her hands on the diamonds," Hicks stated. "They're in a very safe place."

"So is she," Whitney retorted.

"Where is she?" Hicks demanded.

"If I knew," Whitney said with an attitude, "she wouldn't be very safe, now would she?"

"She's got a point," Alex agreed.

Whitney rolled her eyes. "Whenever she wants something, she'll find a way to get it. Listen, Aunt Genie and I really don't get along. I'm through with trying to cover for her. If you really want to catch her, let me go, and I'll help you out."

"If you haven't noticed, that's what we're trying to do here." Hicks leaned over onto his fists. "Only you've got it backwards. First you help us out. *Then* we drop the charges."

Whitney folded her arms across her chest. "I don't know. What's in it for me?"

"Five to ten years in jail." Hicks put up five fingers and then another five to illustrate his point. "Or you walk out of here."

* * *

The old pink Cadillac looked out of place pulling in to the Scott Ranch, and Wesley watched Penny fussing over Dylan, straightening his collar and telling him to remember to tell his aunt about his recent test scores.

"Now we're here for backup if y'all can't convince her. But I think she'll listen to you, Dylan."

"Let go of his shirt, Penny," Walter commented. "He'll do just fine if you let him be."

"I hope she buys this," Dylan said, shaking out his arms and cracking his knuckles to loosen up. It was a rather awkward moment for Wesley. He wanted to wish him well, but he didn't know how to say it.

The doorbell rang, and Wesley hopped over to answer it. Dylan's aunt Jonelle stood in the doorway. Her hair was combed, and she reeked of cheap, flowery perfume, but she looked presentable in dress slacks and an ironed shirt. "Hello, Mrs. Dunford." Wesley gave her a respectful nod and turned her over to his grandparents, who were like two grizzly bears protecting their young.

"Hello, Jonelle," Penny said cordially, and steered her over to the couch. "You remember my husband, Walter."

Walter put out his hand, and Jonelle deliberately avoided eye contact when she shook it.

"Jonelle," Penny said, getting straight to the point. "We'd really like you to reconsider—"

"I know you're good people, Penny, and I know Dylan wants to stay, but you don't understand. I've got a financial situation to deal with."

Penny looked at Walter, and Wesley was wondering if Jonelle was going to ask them for money. "Would you like to see Dylan ride?" Penny tried to stall for time. "He's been such a fast learner. Why don't we take a walk to the barn, and Dylan can fill you in on his schoolwork."

"I got three As on my English and math tests," Dylan blurted out.

"And I suppose those As are going to feed our family for the next three months?" Jonelle said reproachfully. She twisted her hair around her finger. "I don't have time to stay, but I would like to talk to Dylan alone for a minute—outside."

Penny and Walter murmured their consent, and Dylan followed Jonelle reluctantly to the front porch.

After the front door closed, Penny ran to the window and tried to crack it open.

"Oh, no you don't," Walter urged. "If she catches you eavesdropping, we don't have a prayer."

"Where are Alex's spy glasses when you need them?" Penny wrung her hands. "Why do you suppose she suddenly wants him back?"

"Maybe she can't collect her government check if he doesn't live with her," Walter suggested.

"Well, she isn't going to get away with this without getting a piece of me first! Some people can't see past their own selfish little world. Just because she ruined her own life doesn't give her the right to ruin her nephew's, too."

"I think she's leaving already," Wesley said.

A car door slammed, and everyone ran to the window to see the pink Cadillac pulling out of the driveway.

"Wait a minute!" yelled Penny furiously. She hurled open the front door, missing Dylan's face by a few inches.

Dylan took a quick step back and dodged the door. "What is it with you people?"

"You're still here," Wesley said.

"She said I could stay." Dylan shrugged.

Penny heaved a sigh of relief. "I knew you could do it!" She threw her arms around him to give him a hug. Dylan looked genuinely uncomfortable.

"What did you say to her?" Wesley asked.

"Well, I could tell you, S.B., but then I'd have to kill you." Everyone laughed except Dylan, who had a pained expression on his face.

28

 High Anxiety

Jack woke up in the middle of the night with a start. He immediately realized the space next to him was empty. Jumping out of bed, he followed the dim night-light down the hall into the nursery. Maggie was pacing in front of the two cribs, where both babies were sleeping soundly.

"You've got it backwards," Jack whispered. "They're supposed to cry and wake you up, and *then* you come in here."

"I know, but I just can't sleep." Maggie took Jack's arm and led him into the hallway. "Imogene is roaming around out there right now. Until she's behind bars, I don't think I can ever sleep again."

Jack sighed. "The alarm system is on. Nobody can get in this time."

"It's not that. I just can't shut off my brain. I keep thinking she's working on another plan."

"Alex said he and Hicks got some new leads from Whitney. They said they're close to finding her."

"That's what they always say when they have nothing. It could be months before they find her."

"I don't think you can go months without sleep, Mag. Shouldn't you take a sleeping pill or something?"

"How about we put their cribs in the bedroom with us?" she pleaded with Jack. "And we can move the dresser and put Wesley's mattress on the floor."

"Mag, it's one thirty."

"Okay, then I'll sleep on the floor in the girls' room."

"You won't be able to sleep in here."

"Do I look like I'm sleeping now?"

Jack sighed. "Okay, if you'll quit walkin' around, I'll grab some pillows and come with you."

"And bring Wesley too."

"Then you go upstairs and wake him up," Jack suggested.

"You already woke me up," Wesley said as he shuffled down the hall half asleep, holding his pillow, a blanket draped over his shoulder. "I call the playpen."

Jack nudged Maggie. "You want the toy box or the swing?"

* * *

It was barely six in the morning, but Alex was already showered and ready to go. Dylan was tangled up in his blankets over in the corner, tossing and turning and mumbling something in his sleep. Alex pulled a briefcase out from under his bed, set the combination, and opened it up. The sound of the click woke Dylan, who bolted upright and opened his eyes. Alex quickly closed the case.

"What's in there?" Dylan asked.

"Oh, nothing."

Dylan was one of those people who could wake up instantly. He got out of bed and stretched. "Is that some secret agent stuff?"

"Not exactly." Alex turned around to face Dylan. "But if it were, I wouldn't be admitting it, now would I?" He pulled his cell phone out of his pocket and answered a call. "Yes, I'll be there around noon. Everything's set. I'll do that. Later." He slapped the phone shut.

"Are you going somewhere?" Dylan asked.

"Yes, I am," was all Alex offered before he changed the subject. "So I guess Jamal is gone for the summer?"

"Yeah, he got an assistant coaching job."

"That leaves just you and me now."

"Yep." Dylan's eyes darted to the side as if he were extremely uncomfortable talking to Alex.

"And school is over in a few weeks. Penny tells me you're going to stay on for awhile."

"Yeah, well, Grandma Penny's the boss."

"Yes, she is." Alex turned his attention back to the briefcase. "I may be gone for a couple of days, so will you be okay here alone?"

Instead of celebrating that he had the room all to himself, Dylan seemed upset by something. "Where are you going?"

"I can't tell you." Alex started to put the briefcase away and then changed his mind. "Would you like to see what's in here, Dylan?"

"Sure, I guess. If you want to show me." Dylan inched forward, like he thought maybe it was one of those practical joke toys, and a paper snake was going to jump out at him.

Alex opened the case and took out a folded piece of synthetic fabric and rope. He set it on the bed.

Dylan handled it. "It's a parachute."

"Not just any parachute."

"You mean, this is *the* parachute?"

Alex gazed upon it with reserved sentiment. "This little artifact is the only reason I'm alive today. Whenever I start to worry about something, I take it out and remember what it represents."

"What's that?"

"Always be prepared," Alex said as he closed the briefcase.

"Are you going to find Imogene?" Dylan asked.

"Hopefully." Then Alex added lightheartedly, "And if for some reason I don't make it back, make sure you take care of Black Betty for me. Amanda said it's only for a few more days."

Dylan looked at the spider and then at the parachute and then at Alex. "You can't go," he said softly.

"What do you mean? Dylan, I have to."

"No, there's something you don't know, and when I tell you, it'll change everything."

"It sounds serious." Alex sat down on the bed. "So tell me."

"Uh, last week, you know when Jonelle came to get me? She was going to make me go back with her. But then she made a deal with me. She said I could stay if I did something for her."

"And what was that?"

"This is going to make you really mad."

"Now I'm really curious," Alex said. "What did she want you to do?"

"Put a bug inside your cell phone."

"Really?" Alex took in the information methodically. "And where did she get the listening device?"

"I don't know. She said it was from the FBI—that they didn't trust you. And that they would pay her a bunch of money to help them out. She told me if I didn't agree to do it, then she would make me come home with her. I was going to tell you about it sooner, but . . . I just didn't."

"Do you believe the FBI is monitoring me?"

"Maybe." Dylan looked at the floor. "No, probably not."

"Hmmm . . ." Alex mulled over the new development. "Interesting. Is there anything else you'd like to confess?" Alex looked at his phone and then at Dylan.

"No, that's all. I'm sorry—I don't know why I did it."

"Of course you know why you did it. You wanted to stay here at the ranch. And for that, I don't blame you. But being a part of an espionage operation—that's a pretty serious crime, one that could get people killed."

"But now that I told you," Dylan said, full of remorse, "you can scrap the mission or change the plan so that nobody will get hurt."

"It's too late, Dylan. A lot of things have already been put into motion."

"So are you going to arrest me, then?"

"I'm not a police officer."

"But you're going to turn me in?" Dylan challenged.

"No. I don't have time for that right now. I have something very important to do."

"You can't go ahead with your plan!" Dylan panicked. "They've been listening to your conversations, and you'll be walking into a trap!"

"And who might 'they' be?"

"I don't know—Imogene and her people—the bad guys."

"And you're certain that they're the bad guys and not me?"

Dylan studied Alex. "Yeah, I'm sure."

Alex smiled and put his hand on Dylan's shoulder. "I'm glad you told me, Dylan; it was the right thing to do. Now, without giving you any more information than you are cleared to receive, let's just say I would be a pretty inept secret agent if I went a whole week completely unaware that a junior high school kid had bugged my phone."

"So you found the bug?"

Alex shrugged.

"If you found it, and you knew it was me, then why didn't you turn me in?"

"Because, Dylan, I knew you'd eventually come clean. I can see some real potential in you. As a matter of fact, I think you've got some pretty impressive intelligence skills already."

"You do?"

"Yes. But if you tell anyone I said that, I'll deny it. Now, as long as you promise to keep your side of the room clean, I promise not to turn you in to the police or Grandma Penny. Do we have a deal?" He put out his hand.

"Deal." Dylan shook it enthusiastically.

"Good, because this cabin would be lonely with just me and Black Betty."

* * *

Amanda adjusted her empty backpack as she knocked on the barracks door. As soon as her knuckles hit the door, it pushed open. Dylan had probably run off once again, forgetting to close it all the way. She would just tiptoe in, get her spider, and leave. The shutters and one window were open, and the breeze had blown papers all over the room. She noticed that Dylan was already taking advantage of living alone by leaving his junk all over and not making his bed. Amanda wasn't exactly tidy herself, but this place was a pigsty, even by her low standards. She heard the door creak, and someone walked in.

"Just what do you think you're doing?" Dylan bellowed. "You just trashed the place!"

"I did not!" Amanda defended. "I just got here a few seconds ago. You better clean this place up before Penny catches you."

"It was clean when I left it this morning," Dylan barked at her. "You're the one who's breaking and entering."

"It was open." Amanda searched around on the nightstand. "Okay, Dylan," Amanda accused. "Where's Black Betty? I need to turn my project in tomorrow."

"I didn't take your stupid spider; it was on the dresser this morning."

"Well, it's not here now. Not that I would find it under all this mess."

"Get out of my room."

"It's not just your room. Alex lives here too."

"Well, if Alex was here, he'd tell you to leave too," Dylan said angrily. "Why don't you ask S.B. where your spider is? He probably took it for a walk or something."

Amanda picked up on Dylan's distress. "What's going on? Is there something you're not telling me?"

"Yeah, there's plenty of stuff I don't tell you. You couldn't keep a secret if your life depended on it."

"What secret?"

"There is no secret. Just forget it."

Amanda backed away. "I can see that you're having a really bad day."

"You have no idea what a bad day is," Dylan snapped. "You get to live here all the time." He started picking up the loose papers and stacking them in a pile.

"Oh, so that's what this is all about? You're feeling sorry for yourself because you have to go home eventually."

"I didn't say that." He threw his pillow on the bed and pulled the covers up over it.

"Yes, you did. You know, nobody has a perfect family, Dylan. I've never even met my real dad. And if you haven't noticed, Wesley doesn't exactly live in a dream world all the time either. But you don't have to get angry with other people just because their life appears to be better than yours."

"Who are you now, Dr. Phil?"

Amanda exhaled in exasperation. "Never mind. I'll just keep my thoughts to myself." She stormed out of the room and slammed the door.

"And quit messing up my room!" Dylan called after her.

* * *

The armored truck pulled up to the cargo plane parked on the runway of a private airstrip. The warm wind and the smell of jet fuel reminded Alex of another day in the not-so-distant past he would rather forget. He zipped up his flight jacket and stowed his pocketknife in one of his sleeves.

"So Dylan finally confessed about the listening device?" Hicks asked Alex.

"Yeah, he felt pretty bad, but he has no idea how much he helped us pull this operation together."

"Well, we can thank him later by not throwing him in jail." Hicks strapped on his double holster. "If Imogene's been listening in, she has to know we're transporting the diamonds today. This is her only chance to try and get them back. Let's hope she takes the bait."

"So this is only about a third of the real diamonds?" Alex adjusted his belt.

"Yes. But only you and I know it. She thinks they're all in there."

"Is Ramon on the plane?"

"He's part of the flight crew. The pilot is also Air Force. You're in good hands with those two. Now remember, we're expecting her to show up, but we're taking every precaution to make sure she doesn't hijack the plane. I don't think there's any way she can get a fully assembled gun onboard, but just in case, we've got to be ready for whatever happens. The guys in the air traffic control tower are standing by. They can scramble the signal to the cockpit and not allow the plane to take off if you run into trouble. Without your okay, the plane never leaves the ground."

"Got it."

Hicks patted Alex on the shoulder. "Are you wearing your vest?"

Alex shook his head. "It's too restraining. I need total mobility. Ramon and the pilot have guns, right?"

"Yes, but Imogene's people might too."

"So I'll have to disarm them. I've got a feeling about this, and I have to go with it."

"Yeah, yeah, you and your 'feelings.'"

Alex looked at his watch. "I'd better go now." As he headed out to the tarmac, he realized he hadn't told Hicks that he had the feeling that even though he knew he was walking into a trap, it wasn't going to play out exactly like he expected. From the short time he'd known Imogene, he had observed that she was very thorough and always had a backup plan. If they were going to successfully take her down, there would be absolutely no room for error.

Alex watched the armored truck pull away from the plane. By then, everyone should have been in place. He didn't usually get nervous, but he felt suddenly vulnerable, like he was standing in front of a crowd in his underwear. He called the pilot on his phone. "What's the word?"

"Diamonds are a girl's best friend."

The password was correct. "I'm boarding now," Alex said as he slowly ascended the stairs. A gust of cold wind blew over him. Or was it just his imagination?

He entered the small, dimly lit plane, and it seemed to be empty at first, except for the uniformed man who was standing in front of the cockpit door, ready to greet him. "You're headed to D.C. today, Mr. Reid?" he asked politely.

"Yes, I hear it's a bit cooler up north." Alex looked around the interior of the plane. Two rows of six seats faced each other in the middle of the small but comfortable charter plane. Alex was traveling under the guise that this was a business trip. The diamonds were already loaded into the back of the plane with the rest of the cargo. "Will I be the only passenger?" Alex questioned.

"I guess the other two are no-shows," the pilot told Alex, gesturing for him to take a seat. The pilot stepped into the cockpit and closed the door to the cabin, and Alex stood there for a moment, looking out the door across the runway. As the stairs retracted, someone stepped up behind him, grabbed him around the neck, and wrenched his arm into a painful position. He didn't try to fight. He'd expected that this might happen and knew he had two backup men waiting to make their moves. The attacker patted him down for weapons and took the knife out of his sleeve.

"What's the matter, Alex? They don't trust you with a gun anymore?" The familiar voice grated in his ears. The assailant manhandled him over to one of the seats and roughly threw him down.

"I checked him for weapons and recording devices," the man reported to an unseen person. "He's clean. But he was packing this." Alex looked up to see the man throw his pocketknife and cell phone into Imogene's hands. He wasn't nearly as shocked to see Imogene as he was to see his former college roommate and best friend.

"Well, if it isn't my old buddy Peter Jaworsky," Alex said bitterly.

"Nice of you to remember my name, Alex. I heard you've been using it yourself, and I really don't appreciate that."

"And I don't appreciate that you tried to murder me," Alex retorted.

"That was collateral damage—you understand. It was necessary for the greater good."

Alex could now see that Ramon, his former backup, was lying facedown on the floor in the corner. "Is he dead?" he asked in horror.

"I don't know." Peter shrugged. "But it doesn't matter, because he sure will be when he hits the ground at a hundred and seventy-two miles an hour."

"You won't get this plane off the ground," Alex said as the engine started up and the plane began to taxi down the runway.

"Says who?" Peter shoved his face right up into Alex's. "Your Air Force pilot? He's been replaced by a non-union guy. I suppose you think your ground team is going to stop us."

"That's right. They won't let you up without the word from me, and even if you did take off, they have orders to bring this plane down immediately."

"Well, you'll just have to convince them to let us go, then."

"I won't do it, and you know it."

"I think you will," Peter said with conviction. "In fact, I know you will. You want to show him our insurance policy, Imogene? You know, Ms. Vandergrift is a very thorough and generous employer. You really should have worked for her."

Imogene took a few steps toward the back of the plane to a closet that locked from the outside. Imogene pulled out a key and twisted it inside the lock. "We knew you were coming, Alex, so we brought you some company," she bragged.

Imogene opened the door. Alex's heart sank when she roughly pulled Maria out by the arm. Her wrists were tied securely in front of her, and her mouth was gagged. Her eyes met Alex's, and although she couldn't speak, they pleaded with him. Imogene and Peter exchanged a sinister glance.

"I find fear is a great motivator," Imogene expounded as she forced Maria to walk forward. She placed Maria in the seat directly across from Alex. "Love is, too. Put them together and you can persuade anyone to do anything."

Alex tried to stand, but Peter shoved him forcibly back into his chair. "Buckle your seat belt," he ordered. "We'll be taking off shortly." He held the knife he'd confiscated in front of Alex, then picked up a duffel bag and started to rummage through it. He pulled out a length of rope, arranged Alex in a straightjacket position, and tied him to the seat.

"Okay, I think we're ready now," Peter said.

Imogene paced up and down the plane like a lawyer laying out a case for the jury. "Everyone has at least one great fear. For some people it's heights, others water, and some . . . failure. I happen to know what Maria fears the most."

Peter was in the duffel bag again, and seconds later he proudly produced a glass canning jar. Alex didn't need to look hard to see what it contained.

"You never know what you'll find in some people's rooms," Peter said to Alex.

Imogene gloated as Peter held the jar up to the light. "Oh, I'm sorry, dear," she said to Maria. "You can't see very well from over there. You might need to get a little closer."

Peter held the jar close to Maria's face and unscrewed the lid. Her eyes grew wide and terrified when she saw the large black widow inside. The gag muffled her screams.

Imogene handed him back his cell phone. "Alex, now would be a good time to call your friends and tell them we're ready for takeoff."

"They aren't going to listen to me!" Alex couldn't believe what was happening.

"Oh well, then," said Imogene.

Peter pulled a stick out of the jar and gently coaxed the spider onto Maria's arm. Maria shuddered and closed her eyes.

"Don't move, Maria!" Alex told her. He turned to Imogene. "I'll make the call if you take the spider off her now."

"Call first," Imogene ordered.

Alex looked at Maria and knew he didn't have any negotiating power.

"You say anything that even sounds like a code, and I promise to make that spider really angry," Peter warned.

"Push four-nine," Alex instructed.

Imogene put the phone to his ear. "Chief, it's me. We're good to go." Alex kept his eyes on Maria. "Imogene's not on the plane."

Imogene slammed the phone shut. "Now that wasn't so hard, was it? You should have told them to move quickly. I think Maria is hyperventilating."

The spider was working its way up Maria's arm and was nearing her shoulder. It stopped. "I don't blame you, Maria." Imogene backed away. "That is a nasty thing. It makes my skin crawl just watching it. You're probably wondering where we got it. What's ironic is that it's actually Amanda's pet. She has always been such an odd girl, hasn't she?"

The plane started to taxi down the runway, and Alex could see beads of perspiration running down Maria's face. She was wearing a collared blouse, and Alex knew if the spider crawled inside her shirt, Maria would probably start thrashing around and the spider would bite her for sure. "Maria, look at me," Alex said sternly.

Maria didn't take her eyes off the spider.

"Maria, you aren't going to panic," Alex assured her. "Look at me."

Maria finally looked at Alex with sheer terror in her eyes. There was nothing he could do to help her. He knew with time he could free himself from the ropes, but he didn't have time.

The plane started to pick up speed, and the spider crawled slowly up Maria's neck and onto the side of her face.

Peter was laughing and tossing the knife into the air, making it spin and then stick in the seat next to Alex.

The tilted ascent and increased speed seemed to agitate the spider. Suddenly Maria threw her bound hands up to her face, violently slapping the spider away. Alex gasped, assuming the spider had bitten her. Peter must have been distracted by the same thought, because he wasn't ready when Maria kicked his left knee, causing his legs to buckle and sending him stumbling into Imogene, knocking her to the floor.

Maria lunged for the knife stuck in the seat and, grasping it with her fingers, she sawed at the ropes that secured Alex.

"Get the spider!" Imogene yelled as she stared at the arachnid on the ground heading full speed in her direction.

Peter looked around for something to smash it with and, as he did, the spider scurried under one of the seats. Maria had already severed one of the ropes, freeing one of Alex's arms so he could remove her gag and cut the ropes from her hands.

"Okay, enough of that!" Peter pulled a gun out of his pocket and aimed it at Maria and Alex.

Imogene stood and dusted herself off. She was more annoyed than angry. "See, Peter, I told you Maria isn't as timid as she appears to be. She can be rather impulsive when she has the proper motivation." She stepped forward. "But unfortunately for you, Maria, the employment position I was going to offer you is no longer available." She checked the seat for the spider and then sat down. "It really doesn't matter if you're tied up or not. The important thing is that we're off the ground. That worked out nicely, now didn't it?"

Peter walked over to Maria and stuck out his hand. "You want to give me that knife?"

Maria placed it in his hand.

"But your little love story is going to end today," Imogene said with contrived sadness. "It never ceases to amaze me how clever you seem to think you are. This whole time you thought you were going to set me up—get me to fall into your trap—when I've been in control the entire time. You two are my ticket out of the country. And we don't even have to worry about a police escort. Alex will take care of that. Don't get any foolish ideas about commandeering this plane. You know Peter can fly and, obviously, so can our pilot. But unfortunately, none of your linguistic skills will help you land this plane. I don't recall that you have any flying credentials at all, Alex."

"Unless you count jumping out of a plane without a parachute," Peter gibed.

"So where does that leave us?" Alex tried not to draw attention to his right hand as he maneuvered it down by his side, trying to untie the rope that still fastened him to the seat.

That leaves you with a fourth down, fifty yards to go, and two seconds left in the game. Let's see . . ." Peter kicked the air marshal's body onto its side. "Not wearing a parachute, I see. I guess you'll have to pray for another miracle, Alex." He turned to Imogene. "You want me to dispose of them now or later?"

"Wait until we're out over the ocean," Imogene said without any remorse. She locked eyes with Maria. "This is most unfortunate. I let your boyfriend bring you back to the cabin because I believed you had promise, Maria. But as usual, you let me down."

"So kill us." Maria was defiant. "That's what you do with everyone in your life who doesn't do what you want. If Wesley doesn't hate you now, he certainly will when he finds out you murdered two people he cares about."

The muscles in Imogene's face twitched. She leaned forward in her chair. "Wesley has been brainwashed. You have taken my son from me, and I realize it can never be like it was before. I've accepted it." She leaned back and narrowed her eyes. "But I'm not going to go away quietly. Revenge is sweet, and I'm going to savor every minute of it. Peter, I believe you've been waiting eighteen months to finish this job. Throw them out, but don't kill them first. I want them to think of me all the way down."

29

Free Fall

Hicks didn't like the way Alex had sounded on the phone. He hadn't used the go-ahead code, but then he hadn't given the distress code, either. Obviously something was going on, and now he wasn't answering Hicks's messages. When the plane veered off course, he knew they were in trouble.

"Chief," came the voice from the control tower. "The plane is already eleven degrees off course. We're not getting any response from the cockpit."

"I know!" Hicks acted like the control tower was somehow at fault. "Just give me a few more minutes."

"The orders were to send up two planes to try and force it to land."

"You don't need to remind me," Hicks said. "We'll do what we have to."

* * *

Alex kept trying to signal Maria to do something to help them buy some more time. He was working at

321

undoing the rope that fastened him to his seat, but every time Peter or Imogene looked at him, he had to hold still. He told Maria with his facial expression that he was making progress, and she must have understood, because she attempted to get Imogene's attention.

"So I guess you're going to kill us," Maria said bitterly. "Just like you did Nicole Mackey?"

Imogene spun away from Alex and faced Maria. Her words were like a dentist's drill. "You know I didn't kill Nicole."

"I don't know anything," Maria goaded. "As long as you're going to kill us, why not tell us what really happened the day you found Wesley in the ocean?"

Imogene's face grew red, and Alex wondered if Maria was successfully stalling for time or actually speeding up their demise.

"Have you ever stopped to think just how impossible the odds were that I was there at that very moment to save Wesley's life?" Imogene asked.

"Yes, I have," Maria answered. "Why were you there?"

Imogene avoided the second question. "I climbed down a cliff so steep even a professional wouldn't attempt it, and then I swam through water teeming with coral snakes to get to him. I reached him right before his life raft sank."

"And what about his mother?" Maria demanded. "Was she already dead, or did you kill her and steal her son?"

"I never saw her." Imogene stared directly at Maria.

"Then how did you get the locket?"

"Cheap jewelry like that can be purchased just about anywhere."

Alex silently applauded Maria. Both Imogene and Peter were watching Maria instead of him.

"And you just so happen to have that same piece of 'cheap' jewelry in your safety-deposit box?"

Imogene looked as though she might slap Maria for disrespecting her. "Wesley was wearing it around his neck," she said. "Not that I owe you any explanations. You're always judging me, aren't you, Maria? Always measuring what I do against your own little set of rules—against what you think is right and wrong. You can pat yourself on your own self-righteous back, but today will be the last time. I want to thank you for making this easier for me. Peter, we're through here."

Maria had distracted Imogene long enough for Alex to work his last rope with one hand so that he was disconnected from the seat. The rope coiled around his waist made it look like he was still bound. He was at a disadvantage, though, because Peter had a gun and his knife. He'd sparred with Peter enough to know Peter's fighting skills matched his own, and even if he caught him off guard and disarmed him, it wouldn't be easy.

Peter had unlatched the emergency exit door and forced it open. The plane automatically depressurized, and oxygen masks dropped from the ceiling. A tornado of cold air swirled inside the plane as Imogene buckled herself into her seat belt.

Imogene avoided Maria's eyes. "Can we make this as quick as possible, please?"

Peter walked up to Maria and put his hand out. "Ladies first."

Alex aimed for a low tackle and sprung for Peter's ankles. Peter slammed the handle of his gun between Alex's shoulder blades, but the gun flew out of his hand. It temporarily slowed Alex, but he stood up and threw a kick at Peter's stomach. Peter dodged the kick and rammed Alex in the gut with his fist. Alex fell down onto his back and tried to right himself. Peter kicked him over and pushed him until his feet hung outside of the plane. Alex grabbed one edge of the door with his hand.

"What happened to you, Peter? We used to be friends . . ." Alex appealed.

"That's the key term, Alex, *used to be*." Peter muscled Alex through the opening so that his legs were dangling completely outside. Peter let go, expecting the force of the wind to suck Alex out of the plane.

With one hand gripping the door and the other using every ounce of strength to pull himself up, Alex fought to lift his body back inside the plane.

Maria ran over and grabbed Alex's arms with both of hers. Imogene and Peter watched the scene as if mesmerized.

Maria wasn't strong enough to pull Alex up and was only slowing his inevitable departure from the plane. It was obvious that in a few seconds she wouldn't be able to hold on any longer.

"Maria, do you trust me?" Alex asked through clenched teeth.

"What?" Maria's hands were slipping.

"Do you trust me?" he repeated.

"Yes," she cried as one arm broke free and she tried to grab the emergency-exit door handle to brace herself against the inside wall.

Alex could see Peter's face, eagerly awaiting the moment when he would be swept out of the plane as her strength gave out. He tightened his grip on Maria's arm until his fingers dug into her flesh. He shouted in her ear, "Then don't let go of me!" He threw up his free hand and grabbed Maria's wrist. His weight pulled her grip off the door handle and threw her off balance. There was nothing she could do to correct it.

In an instant they were both sucked out of the plane.

* * *

Maria didn't know if her heart had stopped beating or if it was beating so fast that it just blurred into nothingness. Alex was still holding her arms, and she was thousands of feet in the air, free-falling without a parachute. The roar of the plane engine disappeared above them, and everything suddenly became quiet. She felt like she was floating, spinning, and flying all at once.

"Put your arms around my neck," Alex shouted. He carefully shifted one arm around her waist so she could get her arms free. "We're not going to die."

"Yes we are." Maria knew Alex was just trying to make this easier for her. They were tumbling through the sky, and there wasn't anything even a skilled Navy SEAL could do to fix it. She thought about how this day started like every other day. She had no inkling it would be her last. Seconds passed, and she looked down. The ground was getting closer.

She didn't know what he was doing, but Alex had wrapped something around her waist and had tied the two of them together. The force of the wind had torn off his jacket. Maria was too terrified to process what was happening. She prayed that she would black out before she hit the ground. They were close enough to see the shoreline where it met the ocean. How ironic, that she would die somewhere so breathtakingly beautiful with the one she loved. It would be over soon. She thought about the words she never said.

"I love you," she said to Alex, not knowing if he could hear her.

"That's good. Hold on, this is going to jerk," Alex said as he tugged on some sort of rope and a parachute mushroomed above them. Maria felt a strong pull as their rapid descent seemed to halt in midair. Maria still wasn't convinced she wasn't already dead.

Alex was trying to maneuver the parachute to get them nearer to the shore and away from trees and rocks. There was no time for a parachuting lesson, but Maria realized they were going way too fast to land safely on the beach.

"Lean forward," Alex instructed. "And take a breath."

Maria was breathing so rapidly that she didn't think that would be possible, but she tried anyway. In a flash, she felt the cold water slap her as they both plunged into the choppy waves. One of her arms slapped so hard she thought it might have snapped in half. They continued down in the ocean, and the parachute ballooned above them in the water like a giant jellyfish. It seemed like a long time before they started to surface. Because they were tied together, it would be impossible to swim. She looked around under water, but all she saw was a mass of tangled rope and cloth. Now she was drowning.

Alex was thrashing at the ropes and trying to untangle the parachute from the two of them. She needed air right away. She kicked her legs, but it seemed like the surface was so far away. Just when she thought her lungs were going to explode, she broke through the water and gulped a precious breath of air. Somehow she had become disconnected from Alex. She could see the shore, but she was disoriented.

"Swim!" Alex shouted. She obeyed because to do nothing meant sinking to the bottom. The tide was strong, and for every two strokes, she was pushed back one. Alex appeared next to her, urging her forward. After several minutes she was so tired she was sure she'd never make it. Her damaged arm wasn't helping things, and the shore wasn't getting any closer. She swallowed several mouthfuls of water and started to cough. Alex grabbed her and threw her onto her back, pulling her along for what seemed like an hour until she could feel the sand below her feet. She stood up as the surf swirled around her legs. Shaking uncontrollably, she collapsed onto the wet sand. Foamy waves crashed over her, threatening to pull her back out to sea. Alex picked her up and carried her onto the shore, where he set her on the dry sand. It took several minutes for both of them to catch their breath.

"See, we're not dead." Alex hit himself in the chest with his fist. "Are you okay?"

"Am I okay?" Maria repeated as if she didn't understand the meaning of the words. She held up one arm and saw that it was still attached. She started to laugh. "That was amazing." Maria stared out into the ocean. She coughed again, shivered, and tried to warm herself in the soft sand.

"Yes, you were," Alex panted.

"I really thought we were going to die. I had no idea—" She coughed and took a deep breath. "That you were wearing a parachute."

"I would have said something sooner, but that would have spoiled the surprise."

Maria turned and looked at him. He was dripping wet with sand stuck on his face. She was laughing and shivering from cold and exhaustion at the same time.

"No one is going to believe me when I tell them what just happened!"

"What about me?" Alex said. "No one believed the first story, and now I'm going to tell them it happened to me twice."

"I'll believe you. How did you get us untied when we hit the water?"

"Thanks to Wesley, I know a really good knot trick."

"The same one you used on Jack and Maggie?"

Alex nodded. "It's pretty useful in these sorts of situations." He picked up her hand and brushed the sand off of it. "I think you were trying to tell me something right before we hit the ground."

Maria was suddenly embarrassed. She hadn't really expected to live. "Really? I don't remember. I think I was in shock."

"I think I heard you say you loved me . . ."

"Well I was obviously under duress. I can't be held accountable for that."

Alex shook his head. "I think you can. Those were your dying words."

"Well, you could have said something other than 'that's good.'"

"You didn't let me finish. I was going to say, 'That's good, because I love you too,' but I didn't have time."

"Are you sure that's what you were going to say?"

Alex thought for a moment. "Yeah, I'm sure."

"That's good." Maria smiled. "I think this is where you're supposed to kiss me."

30

Disappearing Act

The smell of smoke and burgers cooking on the barbecue wafted through the air as the Mackey and Scott families and all other additional residents of the ranch gathered on the patio next to the pool for a celebration. Even the cat-and-dog duo, Bob and Teddy, decided to get along temporarily as they intently watched Walter flip the hamburger patties off the grill and onto the buns.

"I'm tempted to drop one of these just to see who gets it first," said Walter.

"My money's on the Purrminator," Wesley called out.

"Don't go wasting a perfectly good piece of meat," Penny said.

Amanda and Dylan were seated across from Maria and Alex at the table. Amanda stuffed a carrot stick in her mouth and then tried to talk. "And then when you guys landed in the ocean and walked right onto the beach—that's the best part. I think that's so romantic!"

"That's funny," Maria responded. "Of all the words that were running through my head as I was plunging to my death and then practically drowning, *romantic* wasn't one of them."

"She's lying," Alex corrected. "It *was* very romantic. And much more fun than being shot with a tranquilizer gun."

Jack came over and sat down at the table. "Sounds like another parachute story to me, mates."

"That's because it *is* a parachute story," Amanda reminded him.

Wesley and Maggie finished the barricade to keep the girls from driving their walkers into the pool and then joined the rest of the family.

"I'm really sorry about the spider, Mom," Amanda said for the third time. "I can't believe that was scarier than falling out of the plane."

"I was probably already in shock from the spider, and that's why I didn't pass out when we fell out of the plane," Maria supposed. "Just promise me you won't catch any more of those."

"I don't know," Jack said. "The best way to get over your fears is to face them. Maybe you should get another pet. Start with a smaller, nonpoisonous spider and work your way up."

"A goldfish will be just fine, thank you," Maria said.

"Actually," Penny interjected, "we've already tried that once. Bob ate him."

"Speaking of facing our fears," Alex interrupted, "Wesley and I have a magic trick—one that we've put together for this occasion, and we'd like to show it to you after dinner."

"Is this something dangerous?" Penny asked.

"It's pretty risky," Alex admitted. "But don't worry, Wesley won't be in any danger."

Before they could speculate any further, Chief Hicks walked onto the back patio. "Smells good out here."

"Look who's here just in time for supper," Jack remarked.

"Have a seat, Cordell," Penny said while offering him a plate.

"Thanks, Penny, but I can only stay a minute. I just wanted to give you a quick update."

"Did you find the plane?" Jack asked.

"Not exactly. But we do know where it landed, at least temporarily."

Everyone stopped eating and gave Hicks their full attention.

"One of our men, an air marshall named Ramon, was on the plane. Alex thought he might be dead, but he wasn't. He turned up on an island in the Bahamas. He had no idea how he got there."

"So they didn't throw him off the plane," Alex said with relief.

"Thankfully, no," Hicks continued. "And we don't know why they let him go. But so far we haven't been able to locate the plane, Imogene, or Peter Jaworsky."

"But Imogene is definitely out of the country?" Maggie seemed profoundly disappointed.

"And she's got a billion dollars' worth of diamonds," Jack added.

"She's got a hefty sum, but not that much," Hicks said, trying to downplay the bad news. "We didn't transport them all at once, just in case something like this happened."

"Why didn't you just use fake diamonds?" Amanda asked.

"They had to be the real thing to draw her out," Alex explained. "If anyone had known they weren't real, Imogene would have found out. We really didn't expect her to be able to escape."

"No one ever does," Wesley reiterated. "How did she figure out the plan anyway?"

Dylan gave Alex a nervous glance.

Alex gave Dylan an imperceptible nod. "Let's just say we knew that she knew what the plan was. But we didn't know that *she knew* that we knew she knew."

"Thanks for clearin' that up, mate," Jack gibed.

"But the important thing is," Hicks reminded them, "that Alex and Maria are still here with us, and we *are* going to find her. I don't think she'll try to reenter the country for quite a while, but in the meantime we'll make sure your family has a bodyguard so that your children are safe."

"I don't want a bodyguard," Maggie argued. "I don't trust anyone, and that means she still controls our lives."

"Maybe Alex could be your bodyguard," Maria offered hopefully.

"It's not that." Maggie pouted. "I just want to live like normal people."

"Ah, normal," Jack interjected. "It's something we can only aspire to."

"These burgers are really good, Grandpa." Wesley said as he signaled something to Alex under the table.

"Yeah, horsemeat's not too bad, is it?" Walter replied.

"Walter Scott!" Penny threw a napkin at him. "What a horrible thing to say!"

"He's kidding, right?" Hicks looked disturbed.

"You never know." Jack raised his eyebrows and cocked his head. "He's not *normal*."

Walter wiped his face with the napkin and pushed away from the table. "I'm ready for the fear factor segment. When do we get to see this new stunt I've been hearing about all day?"

Wesley gave Alex a secretive look. "Are you ready for this?"

Alex shrugged. "Ready as I'll ever be." He and Wesley left the group to prepare the entertainment.

"Those two are acting strange," Maggie noted.

"They better not be doing some underwater stunt in the pool," Penny said as she gathered up the paper plates. "Y'all would think everyone here has had enough daredevil adventures to last them a lifetime."

Wesley and Alex returned momentarily, pushing a large wooden crate with wheels on the bottom. The crate, a six-by-four foot rectangle large enough for someone to step inside, was tipped sideways so that the front was completely open.

"Attention, ladies and gentlemen, canine and feline," Wesley announced. "I'd like to introduce Alexander the Great, formerly known as Harry Landini, and his never-before-attempted disappearing illusion. Before we can begin, I must insist on complete silence. C.J., that goes for you too." He shot a look at his baby sister, gurgling in her walker.

"As you can plainly see—" Wesley gestured to the inside of the box. "This crate is completely empty. Through his scientific genius, Alexander the Great has developed a way to transfer himself into another dimension. However, he has not perfected the technique on how to transfer back, so there is some risk involved."

Alex took center stage. "Excuse me, I'll take it from here. The Great Weslini is exaggerating. It really is perfectly safe, but just to make sure, I'll need a brave volunteer to check things out before I actually try it myself."

Dylan raised his hand. "I'll do it!" He started to walk forward.

"He said *brave*," Amanda teased.

"Thank you, Maria." Alex motioned for Dylan to sit down. "For volunteering."

Maria looked around and, before she could protest, everyone pushed her to the front.

"This lovely and extremely brave volunteer will now demonstrate that this box holds magical powers. Step inside, please."

Maria looked at the audience, shrugged her shoulders, and then dutifully stepped inside the open crate.

"And now, Alexander the Great will need a magic scarf to assist him in his journey." Wesley produced a black felt hat, and Alex lifted a silky white scarf from the inside.

"Nope, too small." Alex shook his head. He placed the scarf back in, and Wesley stirred the hat with his wand. Alex pulled the white scarf out again, and this time it had grown much larger. It continued to grow and change colors, from blue to pink to yellow. Alex pulled until it completely covered himself and Wesley. The audience was laughing and clapping.

"It's a parachute!" Amanda exclaimed.

"Not just any parachute," Alex corrected. "This parachute holds the key to changing dimensions." Together he and Wesley draped the parachute over the crate with Maria inside. They spun the box slowly in a circle until it once again faced front. Alex lifted the parachute.

To the surprise of the audience, Maria was gone.

"No way!" Dylan said to Amanda. "That was just an ordinary box."

"He's good, isn't he?" Amanda replied.

"That was the easy part," Alex explained. "Now, bringing her back will be a little trickier." He and Wesley pulled the parachute over the crate again and spun it full circle in the opposite direction. Alex lifted the drape. It was still empty. "Oh dear. That's what I was afraid of. Do not be afraid. I shall simply travel into the other dimension and bring Maria back. Weslini, I'm trusting you to get us both back safely."

Alex stepped into the box, and Wesley draped the parachute over it. He asked his dad to help him turn the box this time. Instead of opening the door right away, he thumbed through a physics book and told the family to be patient for a minute.

"Okay, I've got it," he said before he lost their attention. "There are two people trapped in another dimension, so that means we need two revolutions to bring them back. Dad, can you help me out again?"

Jack complied, and they turned the box twice.

Wesley pulled back the parachute, and Maria and Alex both stepped out of the box. Maria was beaming, and everyone cheered.

Walter seemed disappointed. "Okay that was impressive, but definitely not risky."

"Yeah," Dylan agreed. "What was so scary about that?"

Maria held out her left hand, which sparkled with a diamond ring.

"She said yes," Alex announced.

"You're engaged?" Penny said with surprise painted across her face. "They're engaged!"

"My mom's getting married," Amanda bragged.

Walter threw his hands in the air. "You weren't kidding. That was risky!"

Maggie was the first to run and hug Maria. "Congratulations!" The crowd mulled around to gawk at Maria's ring.

"Wait a minute, Al." Jack raised his eyebrows. "Where did you get that diamond?"

"Not from a coffin, if that's what you think." Alex smiled. "Give me some credit. The Chief is right here."

"Yeah, and maybe Mrs. Hicks is wearin' a brand-spankin'-new diamond ring too," Jack said suspiciously.

"Hey, every once in a while there are some perks in this line of work," Hicks joked.

"So Maria," Maggie asked, "did you know about this?"

"No, he surprised me."

"Then how did you get her ring size, Alex?" Penny wanted to know.

"I am a special reconnaissance operative," Alex noted.

Amanda sported a smug smile. "He just asked me."

"What?" Maria looked at Amanda in shock. "*You* kept *this* a secret?"

"That's more impressive than the magic trick," Dylan remarked.

Amanda slugged him in the arm.

31

Black Widow's Revenge

The nurse sprinted down the hallway in her white orthopedic shoes. "Dr. Xavier, the patient in room 306 is conscious now.

"Did you get any information out of her?"

"No, she's still intubated, so she can't talk. I don't think she has the muscle control to write anything yet. We're not even sure what language she speaks. It's impossible to tell what nationality she might be."

Dr. Xavier followed the nurse down the hall. He opened the door, where a person with a red-flushed face, swollen eyelids, and blue lips was barely conscious on the hospital bed. Her face was strangely contorted. The tube down her throat only accentuated her situation, and she was struggling to breathe.

"Hello there," the doctor said slowly and distinctly. "Do you speak English? I want you to look this way and close your eyes if the answer is yes."

The woman looked at the doctor and forced her puffy eyelids shut.

"Very good then. You're at a hospital in Nassau, and you're very lucky to be alive. We nearly lost you a few days ago. We don't know what your name is or who brought you here, but we do know that you are suffering from a severe allergic reaction to some sort of neurotoxin. Are you in very much pain?"

The woman closed her eyes again.

"I'll increase the dosage of your pain medication. We've had to be cautious, because we don't want to overmedicate you and cause any more seizures. As soon as you're able to speak, we'll need to know your name so that we can get your medical records and call someone from your family. As near as we can tell, you may have been bitten by a spider. Were you hiking somewhere where there could have been poisonous spiders? Do you understand me?"

The patient closed her eyes.

"Well then, I can tell you that the worst part is over. At this point we can only wait for the poison to travel through your system. It looks like you are part of that unlucky five percent of the population that has a very severe reaction to this type of spider bite. But the good news is that the tremors and muscle contractions have subsided, and it's all downhill from here on out." Dr. Xavier smiled and dotted his chart with his pen. He checked the monitors and gave the nurse a list of instructions before she left the room.

"Since you're awake now, would you like to watch TV?" The doctor didn't wait for his patient to blink a response as he flipped on the television and raised up the back of her hospital bed. "It's a lot more interesting than just sitting here. I guess you won't be able to tell me what you like to watch, so I'll just find something for you." He surfed around until he found a program that met his satisfaction. "There you go! This is my favorite show."

He set the remote down out of her reach and left the helpless woman alone to watch the *Snake Stalker*.

* * *

Even though she was attractive, the forty-plus-year-old blonde was much too old to be wearing a tight, black leather miniskirt. She had enormous hair, false eyelashes, and a large, sequined handbag hanging off her shoulder. In her five-inch-heeled sandals, she took quick, short steps toward the reception desk at the hospital and drew stares from people in the waiting room.

"I believe my sister is here," she told the receptionist. "Her name is Harriett Greeley."

The nurse checked the computer. "I'm sorry, ma'am. We don't have anyone here registered by that name."

"But you must! Someone called to tell me she was here. That's Greeley, G-R double E-L-Y."

"Are you sure someone called you from *this* hospital? There are several on the island."

"Yes, yes, I'm sure of it. Oh, mercy me," she said, fanning herself. "I'm so very worried about her. She's had some problems with her memory lately."

The nurse shook her head and typed something on her keyboard. "We do have a woman here who came in without identification. She's been very ill and isn't talking much yet, but she could be your sister."

"Does she have red hair?"

"I don't know, but I'm sure someone on staff does." The nurse stopped a man in scrubs who came up to the desk. She turned around in her chair to address him. "Joel, do you know if the woman in 306 has red hair?"

"That's Dr. Xavier's patient. You might want to ask him."

The nurse swiveled back in her chair. "If you'll have a seat right there, I can get you that information in just a moment." She gestured to the waiting room chairs.

"Thank you so much, sweetie," the woman gushed. "Is there a restroom I could use?"

"Sure. It's right down that hall on your left."

"If you'll be a dear and look up that information for me—I'll be right back."

* * *

Wesley had just sat down to a quiet evening meal with his parents for the first time in weeks. They had no sooner said a blessing on the food when the doorbell rang.

"Don't get that," Jack grumbled. "Whoever's at the door can wait until after dinner."

"It might be important," Maggie said.

Before Jack could heave another sigh, Alex, Maria, and Amanda were at the kitchen window with their faces pressed impatiently against the glass.

"Do we know these people?" Jack asked.

Wesley was already letting them in through the side door.

"To what do we owe this culinary interruption?" Jack welcomed them in and sat them down at the kitchen table.

"Hey, that's one of my vocabulary words!" Wesley noticed.

"I just thought we'd drop by and tell you a little story," Alex said.

"That's nice." Jack put his silverware down. "I always thought eating was pretty overrated anyway."

"If all of you don't think this story is worth a little dinner delay, I'll buy you all dinner tomorrow," Alex promised.

"It's a deal." Jack gave Alex his undivided attention. "Shoot."

"I just got back from headquarters, and I thought you should be the first to know. He pulled out an envelope and set in on the table."

Maggie started to grab it.

"First the story," Alex said. "Then the visual aids."

"Will you just tell us!" Maria said, getting impatient. "Honestly, you can be so annoying."

Alex strummed his fingers on the table. "Okay. This afternoon, Hicks got a call from a hospital in the Bahamas. One of the doctors there is a big fan of the *Snake Stalker*."

"So?" Jack motioned for him to get to the point.

"Several days ago someone dropped a patient off at the emergency room with no identification and then disappeared. The emergency team thought the woman might have a perforated ulcer or some sort of poisoning. Without knowing what was wrong, they didn't know how to treat her at first. Her condition continued to decline, and she went into asphyxia."

"What's that?" Amanda asked.

"It's when you stop breathing," Maggie answered.

"And that's when they noticed the spider bite marks on her back. They ran some tests and are fairly certain she was bitten by a black widow."

"Let me guess," Jack said. "This woman has red hair and recently buried a billion dollars' worth of diamonds in a coffin?"

"Yes, from the photo they emailed us, it would appear to be Imogene." Alex picked up the envelope.

"I have to warn you—this isn't pretty." He pulled out an extremely unflattering photo of Imogene's swollen face.

"And she's still alive?" Maria asked.

"Yes, she is."

"Whoa!" Jack covered his eyes. "With a mug like that, it would be more humane to put her down."

"So far she is recovering, and pending a positive ID, we plan to have her extradited back to the States just as soon as her medical condition allows."

"Looks like Black Betty came through for us in the end." Alex put up his hand for Amanda to give him a high five.

"My spider took down Imogene?" Amanda asked as she slapped his hand.

"Well, I have to take some credit for her boarding school and training," said Alex.

"This is really her," Wesley said after close examination of the picture.

"It could have been me," Maria gasped.

"Not likely," Alex stated. "Even if the spider had bitten you, most people don't have this severe of a reaction."

"I can guarantee you," Maria assured him, "I would have had a severe reaction—even if it had only been mental."

"We're pretty sure with the timing of this and the way the plane was headed," Alex continued, "that they must have landed in the Bahamas soon after Imogene was bitten."

"You don't know what a relief this is," Maggie said. "As soon as she's in custody, I can start sleeping at night."

"So can all of us. I spoke with Hicks, and we're going to do everything we can to make sure she can't get bail. Peter Jaworsky is still at large, and so are the diamonds, and that means she could have access to huge sums of money."

"Do they think they can track down Peter?" Maggie asked. "He sounds every bit as horrible as Imogene."

"He is," Alex agreed. "And he's managed to avoid capture so far, but at least he doesn't have a personal interest in getting Wesley back."

"They actually found her." Maggie heaved a sigh of relief. "Thank you, Alex, for everything you've done."

"Hey, thank Amanda," said Alex. "I'm just sorry we didn't get her sooner."

"Good job, mate. And you were right," Jack admitted. "That was worth the dinner delay. The only problem now is that picture has made me lose my appetite."

32

Golden Shot

Alex and Maria were sitting in the beanbag chair while Wesley, Amanda, and Dylan passed the popcorn around. The rest of the family was gathered in front of the big-screen TV in the rec room.

"Come on, Mum." Jack patted the empty space on the couch next to him. "It's really good, I promise!"

"Watching the father of my grandchildren getting bitten by a rattlesnake is not my idea of entertainment!" Penny said, shrinking away from the television.

"But it's not like you don't already know the ending," Jack argued. "I'm sittin' right here in the flesh!"

"I know, but fangs ripping into flesh makes me queasy." Penny set a pile of napkins on the table. "Especially when it's up close and in slow motion."

"It's starting!" Wesley motioned for everyone to stop talking, and Penny reluctantly took a seat.

A large pile of rattlesnakes filled the screen and everyone, including Jack, was wondering what had possessed him to be so bold. "Penny's right, I don't think I can bear to watch this." Jack hid behind his hands.

"So you stepped back into that gang of angry snakes just to get the picture of Imogene?" Maggie was incredulous. "Are you crazy?"

"Looks that way, doesn't it," Jack agreed.

"But it's the best show he's ever done," Dylan said to stick up for him. "Look at those rattlers!"

"Thanks, mate." Jack nodded. "I thought you didn't watch this kind of stuff."

"Well, I never used to, but it's sort of required around here."

The group watched the hour-long special, occasionally commenting on the action sequences and Steve's editing choices. When it was over, Amanda insisted on replaying the part where the snake bit Jack.

"I think that's enough," Jack begged. "I'm startin' to relive the pain."

"You should have worn long pants," Maggie reprimanded him.

"That would have ruined the whole show," Jack defended.

"So Dylan," Penny said, trying to change the subject. "Alex tells me you've been accepted to Hargrave Military Academy. When does school start?"

"The beginning of September," Dylan replied.

"That's wonderful, Dylan. We're all very proud of you," Maggie said.

Dylan blushed, but his face seemed to light up at the same time. "Alex says I better get some discipline if I'm going to be a CTI."

"A what?" Walter asked.

"You know, a Cryptologic Technician Interpretive," Dylan answered.

"Yeah, Walter," Jack said saucily. "Everyone knows that."

"Oh sure, how could I have been so ignorant?" Walter made a face at Jack. "So Dylan, how did you manage to get in so quickly? Didn't you miss the deadline?"

"Alex knows some bigwig people there, I guess." Dylan looked at Alex for an explanation.

"I do happen to know a certain Colonel Nathaniel Harris, who is best friends with the president of the school. But I'm sure Dylan could have gotten in on his own merits."

"Is that a relative?" Wesley asked.

"I guess my dad could be considered a relative."

"It pays to have connections," Jack added.

"And your Aunt Jonelle is okay with all of this?" Penny asked.

Dylan looked at Alex before he answered. "She thinks it's a great idea. She's pretty happy to get rid of me. I can get some grant money to pay for it and can use some of the money I earn working here this summer."

"That's great, Dylan," Maria applauded. "I bet you're so excited."

"Sure." Dylan tried to downplay his enthusiasm, but everyone could see through the façade. "At least I don't have to worry about having my locker next to S.B. next year."

Everyone laughed. Now that Dylan's broken nose and black eyes were healed, it was hard to remember the incident that brought Dylan to the ranch in the first place. His countenance had completely changed.

"And what about you, Maria and Alex?" Penny pried. "Have you decided if you're staying here?"

"We don't know yet," Maria answered. "We're leaving next week to take a trip to Maryland to meet Alex's parents, and we'll have plenty of time to discuss it. Actually I'm pretty scared about meeting Colonel Harris. From what I hear, he's pretty tough."

"Don't worry," Alex consoled. "Mom is a sweetheart, and Dad will love you."

"Yeah," Jack agreed. "The colonel will appreciate your shoot-first-ask-questions-later philosophy."

"Could we not go into that story?" Maria pleaded.

"He will definitely appreciate Amanda's athletic skills. He's very much into football and baseball," Alex said, skillfully changing the subject.

"Hey, we never got to see you throw," Maggie said. "We only heard about it from Jamal."

"I'm not that good. It's been a while," Alex justified.

"Let's see," Jack challenged.

"You guys don't have a football—that was Jamal's," Alex said, trying to weasel out. "It was a lucky throw. And I was mad at Dylan. I'll never be able to do it with all the pressure you're putting on me."

"C'mon," Jack encouraged. "Face your fears, remember?"

Wesley came running back with a football.

"All right." Alex shrugged. "I'll give it a shot. But if I'm lousy, this is going to crush my self-esteem."

"Do it!" Jack beamed.

Alex walked out onto the Mackeys' front lawn and stretched out his arm. He threw a couple of short passes. Jack caught them and lobbed them back. "Let's see what you got, Al. The big guns."

Alex studied the tree for a moment and then backed up twenty or thirty yards. "You think I can hit that tree trunk from back here?"

"Not likely," Jack said confidently.

"How about this?" He backed up ten more yards.

"That's a fifty-yard pass. It's been done, but they're usually not on the money."

"Okay, let's make this interesting. If I can hit that tree, then you have to agree to be the best man at my wedding, Jack."

"Are you kidding? The only time I ever wore a tux was at my own wedding. I don't plan on doing it again."

"I guess there's no use trying then," Alex said.

"Okay, Al, if you can throw a fifty-yard pass that'll hit that tree, I'll not only be your best man, I'll wear a pink tutu if you want me to."

Alex gripped the football, pulled back, and let loose. It went sailing through the air and straight for the tree. It hit the trunk like a bullseye and bounced off. Alex dusted off his hands. "Thanks, Jack. I needed that." He patted Jack on the back. "I'll be looking forward to the pink tutu."

Jack and the rest of the onlookers stood in awe, their mouths open. The only person who wasn't dumbstruck was Amanda. "Can you teach me how to throw like that?" she asked.

* * *

Later that evening Maggie walked by the photos and magnets on the refrigerator and noticed a new addition. It was the original picture of Imogene and her sister Delphina, only Delphina had been cut from the photo, and someone had drawn vertical black lines over Imogene's face with magic marker, so it appeared that she was in jail.

"Jack!" Maggie scolded when he walked into the kitchen. "What are you thinking? Take this down! This isn't appropriate."

"Where's your sense of humor, Mag?"

"I don't have one when it comes to people who kidnap my children and try to murder us."

"But she's in jail now, Mag. They brought her back from the Bahamas without incident and locked her up without bail. Whenever I think of all we've been through, this picture helps me remember that she finally got what she deserved. Our kids are home. You can sleep at night. She can't hurt us now."

"I know, but this isn't good for Wesley to see. He probably still has nightmares."

"You'll have to tell Wes that—he's the one who drew the bars on her face."

"You both have the same twisted mind."

"It's genetic—we can't help ourselves."

Just then Wesley came in to get a glass of milk. He looked at the picture and smiled.

"See, Mag? Life is good."

"Until the next disaster strikes," she said doubtfully.

"Is that how you look at things?"

"Around here, it's like hurricane season; you have to be prepared for the worst."

"See, Mag, that's why you married me—I'm the optimist, and you're the pessimist."

"You mean I'm the realist and you're the egotist."

"Wes, did you hear that? You better take that back, Mag."

"Or what?" Maggie challenged.

"Or I'll make you."

"I'd like to see you try."

Jack sized up Maggie. "Are you challenging me to a duel?"

"Absolutely not! You know you'd lose."

"Not this time."

"Oh, brother! I've already proved I can take you down. Don't make me do it again."

"That was purely with the element of surprise. Give me daylight and a three-second notice and see who wins."

"One, two—" Maggie grabbed his arm and heaved. "Three!" Jack pulled with her forward motion, took her off balance, and pushed her into the wall, pinning her there.

Maggie was completely taken aback but was visibly impressed. "Wow. Who taught you that?"

"I have some skills—you wanna try that again?" Jack released her and took several steps back. He made a beckoning motion with his hands. "Come on, give me your best shot."

"Jack . . ." Maggie stepped toward him. "This is really no way for a husband and wife to behave. Our children need to see us getting along and respecting each other, not competing all the time. She put her arms around his neck and moved in to give him a kiss. As soon as Jack returned the embrace, she kicked his legs out from underneath him and dropped him to the floor.

Maggie gave Wesley a high five. "Now *that* was the golden shot."

Wesley laughed at Jack and Maggie. They were the two most fun-loving people he had ever known, and he also knew that despite their constant one-upmanship, they adored each other. He wondered if he would have appreciated them as much if he had always grown up with them as parents.

"Let this be a lesson to you, Wes," Jack said. "Never challenge your wife to a duel." Maggie helped him up off the floor. "Especially if you know she can win."

Epilogue

A tan, muscular man sipped his beverage while reclining in a lounge chair on a private cove of a white, sandy beach. He was flanked by two pretty blondes on either side. One woman, who was wearing a wide-brimmed hat and appeared to be at least ten years his senior, was talking on her cell phone. The other woman, who was ten years younger than the man, was rubbing suntan oil on her legs. To anyone who might pass by, they looked like any other tourists who came to enjoy the beautiful waters of Paradise Island.

"I say we propose a toast!" The older woman put her phone down and lifted her icy red drink topped with a miniature pink parasol.

The man lifted his glass. "To getting Imogene off our backs for good."

"To no longer living in her shadow," the woman added.

"To poor Aunt Genie," the younger woman said with mock sadness. "And to not having to hear another word about her precious Wesley!"

The three clanked glasses and sipped their drinks.

"I mean honestly!" the younger woman said indignantly. "The kid's real dad is the Snake Stalker. Who is she to think she can compete with that?"

"Nobody," the man answered.

"So, Mom, can Peter and I get married now?"

"You're still too young, Whitney," her mother answered. "Take it from me—I've been married six times, and I don't recommend it. You should never get married unless it's for the right reason."

"He's very, very rich."

"Permission granted." Delphina Lockhart smiled and stirred her drink. "So Peter, how *did* you manage to get that spider to bite her?"

"I trapped it back inside the jar and waited for her to fall asleep. Then I very cautiously put it down her shirt. I had no idea she would be so allergic to the venom. What a stroke of luck that was."

"We are clever, aren't we?" Delphina scrunched her shoulders. "And the best part is that we all have plausible deniability. She still thinks we came to rescue her from the hospital! She has no idea I told that doctor who she really was."

They all laughed at the thought.

"I have to admit, though, I was tempted to tell her off." Delphina took her hat off and fanned herself. "To think that she would have replaced Whitney, a blood relative, with *Maria* if she had the chance."

"Not only that, she was dumb enough to believe Alex Harris was Peter," Whitney said scornfully. "And she tells me *I'm* not smart enough."

"Well, look who's in jail, and look who's on the beach!" Delphina turned over to tan her back. "Peter, what do you plan to do about Alex Harris?"

"What can I do? The guy has nine lives. I'd have to kill him seven more times to get rid of him permanently."

"But he'll be looking for you—and if he finds you, he'll find us too."

"If he wanted to look, but he won't. He's getting married. The guy is a real family man—he'll have too much responsibility to worry about me."

"Let's hope so," Whitney said with a pout. "Because everything is finally going our way."

"Now that we don't have to give Imogene and that sniveling Richard their cut," Peter explained, "we've got a tidy little sum, even with only a portion of the diamonds."

"But we still have to turn those diamonds into cash," Delphina reminded them. "And it will take some time to set up all our contacts again. Hey, now that we've formed a new group; I think we need a new name." She pressed a finger on the side of her cheek.

"But Colette is famous." Peter furrowed his brow. "You've had that name for years."

"I know, that's why we need to dump it, just like Imogene," Delphina insisted. "She never asked me what I thought about that name at the time, and frankly I've never liked it."

"Let's make it something exotic, like Dominique," Whitney suggested.

"No, no, that sounds like a soap opera star. We need something with meaning."

"I know," Peter said. "Let's be Alexandra."

"That would be too obvious." Delphina thought and then smiled. "But actually, I like it."

"Let's shorten it to Xandra," Whitney suggested.

"That's it," Delphina agreed. "All in favor?" She raised her glass once again. "To Xandra!"

ABOUT THE AUTHOR

K.L. Fogg is a former television news anchor, reporter, and talk show host. She received her bachelor's degree in communications from Brigham Young University and studied for her master's in journalism at the University of Missouri, where she worked for NBC 8. She and her husband, Doug, have three children.